D0049531

Also by Tiffany Trent

The Unnaturalists

THE TINKER KING

TIFFANY TRENT

SIMON & SCHUSTER BFYR

NEW YORK LONDON TORONTO SYDNEY NEW DELHI

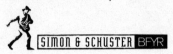

An imprint of Simon & Schuster Children's Publishing Division

1230 Avenue of the Americas, New York, New York 10020

SIMON & SCHUSTER BFYR is a trademark of Simon & Schuster, Inc.

For information about special discounts for bulk purchases, please contact Simon & Schuster Special Sales at 1-866-506-1949 or business@simonandschuster.com.

The Simon & Schuster Speakers Bureau can bring authors to your live event. For more information or to book an event, contact the Simon & Schuster Speakers Bureau at 1-866-248-3049 or visit our website at www.simonspeakers.com.

Book design by Chloë Foglia

The text for this book is set in Weiss.

Manufactured in the United States of America

10 9 8 7 6 5 4 3 2 1

Library of Congress Cataloging-in-Publication Data

Trent, Tiffany, 1973—

The Tinker King / Tiffany Trent.—First edition.

pages cm

Sequel to: The unnaturalists.

Summary: With rebellion brewing in the far-off city of Scientia and dark Elementals plotting war in the ruins of New London, Vespa, Syrus and their friends are plunged into a new swamp of intrigue, deception, and magic.

ISBN 978-1-4424-5759-1 (hardcover)

ISBN 978-1-4424-5761-4 (eBook)

[1. Fantasy.] I. Title.

PZ7.T73135Ti 2014

[Fic]—dc23

2013006018

To the true Princess Olivia—long may she reign

CHAPTER 1

I am up to my elbows in green-black grease when I realize I've forgotten something.

My favorite spanner.

I curse under my breath. I climb back out of the boiler, my arms stinging faintly from the cold grease.

I'm fairly certain this gunk is the residue from burning *myth*. Even with so much changed, the remnants of the old Empire still bear painful reminders of a time when Elementals were shoved into the great boilers of the Refineries and "refined" for their magical fuel. My people serviced those boilers, their own gifts and talents twisted by the Emperor.

Sometimes the memories make me want to tear all these machines to bits. But when I think about finding a way to make them work without causing harm, then I think maybe that just might be the best kind of revenge.

The grease is so caustic that it's eaten holes through the iron. The boiler will have to be patched, but I'm beginning to wonder if I can get the thing running even if it is patched. And on some other fuel besides *myth*.

Engines have never been my strength. I've always done finer work—gearboxes, clocks, that sort of thing.

Part of the problem is just the design. There must be a better way to make this. A different way. It looks like the Refiners were well aware of the corrosion problem but apparently were unwilling to figure out how to change things. *Myth* hurt as much as it helped, in more ways than the obvious.

Whatever the case, it needs to be done as soon as possible. Winter is on its way, and I promised the Empress that I would have the boiler ready before then. I just didn't expect it would be this hard to manage.

Empress. It's still odd to think it, much less say it, in connection with Olivia. Even odder to believe I work for her, but I do.

As I riffle through my tool chest, Piskel drifts down from the rafter where he's been sitting. He holds a tiny hanky over his nose and mouth to keep out dust and fumes. Truffler won't even come here because of all the iron.

Zao gao. It's not here.

"Piskel, I don't suppose you would . . ."

He backs away a little bit, gesturing toward the iron all around us and grumbling.

Ah well. It would probably be too heavy for him to lift anyway. Sighing, I wipe my hands as thoroughly as I can. I'm sure the spanner is on my workbench, probably somewhere obvious.

"I need to go back to the workshop. I forgot something."

Piskel dances around me in obvious joy, nearly blinding me in the basement gloom.

"All right, all right. Calm down! You don't have to come back if you don't want to, you know."

He calms but mutters at me as he floats off toward the stairs. Light, broken occasionally by shuffling feet, trickles through the cracks of the warehouse floor. It gleams on a maze of dusty pipes and fittings, vats and pressure dials. Truthfully, there's more than one boiler I need to fix. But this one keeps the sleeping quarters warm at night, so I'm starting here first.

Or I was. Until I realized I was missing my spanner.

I follow Piskel up the stairs and out through the warehouse loading dock. This building does have some attractive features— the fanciful towers with their slate roofs at the corners, the rows of wheel windows. But many of the windows are out, and some of the brick is crumbling from *myth* exposure.

I wish Olivia had chosen some other place to set up her household. The Tower fell after the Rousing, as did many of the fine estates in Uptown. I doubt Olivia would have wanted to stay there anyway. Virulen is overgrown with vines and ghosts. It would take a great cleansing before it would be suitable.

Besides, Olivia swore that she would not take up a permanent residence until all who had remained in New London had housing. After a year that time has nearly come. But we're still not quite there, which is why I must trudge back across the new City in search of a spanner.

The streets of New London will never be as they once were, but on this side of the River nearest the Forest, we've rebuilt it as well as we can. The smell of deadwood and dried brick drifts on the air, laced with the smoke from the blacksmith's forge. Boarding houses have gone up for the builders, interspersed with the remains of old houses and buildings from Lowtown. Shops and offices have slowly returned as well, though there are no hexshops. There's no longer any need. The gin palace and other such places, though, have returned with a vengeance.

We were fortunate to be given one of the few standing houses left in the City for the offices of the Imperial Unnaturalists, but between Vespa and Bayne, it's not always the most comfortable of quarters. Sometimes, especially when the wolf seizes me, I prefer to sleep in the Forest.

I'm halfway there, picking my way over a boardwalk laid down to protect those on foot from the sucking mud of the streets, when I notice a crowd has gathered across the way. Piskel, who was floating in lazy circles around me, goes over to investigate, making halos over the heads of both Elemental and human.

He returns to me like a shot, buzzing in my face like a golden hornet. I can make out nothing, except that he thinks I have to go over there. I check my sigh, squinting up at the angle of the sun. If I don't hurry, it'll be evening soon. I'm not overly fond of working in dark cellars alone.

Piskel is insistent. Into the mud, then.

I wade into the street, nearly sinking up to my ankles in filth. This is the worst problem we face now, and I've been wanting to figure out a better way to deal with it, by putting down either cobblestones or paving stones as in the few remaining old parts of the City on this side of the River. We would have to install drains and sewers here, which will be a great undertaking with only our own ingenuity to help us.

I suppose magic could help us, though I somehow doubt either Vespa or Bayne would be inclined to use it in favor of a sewer.

I dodge carriages and wagons, though one splashes my trousers up to the knee with black sludge.

This day is not ending well at all.

The crowd parts enough for me to slide in. I realize then that my day has been perfect compared to the day of the one who lies before me.

It's a kinnon, an Elemental of the air, a creature rarely seen around these parts. His brilliant feathers are already dimming, and many of them have fallen in a pile around him.

Piskel is in his face, trying to revive him, but the kinnon moves his head away and gasps for breath.

I kneel next to him, sliding my hand under the feathered neck.

"What happened?" I ask the crowd.

"Well, one moment he were flyin,' and then the next he were fallen onto the deck," an old salt says around the pipe in his mouth.

"And why didn't you send for the Imperial Unnaturalists?" I ask through gritted teeth.

"It just happened a moment ago," another woman says.

"Piskel." I don't need to say more than his name. He is off, buzzing down the streets, skipping over the new roofs toward our townhouse.

The kinnon is trying to lift his head, to speak, to get away. His eyes are wild. His shoulder and neck are wet with silver blood.

He is murmuring something, and I can barely understand him.

"I cannot hear you, brother," I say, leaning close.

He takes several shuddering breaths. I am not sure if the touch of my fingers hurts him. Sometimes the touch of human hands is as awful as iron to the Elementals. Though my hands are not entirely human anymore.

There is blood, but the wound itself is not as severe as I would have thought. It's a puckered sore, like a bite.

"They are in the City," he says. "The . . . the Dark Ones."

I frown. I don't know what he means. I have seen no darker Elementals in the City since Vespa and Bayne asked a coven of vampires who were attempting to set up a blood racket to leave.

But the old City across the River has seemed increasingly hostile of late. The salvage crews have stopped going there, claiming a darkness has driven them off, a feeling of terror they can't explain.

Olivia has been certain that it's all old, dark magic of her father's still leaching out from the Tower and the Refineries. Nothing to be too alarmed by. Vespa and Bayne have been planning a cleansing, once the next Council of Elementals meets.

"Rest easy, brother," I say. "We can talk of this when you're healed."

But he shakes his head, his once sky-blue skin dull as lead.

"The Dark . . ." And then I would swear he whispers a word that I've not heard since childhood, since the terror tales that Granny would tell around the fire after a Gathering.

"Ximu," he gasps. The name leaves his mouth with his last breath. The skies have been clouding over since he fell, and now, with his death, rain falls on him and me and the people all around us. It dissolves him in my arms until there's nothing but a silvery powder.

I think of the wound on his throat that must indeed have been a bite and the whispered name he spoke.

I'm still on my knees in the rain shaking all over when Vespa and Bayne come.

Vespa helps me up and surrounds me with a coat she thought to bring.

"He's gone, then?" she asks.

I nod.

"I wish we could have helped him," she says. "I've never seen a kinnon before. They're quite rare here. I wonder what he was doing this far north."

"What killed him?" Bayne asks.

Ximu. I shake my head, because I just cannot believe it. I just cannot.

"Syrus?" he asks.

Vespa looks sidelong at Bayne. "I think perhaps he might need some tea to ease his shock, Pedant."

Bayne takes her ribbing with good grace. "Very well, but we may as well go on to the warehouse instead of returning home. The Empress will need to be made aware of this, I'm certain. That way, you'll only have to tell it once," he says, looking at me.

I nod again. That much is true.

We all try not to see the silver trails fleeing like mercury under the boardwalk as the rain grows heavier.

By the time we arrive at the warehouse, it's pouring. The towers with their rain-slick roofs are forbidding as a fortress.

The faun sentries standing in the foyer look at us with curiosity as we pass. They've felt the reason for the change of weather, but they know better than to ask.

We take the elaborate wrought-iron staircase, escorted by a human steward who can withstand the presence of iron better than the Elementals can. This was once a draper's factory, built in grand style to accommodate all sorts of customers, even in the midst of Lowtown. Each floor has a different decorative theme, though I have no idea what distinguished any of them from one another. The manner in which it was built allowed the most wealthy patrons to peruse the wares free from mixing with folks of lower stations—four internal wells of stairs allow people to pass largely unseen by others.

It's a grand place to me, but it's still no palace.

Olivia receives us in one of the many chambers that I suspect were reserved for the Uptown folk. It's a bit ragged around the edges—the gold-embellished wallpaper is peeling, and there are water stains on the stamped ceiling tiles. It reminds me a bit of Virulen and its tattered glory.

Olivia rises from her chair as we enter and stand dripping on the fine carpet. Her pale hair is swept up in a simple knot at her nape, but little bits of it escape, framing her face. Her gown, as always, is plain but well made. She regards us with the grave, gray gaze that makes my heart squeeze every time I see her.

She had that same look when I found her in Fauxhall Gardens after Tianlong had gone. The Phoenix sheltered her under his wings as the last of the Creeping Waste dissolved into air. I took her hand and helped her up, and together we looked across the smoke of her devastated but free realm.

That day, she kept hold of my hand, saying, "Thank you, Mr. Reed."

I think it might have been then that I fell in love.

Today she's just as concerned as she was then. "I suspect by the weather and your faces that your news is not good."

Vespa shakes her head. "I'm afraid not. But we will let Syrus tell you."

Olivia holds up her hand before I can speak. She pulls a sash by the door where I presume she must have entered, and I hear a distant ringing. A human maid is soon at the door, bearing tea and the wheaten cakes from the new bakery.

I try not to show any sign of hunger, but Piskel marches straight toward the tray and looks up at Olivia with adoring eyes.

"Please," she says, smiling as she gestures us all toward the tray.

Piskel is trying to grab one of the cakes and drag it away himself, but it overburdens him and he falls flat on his back, pinned under the cake. I peel it off him. "Let me help, little brother," I say, and pinch off a few bits for him to stuff into his cheeks after he manages to get back to his feet.

The Empress laughs, and the sound reminds me of Granny's water chimes—tiny bells she hung outside the train car in the rain to bring us luck.

The tension in the room relaxes somewhat, but I'm still sad. I can't help thinking about those magnificent feathers fading into dust. I never thought I'd see that again.

"Tell me what you saw, then, Mr. Reed."

I tell her of the kinnon and how he dissolved into dust in my hands. I tell her of the puckered wound. "I know who made it."

I look down at my hands and notice the dirt beneath my nails. I'm trying to distract myself from saying what I have to. I don't want to believe it.

"Who?" the Empress asks. Bayne and Vespa are poised on the edge of their seats; Vespa's cup is halfway to her lips, a curl of steam rising like a question mark off her tea.

"*Ximu*," I say.

Their faces are blank.

"Queen of the Shadowspiders."

Chapter 2 —

Vespa put her cup on its saucer very carefully and set it on the table. "Queen of the what?" She thought of the dusty exoskeleton in the storage rooms of the Museum. While she owned that the shadowspiders might be social insects like ants or bees, she had a feeling that Syrus wasn't talking about that sort of queen.

"The *xiren*. What you call shadowspiders."

"Hang on—since when do shadowspiders have a *queen*?" Bayne asked.

"Since the beginning of time," Syrus said. He still had a bit of the silver dust of the kinnon sparkling around him, in addition to the grime of work and the streets smeared across his cheeks. Vespa had wanted to tell him to clean up a little before they entered the reception room, but she also hadn't wanted to embarrass him. He could certainly be sensitive about such things, especially in front of Olivia.

Olivia frowned. It looked as if she was trying to simultaneously concentrate and replay in her mind every word Syrus had said.

"You've never heard of this in the Architect histories?" he said, looking over at Bayne. "You have most of our old texts."

"Yes, but we can't read most of them, if you'll recall. Refresh my obviously flawed memory." Bayne's gaze was fixed on the boy, and Vespa felt almost sorry for the intensity of such scrutiny.

Syrus sighed, as if he wished he didn't have to be the one to do this. "This is one of the tales my Granny told me, when I used to huddle with our family around the potbelly stove in the winter. The tale of Ximu is one of the tales we loved and feared most, the one she told to remind us that there were worse things than the mad Cityfolk."

"Hmph," Vespa snorted.

"Well, they were mad, you know," Syrus said defensively. He shook his dark hair from his shoulders, and silver dust glittered around him.

"Go on," Olivia said.

"Ximu was the great enemy of our people, perhaps the only Elemental who hated us with a passion and sought to exterminate us as much as the Emperor did," he began. "Far in the north and west, she and her people lived in a city of bone. Her poison could make the most resistant man her slave, and her magic was some of the strongest and darkest this world has ever seen. Far worse than the Grue, if Granny's tales are true. When our people came here, the leader, Blackwolf, challenged her. He was a warlock and, after much strife, he was able to drive her from the City. Their battles are tales of legend. Sometimes he would win the upper hand; others she would return to defeat him. At last he built an army of mechanical warriors who could not be defeated by her poison or magic. In one final battle our people and the mechanical warriors pushed Ximu and her people into the sea."

Vespa heard Olivia gasp. She saw the Empress's pupils dilate, and the shadow of something—a vision or a dream perhaps—flitted across her pale face.

Syrus continued as if he hadn't noticed. "Blackwolf spent much of his magic placing wards all along the coast to keep her from returning, and his City fell into ruin and disrepair with so many of his people scattered in the war. It's then that we began wandering over the land, seeking the protection of Greater Elementals, splitting into ever smaller clans.

"When your people arrived and eventually sailed to the island where the *xiren* had fled, we said nothing. We half hoped it would lead to your deaths. But all it led to was yet more exploitation of the Elementals. We watched and waited to see what would befall you for your foolishness. As Granny often said, 'We thought then that perhaps our greatest enemy would become our greatest friend.' Then, reports came that the shadowspiders were no more and that the trade had dried up. Our elders said then that old Ximu had died at last, her magic unwound by being cut off from her palace of bone too long."

"You're talking about Scientia, aren't you?" Bayne asked. "My family's palace is made of bone and ancient beyond reckoning."

Syrus nodded. "You call it Scientia now, yes."

"So," Vespa asked, "what are the shadowspiders, exactly? I always thought they were just lesser elementals who wove particularly strong silk!"

Syrus shook his head. "My granny always said that the most powerful of the *xiren* could take human as well as spider form, if they wished. Her Captains can walk in human form and turn others to do her bidding. And that is why it is never wise to taunt a spider."

"Ah," Vespa said. "Werespiders."

"Of course," Bayne muttered. He twitched his coat closer around his shoulders. Bayne wasn't overly fond of arachnids to begin with.

"But they have been thought dead for centuries," Olivia said. "How could they possibly be here now? Are you certain that's what the kinnon said?"

Syrus nodded. "Her name was his last breath. And the wound on his shoulder looked very much like a spider bite. While I haven't seen Ximu myself, kinnon do not lie. It's not in their nature."

Vespa noticed everyone's eyes on her. "Yes," she said. "So all the bestiaries and codices I studied at the Museum said. Their blood, if it can be preserved, is a powerful truth serum."

"Whatever the case, perhaps we should send an envoy to investigate and to offer the hand of friendship," Olivia said.

Syrus's eyes went wide, but it was Bayne who spoke first. "Your Majesty, I really don't think—"

Olivia's glance cut him off. "What, Pedant?"

Bayne shook his head. He and Olivia had argued many times before. Both Bayne and Vespa had sensed a growing darkness in the old City, and had tried to persuade Olivia that danger might be present. But she had heard none of it, convinced that it was merely toxic magic of her father's at last coming to light. "It will be swept away by the new realm of peace we're creating," she'd said the last time they'd spoken of it. "Pay it no more mind."

"Majesty," Syrus said, his voice soft and deadly calm, "if indeed we are dealing with Ximu, please do not send someone to treat with her. Whoever you send will not come back alive, I promise you."

Olivia rose, clearly discomfited. She went to the window and pushed away the draperies with a pale hand, looking out onto the dismal sky. "But surely," she said, "since the New Peace, all has changed. Perhaps she is different. I do not care if she takes the old City. I have no use for it. I am happy to offer it to her."

Bayne seemed as though he might implode. He threw Vespa a pleading glance.

Vespa rose and went to stand beside Olivia. Vespa looked out across the new City with the muddy streams of its thoroughfares now running through it. She looked beyond it to the treetops of the New Forest and the green edge of the Euclidean Plain. No longer did a Wall shut these things from her sight, and the beauty of it was breathtaking.

Olivia's gaze drew her back. "You think I am foolish too, don't you, Vee?"

"None of us think you are foolish, Majesty. Just . . . perhaps . . . a tad naive." She winced a bit at having to say it aloud, but there it was.

As if catching her thought, Olivia turned, letting the curtain fall, and took her hands. "You know I've always valued your honesty." She looked at Syrus and Bayne. "From each of you, actually. But if we are to have peace, I don't see how this can be done any other way."

Bayne stood and bowed. "Majesty, none question your desire for peace. But as I've often said, inasmuch as we desire peace, we must also be prepared for its opposite."

Vespa glanced at him. His restraint was admirable, considering how he'd sometimes ranted to her in private about Olivia's obstinacy.

Olivia frowned. It was a tiny frown, barely noticeable as frowns go, but Vespa knew what was coming. "Often have we discussed your admonishments that we have a standing army and fortifications, but I ask you: Do not those very preparations declare the opposite of peace to all who observe this new Empire? I do not want it said of me that I promised peace with one hand and gave war with the other!"

Bayne sighed. "Yes, Majesty, we have indeed often spoken of this. And each time I've hoped that perhaps some bit of logic or reason would reach your ears . . ."

Olivia stiffened. She dropped Vespa's hands. "Logic? Reason? Was it not these very things that brought us to where we are today? What of Compassion? What of Honor?"

Emotions chased across Bayne's face like clouds. "Those are also important, but—"

"Those are the foundation upon which my realm rests, Pedant," Olivia said. "See you remember it."

Bayne bowed his head. "Your Majesty."

"That does not mean, however, that we should not call a Council to learn more. I know the Council of the Equinox was scheduled soon, but I think we should hasten it. Please convene it. In the meantime I will send an envoy across the River. Whom would it be best to send?"

"If you must send someone, let it be us, Your Majesty," Bayne said. "We are your Unnaturalists, after all. If anyone should investigate such a rumor, it should be us."

Olivia shook her head. "I would prefer to reserve your skills in case they are needed for further negotiations. And as well known as you are, your presence may threaten whatever is in the old City. You defeated the Grue, after all. You may have enemies."

"But . . . Majesty, this is preposterous!" Bayne said. "We are the most accomplished, the most powerful—truly the only people in your realm qualified to handle such a creature. Why would you send anyone else?"

Olivia's mouth was hard. "Because I wish to, Pedant. That is all the answer you require."

Everyone was silent, not knowing what to say. Vespa saw that Syrus's head was bent, his hands resting across his knees in defeat.

"Mr. Reed," Olivia asked. His head snapped up at his name. "Whom shall I send?"

He sighed. "You'd best send someone you don't mind losing, Majesty. That's all I can say."

"No one is expendable, Mr. Reed."

He stood and looked Olivia in the eye with an expression somewhere between sadness and yearning. "Whoever you send will be."

Olivia's mouth thinned. "I am sorry this distresses you, Mr. Reed. That is certainly not my intent."

He nodded, and the painful silence descended again. Then he said, "I will go, if that is your wish."

Olivia half smiled. "No. I have need of you here." A look shot between them, something that Vespa thought she recognized all too well. "There is the matter of that boiler, after all. Is it fixed yet?"

Syrus blushed. Vespa didn't recall that ever happening before.

"No, Majesty. I'll get back to it right away."

"Thank you. Winter is on the march, so they say."

Syrus bowed.

Vespa feared Ximu wasn't the only trouble coming their way.

Chapter 3

Olivia sends us back to our townhouse in one of the few remaining carriages in the City as a kindness. I'm distressed that a driver and horses must get utterly soaked for us, though I suppose I'm glad it's not a wight and animals driven by *myth*. And that the rain that falls isn't tinged sickly green with Refinery smoke.

Vespa sees my discomfort. "It's what he does," she says, speaking of the driver. "And it gives him employment that he might not otherwise have."

She's right, after a fashion. But it's that kind of thinking that allowed so much awfulness to go on before. Everyone turned a blind eye to suffering. I don't entirely know the world I want, but I wonder, as I look out through the rain-streaked windows, whether I'll have the chance to find out.

Telling the story of Ximu in that dim room brought it all home to me. The Queen of the Shadowspiders has always been a faraway legend, a being of wonder and terror. The Manticore had been the reality and Ximu but a strange, twisted nightmare of the past. But now, to think that they have somehow reversed . . . It fills me with fear.

I long to know what *Nainai* would have said about all of this.

She liked talking about the various ages of the world, and she was certain that we were on the cusp of a new one. If she'd managed to live, I can only imagine what she would have thought of now.

I often wonder about the others—my cousins and aunts. All those taken in that last Cull. What would they think of the boy who freed Tianlong? How often I've wished for the help and humor of all my kin, with so much still to be done to make this a truly working City again.

I looked for them. I truly did. I considered leaving and searching for them. But I couldn't quite bring myself to do it. Every time I would go to the edge of the City and stare out across the new Plain, I'd just turn and walk back again. This City needs me, and I'm responsible for that need. After all, we woke the Dragon from his slumber and restored his lost Heart to ends both dire and good. The least I can do is try to help build life here anew. And I have no idea where to even begin to find my people. This City has problems I can solve.

Piskel huddles close to my face on the carriage frame and stares out the window too. He keeps clucking and shaking his head, muttering to himself about how if he'd just stayed in his favorite tree that day, none of this would have happened.

"I'm glad you didn't, though, little brother," I say.

Hmph.

I don't think he agrees. But he nestles closer to me, all the same.

Bayne and Vespa are silent, each lost in their own thoughts. I think we hardly know what to say to one another. What can we do if Olivia doesn't want to listen to our warnings? What should we do?

At last we pull onto the cobble of the one intact row of houses in the City. The sign bearing the winged-clock emblem and the gold-painted letters LUMIN & NYX, IMPERIAL UNNATURALISTS blows back and forth in the rain. I can finally read it after a year of forced training by Vespa. Unfortunately, my attempts to help her read my language haven't met with as much success. She has no musical ear whatsoever. Can't hear the tones and can't write the proper brush-strokes to save her. But I'd never tell her that.

The door is charm-locked, and I let Vespa handle it, since I'm always getting stung whenever I try to open it.

Sometimes it still alarms me how comforting and familiar this place smells, how in just a year it's become home. I would never have guessed that anything but the clan car would be home. And to have a place that is relatively solid and free of drafts with a real working hearth, a kitchen, and separate rooms is an unheard-of luxury. It still sometimes feels crowded, though.

I move toward my workshop, a room off the parlor that was full of skeletal plants and broken pots when we got here. Vespa said it must once have been used like the solariums in the great houses, a place where you could sit in the sun and be surrounded by exotic plants. Though why the owners wouldn't just take a walk in the Forest is beyond me.

Truffler stops me. He's been stirring something on the hearth—another of the interesting dinners he sometimes cooks. He holds up a bowl of dark liquid that smells promisingly of mushrooms.

"Eat," he says.

In the dining room that doubles as a library, the hob sets bowls on the scarred table amongst all the books and papers scattered across it. He can barely see over the edge of the table, so the bowls settle precariously into their places. He hands out spoons, then disappears into the kitchen.

We sit. None of us wants to be the first to speak. There seems to be nothing to say. Olivia is determined not to believe the seriousness of our situation.

Truffler returns with a steaming bundle. He grins when he whisks the cover off a basket of fresh bread.

"Butter, too," he says, setting a pot and butter knife out on the table. Piskel's eyes are like saucers, and he wipes the drool from his mouth, even though his belly is still round with wheaten cakes.

I am the first of us to speak. "You're turning into a regular house brownie, you know that?"

It's hard to tell when the old man blushes, he's so hairy. He shrugs. "Bread makes it all better."

Piskel nods vigorously.

We dig into our stew. Truffler has a special seat he uses to help him sit at the same height as us, and it makes him look even more like a child than normal.

"This is delicious, Truffler," Vespa says. "What's in it?"

"Mushroom. Barley. Eye of newt and wing of bat."

Vespa's mouth screws up, and she sets her spoon down carefully. "You're joking, right?"

We both look at her solemnly.

"Ancient hob recipe," Truffler says.

"I don't think it's a joke," Bayne says, scooping up another spoonful with all due ceremony. "You know Elementals and their strange brews." He buries his smile in his spoon.

Vespa looks almost green as she pokes at her stew. "So . . . not all of these little white things are barley?" she asks, looking at me for some reason.

I shrug.

Truffler winks at me. I try to hide my smile.

She glowers. "You are all having a laugh at my expense." She can still play the haughty prig as well as ever, though these days it's largely an act.

We can't hold back anymore. Truffler bursts into snorting laughter. Piskel spits crumbs everywhere, holding his sides. Bayne chuckles.

"Melonhead," I say, ruffling the hair on Truffler's crown.

"Well, even if it's made of the fabled crocodiles of the Apocalyptic Isles, it's still delicious," Vespa says. She jams the spoon in her mouth, daring us to poke fun at her further.

After we push our bowls away and Piskel is lying on the table holding his tummy and groaning, Bayne begins the conversation we've all dreaded.

"What shall we do now?"

"What do you mean?" Vespa asks, a line appearing between her brows.

"Well, you can't really plan to just sit here and wait to see what happens! This is quite possibly the largest case we've ever encountered, perhaps the greatest we ever will encounter!"

"So you think we should just march across the River and investigate for ourselves?" Vespa asks.

Bayne smiles. There's more mischief in that smile than I've seen in months. "Of course."

"But Olivia specifically told us not to! She said to call Council, and that she would send an envoy."

Bayne and I are silent.

"You don't really think . . ." Vespa trails off.

"Who better to do it than us?" Bayne asks.

"There's no question of that. But she forbade it, Bayne!"

"Look, we can take a few potions and other defensive items I've made. And we can use magic to escape quickly if need be." He doesn't mention the thing that is probably troubling her the most—the unreliability of her magic these days. He feigns disinterest by scanning some of the papers near his bowl.

"Still . . . ," Vespa says.

He looks up at her. "Since when do you follow the rules?" he asks.

They grin at each other.

"Not to interrupt your scheming," I say, "but I feel I should mention that this isn't like rousting a coven of vampires. It isn't even like dealing with the Grue, who nearly killed us all. This is Ximu we're talking about. She's been here since the beginning of Time. She can't be defeated by simply knocking on her door and asking her to leave."

Vespa's gaze is sympathetic. "We understand."

"But you're going anyway?"

They both nod.

"Then I'm going too." Magic or no magic, I'm not letting them do this alone.

CHAPTER 4

Bayne decided that they should go as early in the morning as possible. Though Vespa was generally averse to anything that involved rising from her bed before the sun had risen from his, she agreed that going deep in the night, when the dark powers for some Elementals ran strongest, would be stupid. The dawn might give them at least some magical advantage.

Magic. She gritted her teeth, thinking about it as she gathered her clothes to get dressed.

Ever since she had given over the Heart, Vespa's magic had been increasingly faulty. It had gotten to a point where she didn't know what would work and what wouldn't. One day she could easily manage the flow of etheric energy and could manifest that into whatever the spell required. Others it was as though something in her was broken.

Bayne likened it to an everlantern with faulty wiring. It didn't happen often, but when it did, the magic that kept it eternally lit stopped working. "You've got a wire loose in there somewhere," he often said.

Vespa still didn't much appreciate the analogy.

She sighed as she hooked her corset laces over the doorknob and bent forward, while simultaneously reaching around to pull them tighter. Not having a maid for a year had taught her to be ingenious. She could now be properly dressed and ready for adventure in about five minutes.

Vespa wished magic was that easy.

She hadn't asked for the magic that had ultimately spelled the end of New London and life as she had known it. But when Bayne had revealed that Vespa was the first witch in centuries and that only she could end the slavery of the Elementals, she'd embraced all that, frightening as it had been.

She realized now, a bit ruefully, that much of her acceptance had come because of Bayne, and the chance it had offered her to be near him under his tutelage.

And then all of that had fallen apart when she'd discovered he was a Duke's son masquerading as a Pedant. He was a spy for the Architects, a secret society of warlocks trying to restore magic to the world. And he was also running away from the marriage his parents were arranging for him.

She'd had an unfortunate hand in that, too. As she pulled on her warmest wool dress, it still made her squirm a bit to think of how Lucy Virulen had manipulated her into charming Bayne and how, despite her own desires, Vespa hadn't been able to release him.

She supposed she'd expected that when the dust settled from the Rousing of the Dragon, that things would pick up where they'd left off after that long-ago kiss in the storage room of the Museum. She couldn't see how it could go otherwise. But in the last year, though they'd shared quarters and he'd mostly been kind, there was still a shadow of something—regret, anger, revulsion?—when he looked at her.

She checked herself in the floor-length mirror they'd managed to salvage. It was cracked at one corner, so sometimes her reflection wavered. But, as she swiftly pinned up her hair, which was darker now that the sun was weaker with the onset of winter, she couldn't really see what he objected to. Certainly she was no Lucy Virulen, but neither was she a warty troll woman.

Whatever it was, that shadow had gotten in the way of everything. And she didn't know how to make it vanish. The more she confronted it directly, either by asking him what was wrong or how she could help him, the worse things became between them. She had learned to say nothing for the most part, except when she couldn't help herself.

The shadow was in his eyes this morning when she finally went downstairs to put on her boots. Truffler, who had appointed himself official housekeeper, objected to shoes being worn about the house. They tracked in mud and dirt.

"Are you sure you want to go? This could be dangerous," Bayne asked as he packed a satchel with glowglobes and paralytic grenades.

"And miss out on the adventure?" she asked as she laced her worn boots. She really hoped a cobbler would set up shop in town again soon. "I hardly think so. You can use my power, yes?"

He glanced at her. "I suppose."

Guarded. Always the answer was guarded behind some wall she couldn't quite understand, though this sounded very like he was anticipating disappointment.

She pursed her lips and decided not to air her frustrations now. Later perhaps, if all was well. She didn't want to think about what would happen if all *wasn't* well.

Syrus came in from his workshop, his hair tousled from sleep. "You're sure your power's up to it?"

He was much more direct.

Vespa didn't truly know the answer, but she wasn't about to say no. "It seems to work best when I just feed it to Bayne and he controls it. You were planning on doing that anyway, so it should be fine."

"I was planning on that, yes, but you need to learn to control it on your own."

She could almost hear the words he didn't say. *Because someday I may not be here.*

"I'm working on it," was all she would say.

"I still think it is a bad idea, you know," Syrus said. "Going in there." He yawned. Piskel, who had just poked his head up out of Syrus's collar, yawned after him.

Coffee and tea were scarce these days, but Truffler had pilfered their small store of coffee and made some for the occasion.

The hob handed Vespa a cup. "Thank you, Truffler. You really didn't have to, you know."

He shrugged and carried his tray over to Syrus and Bayne while she sipped. The coffee was sweet and rich. Perfect.

Piskel turned his nose up at the coffee. He hated the smell. He drifted into the parlor, and Vespa supposed he would curl up in his little basket by the fire and fall asleep. Piskel was not a morning sylph.

"You don't have to go, if you'd rather not," Bayne said to Syrus.

Syrus stared down into his cup. He sighed. "I'll go," he said.

"We'll leave at the first sign of trouble," Vespa reassured him. "We're just doing reconnaissance, I promise."

Syrus looked at her in confusion. He often accused her of being a walking dictionary.

"Spying," Bayne said. "We're just spying. The gear I'm taking is defensive only."

"Where have I heard that before?" Syrus muttered into l
They were soon ready.

"All right, then," Bayne said. "Take hold of my sleeves."

Vespa and Syrus did so.

"Be ready for anything," he said.

"I think that really goes without saying," Vespa said.

He looked down at her with a raised brow. "Are you stalling

Vespa coughed slightly. "Possibly." Because who in their rig
mind would be eager to transport themselves straight into a spide
web? If that was indeed what they were headed into. Syrus wa
sure, but Vespa needed more proof.

Bayne was still looking at her.

Vespa sighed. "Just go."

The next moment, they were dissolving into air.

Bayne took power from her easily. The stretch and pull of her
body from one place to the other was familiar and almost pleasant.
Slowly she began to feel that it was taking much longer than it
should for them to materialize.

It had always been habit for her to close her eyes before the magic
took hold; she supposed for the time they were suspended in space,
she truly had no eyes, which was a strange and disturbing thought.

There was a terrible pressure and a rushing sound. Vespa opened
her eyes involuntarily. Dark, sticky webs reached out, threatening
to entangle her. Something vast and spiderlike moved beyond it,
but she honestly couldn't see much.

Vaguely under the roar she could hear Bayne shouting. And
then the next thing she knew, someone had dropped her from on
high into an icy bath.

Or at least that's what it felt like. At first she was so shocked

as she spluttered and reached for air that she wasn't sure what had happened.

Then she understood. She was in the River, and speeding quickly toward the pilings and ruins of the old Emporium bridge.

Vespa had never been the strongest swimmer. She had only been a few times in Chimera Lake near the University, which had been rather like swimming in a large, warm bathtub. This raging cataract was far from that.

She thought she heard Bayne shouting for her when she could manage to keep her head above water. It sounded like he was yelling at her to get rid of something.

". . . petticoats!" he screamed. He was swimming toward her but not fast enough. She tried swimming upstream, but there was no way that she could fight the current. In one glimpse before she was pulled under again, she saw Syrus crawling from the River on the new City side.

As heaviness encircled her waist and legs like a coiled snake, dragging her down, Vespa understood that Bayne wanted her to remove her petticoats.

She just wasn't sure how. She tried pulling up her skirts and finding the strings, but her hands were numb and freezing, and the waterlogged wool confounded her efforts. When she bobbed up again, she saw that she was about to pass into the ravine that the old bridge had spanned. The bridge pilings and broken remains of the Night Emporium were looming quickly.

Vespa tried magic, thinking perhaps she could transport herself out of the River, just to the bank. Nothing. There was absolutely nothing there.

Through a haze of water droplets she saw Syrus running along

the jagged shore. He gestured that she should swim toward him, rather than trying to swim upstream toward Bayne.

She tried it, striking out as best she could at an angle to the heavy current. She was making strides but not fast enough.

Bayne swept into her then with such force that she rolled back underwater. He grabbed the back of her dress and managed to haul her toward him.

"Magic . . . won't . . . work," she said through stiff, almost frozen, lips.

"Rivers are null spaces. Can't use magic in them," he said above the roar.

Of course.

"I'm sorry," he said next. Before she could wonder why, he grabbed hold of her collar and ripped the wool dress from her body.

"Hold fast to me!" he shouted.

Vespa put her arms around his neck. She realized then that he had no coat. She was not going to wonder about the state of his trousers.

He fumbled with her petticoats, and then they also slipped off her.

"This is a most distressing situation to be thrust into, Pedant," she said, looking up at him as they were swept toward the rocks. His dark hair was plastered against his head and neck; droplets of water glittered on his eyelashes and lips. But there was that light in his eyes that she had missed, the joy he often took in defying danger.

"That all depends on your point of view," he said, half smiling. "Hold fast!" he said suddenly.

She braced herself against him, trying not to get in the way of his arms or legs. He reached and seized something with all his strength. The water roared around them and she was nearly torn from him, but she clutched at his waist with her numb arms until she felt her feet touching rock near his. He held her around the waist with the other arm. He had seized an iron spike as they were about to pass it, and brought them into an eddy around the old bridge piling.

"Can you climb up on your own?" he asked. "I'll help push."

Vespa nodded, unwinding her arms from his waist and finding handholds in the rock under the water. He boosted her with his arm, and she managed to haul herself up onto the old piling.

He came up after her.

Shivering in her soaked underthings, she collapsed on the nearest rock and took several gasping breaths.

"Sorry about your . . . erm . . . gown," Bayne said as he wrung the water from his hair. His once-white shirt was stuck to his skin. Vespa forced herself to look away so that she wouldn't see the definition of muscles, the dark hair of his chest. Her hair was straggling out of the careful pins, so she finished it off, uncoiling it and wringing it out between her hands.

"It's all right," she said. "I'm sorry I didn't understand right away. I tried to get the petticoats off myself, but couldn't do that and swim, too."

"Wool can take on a lot of water. You'd likely have sunk if I hadn't . . ."

"No, really," she said, "no need to explain."

Vespa looked up at him again and wished she hadn't. He was beautiful with the morning sun touching his face and that look in his eyes that she could never quite understand. But she felt decidedly naked under his gaze and wished for all the world that she had enough magic to provide herself with a cloak. The magic simply wasn't there, though. Whatever had happened that had forced them into the river had drained her completely.

She heard Syrus shouting distantly over the cataract and realized he might not be able to see them. Bayne climbed to the other side of the piling and waved, shouting, "We're all right!"

Vespa rose and went to stand beside him, waving at Syrus. He'd gone as far as he could before the sheer walls rose up and the rocky shore disappeared into them. There were quite a few more pilings and turbulent river channels to cross before they could even get to where Syrus was.

Syrus's face went white then, and he pointed behind them. They both turned and looked over their shoulders.

"Bayne," she whispered, though she knew he couldn't hear her.

On the opposite bank, where the rocks rose into dark cliffs, a scarlet-robed figure stood. It had a human shape, but Vespa couldn't tell what it might be. As it turned away, she caught a glint of gold deep in its hood, but that was all.

"They will come back!" Syrus shouted across the water. "Hurry!"

Without a word, Bayne pulled Vespa close.

"I thought . . . ," she began.

"We're not in water now, are we?"

Before Vespa could even shake her head, Bayne pulled them from the piling to the bank next to Syrus.

"Take hold, Syrus," he said. "I think I can get us home. Just barely, but I think I still can."

Syrus nodded, and then they were dissolving again; this time, Vespa hoped, with a different result.

CHAPTER 5 ——

I'm gasping for breath as if I'm still in the water as we come to form in the parlor. Truffler enters, muttering and clucking as he sees what a state we're in. Piskel climbs from his basket, scolding us for waking him until he realizes that something is amiss. He floats over to me and puts his fingers over his nose. I guess I stink of the River too much for his liking.

"Hot water at stove," Truffler says, indicating we can bathe if we'd like.

We each go to our rooms to find fresh clothes. Gentlemen that we are in manners if not in title, we let Vespa bathe first.

"What happened?" I ask as we sit shivering by the parlor fire, waiting our turns at the bath.

Bayne is practically green with exhaustion. "If it is Ximu, as you say, then she's got a field surrounding the old City now. I can't transport us in there without getting stuck in her energy web. I'm wondering if that's how the kinnon got bitten—he may have flown into it accidentally and gotten stuck."

"And then somehow he managed to get free, only to die of his wounds. Poor chap."

Bayne nods.

"It's Ximu, all right," I say.

"What's confirmed it for you, since we couldn't manage to actually see her?"

I think about the scarlet-robed man and shiver. "The *xiren*. The man who was watching us—he is one of her Captains who can take human form. They wear robes like that, woven of their scarlet silk. And I saw the gold markings . . ."

Nainai always warned us to beware those who walked in scarlet. "Shoot first, ask later, where they're concerned," she said. I had always thought her advice so funny. What if the *xiren* changed colors on occasion? And why should I worry if they were extinct anyway?

I didn't worry until today.

Bayne nods.

Vespa opens the kitchen door then, patting her hair with a towel. She's dressed again in what I think is probably one of three gowns she owns, now that one of them is at the bottom of the River along with her petticoats.

"I . . . hmmm . . . have no other petticoats, so I suppose this will have to do for now," she says. "Else I shall have to resort to wearing trousers."

Bayne looks up at her, and something passes between them— that age-old something that I wish they would just resolve. She blushes and looks away from him. I often feel like I'm in the way, that so much is unspoken because of me, but then and again, I also know that it's much more than that.

"Your turn, gentlemen," she says.

I defer to Bayne. He looks far more uncomfortable than I am. "Your lordship," I say, gesturing toward the kitchen. He glowers at me, gathers up his fresh clothes, and enters the kitchen.

Truffler is toasting bread on the hearth in the parlor, and Vespa goes in to sit with him. I don't move, not wanting to soil anything with my wet clothes or offend Piskel with my stench.

Bayne is quick, and soon it's my turn. Good man that he is, he's refreshed the water, so I don't have to wait too long before I can pour it into the beaten-brass tub. It's not the most comfortable way to bathe—certainly not like the bathing rooms I glimpsed in the Grimgorn estate or Virulen Manor—but it'll do.

I don't want to think about anything as I scrub the River from my body, but one persistent thought worms its way in. If Ximu is in the old City, and I've no doubt of that now, then she apparently has something to hide. Something big.

When I'm clean and dressed, I return to the parlor just in time to see Bayne tucking an old quilt around Vespa, who's fallen asleep on the settee. He reaches out a trembling hand toward the curls that fall around her shoulders, but then he withdraws as if he's touched fire.

Those two. I clear my throat softly.

He turns. "I was just . . . making sure she sleeps. She needs rest after all that."

"Mm-hmm." Piskel is laughing behind him and making crazy, lovesick faces.

Bayne jerks his head toward the library. "Let's go in there. We'll catch her up when she wakes."

We go to the scarred table with toast and tea. Bayne clears away maps and books, except for an old map of New London, which he unfurls before us.

We both stare at it a long time. I'm looking at the curve of the

River, wondering if and how we can defend our side if anyone tries to cross it. The ravine gives us some advantage.

He's thinking the same thing, because he finally points to a place upstream near the old Tower.

"There," he says. "I think if it came to it, they would cross there. It's shallow there and not as wide, yes?"

I nod, thinking of the time when I swam the River against Truffler's urging and freed the Harpy. Bayne had been there. I never imagined when I hid under the Harpy's cage with him that we would one day be living in the same house, plotting how to defend the Empress against Ximu.

"You think there's an army, too?" I ask.

"I'm almost certain of it," he says. "What else would she be hiding there?"

"My thoughts exactly."

"We must tell the Empress," Bayne says.

I remember their exchange yesterday. "Won't she be angry that we disobeyed?"

"Perhaps," he says. "But I hope the information will finally open her eyes. We must have better defenses."

I ask the question I'm sure neither of us wants to contemplate. "Is it already too late?"

Bayne stands and begins to pace. He always paces when he's thinking or nervous. "It may very well be."

"Then . . . what can really be done? Can you and Vespa make a field like hers to protect the City?"

Bayne shrugs. "We could try. I'm not sure how successful it would be unless we could convince some Elementals to help us keep it going. And we obviously can't live this way forever, can we?"

"No. Ximu won't rest until everything belongs to her. That's always been her way in all the stories. I can't imagine that has changed."

"Olivia is right in one thing, at least," Bayne says. He opens a cabinet and fishes out paper, pen, and ink.

"What's that?"

"It would definitely be easier if we could all just learn to live together in peace."

I nod. "Yes. Yes it would."

But somehow I don't think that's going to happen.

While Bayne writes his letter, I fidget with the need to do something. I decide to go work on the boiler. It will take my mind off things, and it's something that I know will please Olivia if I can manage to fix it. I try not to think about whether soon it may not matter if I fix it.

I go to my workshop and find my favorite spanner on the bench right where I left it. I pull on the one dry coat I have left and return to the table.

"Are you off?" Bayne asks.

"Back to the warehouse to fix that boiler if I can." *Beats sitting around here fretting*, I want to say. But I don't.

He nods. "If you don't mind, carry this letter and ask that it be delivered to Doctor Parnassus."

I take the letter and put it in my pocket. Piskel floats over and settles in my collar. "Ready for another day in the dungeon?" I ask him. A resigned squeak is my only answer.

"What will you tell them about what we encountered?" I ask Bayne.

"Only the bits that are relevant, of course." He smiles, but it's brief and troubled. He looks down at the map again. We're still thinking the same thing. How can we defend what we've rebuilt, if it comes to that?

I think about it as I pick my way across town, the letter snug against my chest in my jacket. The rain from the kinnon's death and the autumn chill have made the streets into channels of cold, sucking mud.

It's an unpleasant journey, but I at last arrive at the warehouse and find a faun courier who's warming himself by a brazier outside. He agrees to take the letter to Doctor Parnassus, the satyr doctor who is head of the Elemental Council, and receives the letter with all due ceremony. I don't envy him the trek through the mud.

Back into the warehouse cellars I go, with Piskel muttering against my ear.

The boiler squats in the half light, taunting me. I eye it the way I would one of the boys I used to box in Lowtown as I take off my jacket.

I light my oil lantern and crawl inside very carefully. I will never wish for an everlantern, but I do wish for a thing like it that could produce light without the potential of catching everything on fire. It's a strange idea, I know.

I'm up to my elbows in grease again, and just thinking that Piskel is awfully silent when he comes zooming into the boiler. He bounces off the walls, sparking so hard, I'm afraid he'll blow us through the roof if he manages to ignite any of the fuel. I clap my hands around him.

"Stop! Before you blow us to bits!"

The buzzing in my hands calms, and when I open my hands, he is glaring at me. He wipes a smear of *myth*grease from his face.

"What?"

He tilts his head toward the outside and floats upward, gesturing that I should climb back out.

"But I just got in here. Is it really important?"

He stares at me with those gimlet eyes and nods slowly.

"Is it dangerous?"

Piskel shrugs.

I can't help but roll my eyes.

I climb back out carefully with the lantern. "If this is a prank, I'm not going to be happy about it."

I wipe my hands again on the rag and glance at my patched coat. I'd put it on, except that I'm still so thick with grease that I'd rather wash off first. But, thinking about the *xiren* I saw on the riverbank, I pick up the knife I keep nearby.

Piskel tugs at me, gesturing and buzzing toward the stairs. I follow him up out of the cellar and into the hall, which is crowded with people trying to get out into the courtyard.

I blink once I'm out in the midmorning light. Everyone's here—Councilors, guards, tradesmen, Elementals. I'm certainly not the only person with patched clothes. (Though I do seem to be the only one covered in grease). Gone are the eversilk coats and trousers, the elaborate wigs and beauty marks of days past. This New London is new indeed.

I'm not sure what they're all looking at until I notice the edge of a silver cloud above the building roofs.

It can't be.

Piskel makes a noise like: *Now do you believe me?*

Not yet. I let the crowd push me down the cobbled street until we get a clear view.

The airship floats at the edge of the Euclidean Plain like a dream. It's vast, bigger than anything I've ever imagined. It holds all of my attention, such that I don't notice the crowd is moving again until someone next to me jams their elbows into my ribs and smashes my toes.

I curse under my breath and am about to say it louder when I look round. The Empress walks down the makeshift aisle to stand beside me. I shut my mouth.

The morning sun lights her pale hair, much as it did yesterday when she stood in the window. I feel guilty that we disobeyed her and have the sudden urge to tell her everything that transpired earlier this morning. But I have a feeling that would be a very bad idea. I drop my gaze, afraid something on my face will betray me.

She smiles shyly. Her guard—a contingent of fauns—makes a small circle around just the two of us.

"Mr. Reed, I see you have been hard at work." I look up for a moment, and her gaze takes me in. I'm both embarrassed and proud at once.

"Yes, Your Majesty."

"And what have we here?" she says, looking toward the airship.

"No idea, Majesty."

A line of people moves down the gangplank, a parade of brightly feathered birds.

From a little pouch at her waist the Empress takes a pair of old opera glasses and looks toward them.

"Ah," she says. "I think perhaps we should summon Pedants Lumin and Nyx."

"Your Majesty?" I'm thinking of the boiler still half fixed, my tools scattered everywhere in the cellar.

"It would appear the Grimgorns have finally answered my letter."

• • •

When I tell Bayne the Grimgorns have sent an airship, I worry for a minute that I've made a mistake. He has that lightning-eyed look that I've come to dread. Though he's no longer the fine lordling with his heeled shoes and brocaded coats, he can still play the part. Piskel thinks I've slipped up too, because he cowers behind my ear, peeping out when it seems that Bayne is taking a while to answer.

Truffler enters from the parlor, trailing Vespa behind him, who has apparently just woken from this morning's nap. Truffler comes to stand beside me, patting my hand.

"And?" Bayne says.

Vespa's avoiding Bayne's gaze, probably for the same reasons I am, but that's not hard because all his attention is on me. I'm surprised I don't go up in a puff of smoke.

"Her Majesty asked that you both attend her," I say.

"Well, I suppose we should be off," Vespa says. "We wouldn't want the festivities to start without us." The false cheer is obvious in her voice as she bundles into her overlarge Pedant's robe.

Bayne's brow rises. "No, I'd imagine not."

"Do you think your father . . ." Vespa trails off as Bayne's expression hardens again.

"He is not my father," Bayne says. He throws on his Pedant's robe and digs out warding stones from the drawer in the library. He turns to me as he pockets the stones, and says, "You did get my letter off to Doctor Parnassus, yes?"

"Yes. A faun courier has taken it to him."

"Good. Council certainly has many things to discuss now."

Nothing to argue with there. I glance at Truffler to see if he wants to come along, but he shakes his head.

"Brownie," I taunt.

He shrugs. He much prefers forest and hearth to crowded streets or warehouses. He salutes me as he steps aside into the workshop, shedding clouds of hob hair as he goes. I try to keep myself from wishing I could just stay here with him.

We go back the way I came, and there is little discussion as we make our way. Vespa tries to draw Bayne out of his shell, but he doesn't really answer. Eventually, she gives up. He's strung tight as a bow. I'm almost glad that I'm not a Council member, and therefore will not have to be present when he and the Grimgorn entourage meet. I suspect it won't be pretty.

We part ways just beyond the doors. Bayne takes me aside and says almost in a whisper, "Say nothing to anyone of the *xiren*, do you hear? Now is not the time. It will be discussed in Council. For now, silence."

I nod. This is confirmation of what I felt earlier, and it's not like I come across many people in the cellar anyway. I make my way back down to where the cursed boiler sits like some dark Elemental. My stomach protests; I've had nothing to eat since our bit of toast, and I'm not likely to get anything until either I defeat this boiler or it defeats me for another day.

I knock at the boiler with my wrench, thinking of the old Tinker songs my uncles would sing outside the train cars as they worked on fixing anything from leather harnesses to small engines. Elder Ji told me of the great engines he'd worked on back when the trains ran from Scientia through Euclidea to here. The steam engines had run on coal, and he could remember shoveling coal into the boilers to make the engines run day and night. Back then, Tinkers worked on the engines and in the northern mines. It didn't sound much different from working for the Refineries, but my uncles always assured me that it was.

"There was nothing like the thunder of the iron horse across the Plain," Elder Ji used to say.

I wonder sometimes if that's why my people clung to the train-yard. They were nostalgic for that life of wandering on the iron horse, for the minesongs, for the Elementals they met on their journeys. But then there was always the Manticore to consider.

And now I am thinking of converting this boiler back to coal and wishing that I didn't have to. Coal may be better than *myth* in many ways, but it's dirty and causes disease, even if it doesn't directly take the lives of Elementals. I can't help but wish I could harness the sun's light as easily as Vespa and Bayne harness their magic. If I could convert sunlight into energy, there would be no end to it. Except when there's no sun, of course.

Piskel squeaks at me to stop dawdling and finish the thing. He's hungry too, I reckon. He could leave in search of food, but he stays, lighting my work with his golden glow so I don't have to use the oil lantern.

In the end, the boiler wins. Just as I'm attempting to reroute a major pipe, it falls apart in a shower of rust and unmoored fittings.

"*Hozide pigu!*" The old language is as good for cursing as it is for blessing.

Piskel holds his sides and laughs, his light fitful between gales of laughter.

I'm half-in, half-out of the blasted thing, spitting rust and *myth* residue out of my mouth, when I hear a slight cough.

"Sir Artificer."

The voice echoes through the maze of pipes. I haul myself from the boiler. It's gotten so dark now that I can barely make out one of the Empress's faun guards standing nervously nearby. He doesn't like the iron or the *myth* residue any more than I do.

"The Empress has requested your immediate attendance in the throne room."

I nod. Once again, I am covered in grease and rust. I wipe myself down with the rag as best I can, glaring at the boiler. I had no idea it was this late. We will meet again, and next time I will triumph. I hope.

Piskel follows behind us, humming to himself through the maze of pipes.

Upstairs there are smoking torches and lanterns, the result of a city now utterly devoid of *myth*. I am wishing we could somehow get a gas line in here and wondering how that might be possible. Then I think about the *xiren* I saw and wonder if anything will be possible soon.

The faun ushers me into the throne room, one of those galleries created to show off the merchants' wares to best effect. Banners of silk have been hung where the old drapes used to be. No one is about except guards and servants; the meeting regarding the arrival of the strange airship must have concluded.

The Phoenix Throne on which the Empress sits for Imperial business is ablaze with the failing sun's light. It was carved from deadwood by the dryads, inlaid with salvaged gold and precious stones by hobs and gnomes. Olivia sits in the center of all this richness.

"Forgive me if I'm blinding you, Mr. Reed," she says, getting up and coming down off the makeshift dais on which the throne rests.

It's then I notice the strange golden egg on the last step. She scoops it up and brings it to me. "I thought you might like to see this."

The egg is so large that I'm afraid she'll drop it when she opens her hand. I reach to catch it. She smiles because the egg is already unfolding itself, having put down tiny golden feet that clutch the edges of her palm. With unbelievable smoothness, a long, elegant neck unfolds, and jeweled eyes peer at me. A long, filigreed tail spreads across the Empress's wrist.

It's a mechanical Phoenix, very nearly an exact replica of the throne in miniature. Except that it can move, of course.

"The Grimgorns gave it to me," she says. "As a sign of faith and goodwill."

I am curious to know more, but she stays silent on that subject. I suppose I'll wait until I see Vespa before I get answers. Bayne isn't likely to want to talk about any of this. For reasons I can't explain, I feel uneasy about the little Phoenix, though I won't say so. Piskel does too. I can tell from the way he's frowning as he checks it out from every possible angle.

I reach out to touch it, and it snaps its tiny golden beak at me. In fact, I'd almost swear it hissed when it did so.

"What the . . . ?"

The Empress strokes it with her free hand, and the thing calms. "I think perhaps it only likes me," she says. "Though I can't quite fathom how that might be so."

I bite my lip. I don't either, but I don't want to say so. If it had been built with *myth*, there'd be no question. But I sense no magic, and neither does Piskel, much to his consternation. It doesn't look like any of the antique clockwork I keep in my workshop. Piskel's frown deepens; he pokes and prods at the Phoenix.

"Gently, Piskel," she says. She puts her other hand over the Phoenix to protect it, closing away all but the tail trailing across her wrist. Piskel grumps over to my shoulder and hides in my hair.

"It's like nothing I've ever seen, Majesty," I finally admit.

"Me neither," she says. "Would you like to take it with you and try to figure out how it's made? I would very much like to know who in Scientia is capable of making such things without magic."

I nod. I open my hands, and she places the Phoenix in them.

"It'll be all right," she says to the Phoenix. "Go with him." It bows to her and then folds itself back into an egg. Olivia's cool fingers dance across my skin, and it's all I can do not to shiver. I look into her eyes and see she's smiling. I want to ask her a million things, but my tongue seems to have tied itself in knots.

"Let me know what you find out, Mr. Reed."

It feels as though her fingers are still on my skin. Somehow I manage to untie my tongue. "I will, Majesty."

I shift the egg to my jacket pocket and bow. She holds her hand out to me then, and I realize I am meant to kiss it.

Praying I don't mar her with rust or grease, I take her hand in mine. I bend and press my lips just above her knuckles. I can't look in her eyes, though I feel hers on me. The skin on the back of her hand is as cold as her fingers. There's even a metallic tang against my lips, a charge like the spark off an old *myth* cell.

A deep shiver moves through her as she withdraws her hand, and it makes me smile just a little. I can give as good as I get. I risk a glance into her eyes and find mirrored there all the things I feel in her presence before she shutters them and steps away from me.

"Tell me what you learn."

"Of course, Your Majesty."

The gold egg is heavy in my pocket as I return home.

Chapter 6 ━

When Syrus entered the townhouse covered in grease, Vespa couldn't help but breathe a sigh of relief. It had grown dark since they'd returned from their impromptu meeting, and, after this morning's adventure, she was now more worried than usual for his safety.

"Any progress with the boiler?" she asked.

Syrus frowned and shook his head.

"Sounds rather like our meeting," Vespa said.

"What happened?"

Vespa looked him up and down. "Perhaps you'd like to wash up and eat first?"

He grinned, and Vespa smiled back. Food was always the way to his heart.

"Water's heating in the reservoir, and dinner should be ready by the time you've finished."

He nodded. She heard him shut the door as she went to the library that also doubled as a dining room and began clearing space for plates. She'd managed to get a good bit of mutton and late greens at the market today, since it had been her turn to do the shopping. Farmers had had a difficult time of it since the Rousing, and with trade routes all but dissolved or vastly reduced, anything exotic—oranges from Newtonia, spices from Babbageburg—was practically nonexistent in the New London market.

As she placed a battered fork, Vespa was struck by the oddness of her life. A year ago she had never expected to leave her family, certainly not for an arrangement as unconventional as this. What would her Aunt Minta think of the fact that she lived with two strange men, married or related to neither of them? She sighed and tried to ignore the inevitable path of her thoughts by returning to the parlor and building up the fire a bit so that Piskel's nearby nest would be cozier. He snuggled into the blanket she'd knitted for him inside his basket and fell asleep.

Dinner was finally served in the library. Bayne came down from his room, his face a bit less stormier than earlier. Truffler emerged from Syrus's workshop, his hairy hands dirtier than Vespa would have liked.

Syrus, on the other hand, was so clean, he almost shone. Two baths in one day was a record for him. He had washed his hair again, for it hung to his shoulders in long, raven ropes. Vespa was surprised at the realization that in just a year he'd become a young man.

He still wasn't the most polite eater, though. He slurped rice, greens, and mutton from his bowl with Tinker eating sticks so loudly that the noise echoed in the library. Vespa had tried to learn to use the eating sticks but found them nearly impossible. She'd dropped everything as soon as she'd managed to pick it up.

"What?" Syrus asked when he noticed Vespa staring at him.

"You're a bit noisy."

Evidently she wasn't the only one who thought so, because

Piskel floated in from the parlor, rubbing his eyes and grumbling. He plunked down on the table and fished a grain of rice out of Syrus's bowl, shoving it in his mouth with an expression of utter annoyance.

Vespa ignored Bayne's half smile as he pushed his mutton around with his fork.

"Just my way of complimenting the chef." Syrus smiled and slurped some more. "But if you don't want to hear it, talk. What happened at the meeting?"

Vespa was about to speak when Bayne said, "My erstwhile family have invited the Empress to join them in Scientia. They say there are urgent matters to discuss that can only be done in person."

"Why didn't they come here?" Syrus asked.

"Well, in point of fact, they did. They sent their envoy with gifts and an invitation. It would have been rude to just appear."

"But Olivia has written to them many times inviting them to visit, and each time has received no word," Vespa said. "They've known the invitation has been open for at least a year."

"Perhaps those letters never reached them."

"Wouldn't there have been news of a lost courier, though?"

Syrus coughed softly into his sleeve.

"It's likely a way of sparing the Empress embarrassment. She can barely lodge her staff and the envoy's entourage as it is. A full contingent from Scientia would overwhelm her. This is a matter of etiquette."

Bayne's voice was taking on that entrenched, level tone that Vespa dreaded. But she couldn't just let this go. The safety of the Empress and all they'd fought for might rest in the balance if Olivia went to Scientia.

"I still think it's a trap," Vespa said. "Especially considering what we saw this morning. It seems far too much of a coincidence, if you ask me."

"I know. I'll concede it's possible. But after a year's silence and no aggression from Scientia, I highly doubt that's likely."

Syrus quietly set the golden egg on the table. The Phoenix unfolded itself and glared at them with topaz eyes. Vespa remembered the envoy giving it to Olivia as a gift. She was still perplexed by the fact that it worked without magic and seemingly without recognizable gears.

She could see that Piskel was puzzled as well. He marched over with one of Syrus's toothpicks under his tiny arm to where the Phoenix sat. The Phoenix snapped at him when he tried to approach it. Piskel jabbed at it, poking it beneath one of its wings.

"Piskel!" Vespa reached to scoop him off the table.

But Bayne held up his hand. For the Phoenix, instead of snapping at the sylph again, reached under its wing, where an apparently secret compartment had slid open. It withdrew a small scroll of paper and threw it on the table. Then it folded back into itself, a lifeless egg once again.

Bayne reached across and unrolled the paper.

Written across it in neat letters was a long series of zeros and ones that seemed to stretch forever.

CHAPTER 7 ▬

Bayne whistles long and low.

Vespa frowns. "What is it?"

"If I'm not mistaken, that is the sacred language of Saint Boole," Bayne said.

"Saint Boole, who revealed the Doctrine of Logic?" Vespa asked.

"The same."

I shake my head. "I have no idea what you two are talking about."

Bayne spreads the paper in front of me. "These groups of ones and zeros mean something in the language of Logic and Mathematics."

"It's a code," I say.

"Yes. Someone is trying to send us a secret message."

"The Empress must be told of this," I say, rising from my rickety stool. I lean forward to scoop the egg and the scroll off the table, but Bayne stops me.

"Leave it here, if you please. I'd like to examine it further. Perhaps there are other compartments with more hints as to this note's origin. We may even be able to detect who wrote it." He glances sidelong at Vespa in challenge, and she raises her chin a bit. There will be a competition when I leave.

"Hao bao," I say.

Piskel refuses to go along this time, yawning and crawling into his little basket without so much as a "good night." I would go as a hound, but the embarrassing circumstances it leaves me in after transformation are less than desirable for talking to an Empress. So I run. Back through the dusk, with Truffler at my heels. As long as we won't be touching iron, he's fine with a bit of night air.

When I arrive at the warehouse, the guards recognize me, but they still cross pikes over the front door.

I pretend I'm Bayne with all his lordly ways. "I'm here to see Her Majesty on a most urgent matter!" Perhaps if I'm more businesslike, they won't question further.

And they don't.

They nod and slide the pikes aside. A satyr chamberlain leads me up to the Empress's receiving room, the one we saw her in just yesterday. It's chilly in here, and I feel chagrined. I need to get that boiler up and running.

When the Empress enters accompanied by one of her maids, I have the distinct feeling that she had already been undressed for the night. Her hair, usually pinned up in some fashion, is down across her shoulders. Her gown is very simple—at first I think it's a nightgown—and she walks without the stiffness of a woman in stays.

She notices me watching her. "It's a new fashion I'm trying, do you like it?"

I blush. "I suppose so, Your Majesty." I don't know what to say. All the girls in the Forest wore patched skirts and checkered head-bands, the symbols of their clans. The old ladies wore hats with the white chicken feather to symbolize the day we escaped marauding shadowspiders, because of the white rooster who crowed at dawn. Our women have been wearing that without variation since we can remember. I do not understand this thing called fashion.

She purses her lips, and I have a feeling I was meant to say something else. "I would guess you didn't return here for viewing gowns, though. What's so urgent, Mr. Reed?"

I tell her about the note that Piskel found.

"May I see it?"

"Vespa and Bayne wanted to try to find out more about its origins, but they thought you should know immediately."

She begins to pace, the white gown swirling around her like moonlight on leaves. Perhaps I do care a little for fashion after all. She doesn't say anything for a few minutes, and I'm unsure whether she even remembers I'm here.

Then she turns to me, her gaze deadlier than any of my darts. "I'm going back with you."

"But Majesty . . ." I can't tell her what I want to say. That there may be dangerous *xiren* walking our streets even now. Bayne forbade me to mention it, and I must hold to that. Perhaps I can convince him to tell her the truth once she's in the townhouse.

Under that gaze I fall silent. Truffler clutches my trouser leg.

"I'm going along, Mr. Reed. I need to see this for myself." After a breath she asks, "May I call you Syrus?"

You may call me anything you like, I want to say. But I nod instead.

She comes closer. There is again that light, clean, almost metallic scent. She smiles and says, "And you may call me Olivia when we are alone like this."

When we are alone like this. It echoes in my head until I can feel it radiating out through the blush in my cheeks. Will we be alone like this often? It is only for her to say.

She seems to be waiting for me to say something.

"Thank you, M—Olivia."

The smile lights her eyes as she nods. "I'll just get them to fetch my cloak and alert the guard to escort us," she says. "Meet me by the doors."

A contingent of faun sentries escorts us from the building. I'm glad of them. Even if I can't tell her why.

It's full night. The moon is obscured by webs of cloud, and a stiff breeze nearly puts out the torches the guards are carrying in addition to their pikes. I turn to the Empress and almost tell her to go back inside, so filled am I with foreboding, but she has already gestured the guard forward.

Truffler is clutching my trouser leg again and muttering. "All will be well," I say, but it really comes out as more of a question than a statement.

He looks up at me, and I don't like the fear in his eyes.

It's when we turn down an alley not far from the townhouse that I know something is very wrong. The moon disappears entirely. A nasty, skipping breeze blows out all the torches. The fauns sense the same wrongness I do, and the Captain calls for them to drop torches and ready pikes. Olivia looks over at me, and her eyes shine eerily despite the lack of light, like I imagine mine do when I'm in houndshape.

"We're nearly there," I say, trying to be encouraging. But I'm cut off by the whisper-sound of things dropping to the ground, the stuttered cries of fauns as their throats are cut. I drag Olivia with me against the wall so that our backs are against something. I look up and see eyes for just a moment. Spider-eyes. And the golden markings of the shadowspider glimmering on its forehead. *Xiren.*

"They've crossed the River." I hear myself say it as if from a distance. I can just about hear *Nainai* saying, "You can bet sure as sure that Ximu has something up her silk sleeves. She'll be back, have no doubt."

How right she had been.

"What's happening?" Olivia asks, huddling close.

I don't answer her. "Truffler . . ." I start to tell him to take Olivia and run as I draw my knife. But there's no time. The *xiren* falls upon her, and I hear her gasp.

I leap onto the back of the thing, trying to stab through its heavy cloak.

Truffler moans and wrings his hands behind us. There is nothing he can do.

The *xiren* has Olivia by the throat. It tries to throw me off its back but can't quite manage it. Finally it lets go of her to deal with me.

"Truffler," I shout, "take her and run!"

That at least the hob can do. I see him help her to her feet, and then the *xiren* takes up all my vision. The moon escapes the web of cloud then, and I am left gasping.

The *xiren* who has turned to face me stops.

Everything stops.

I'd know that face anywhere. It's engraved in my dreams. I still see it, telling me to go right before I dive through the window and the thunderbuss blast shatters behind me. Even despite the golden markings and the blackened skin, I know that face.

Uncle Gen.

"Syrus."

I can't speak. All I can do is gape at him. I am a fish slung from water to stone, desperately trying to breathe.

"You must come with me."

I flex my fingers on the dagger hilt. I don't want to kill him—not that nightmare again—but I also am fairly certain that I should.

I finally find my voice. "Why?"

"Because our Queen commands it."

"And my Empress forbids it."

He takes a step toward me, and I raise my dagger, stepping back. Uncle Gen makes a slight nod, and I realize my mistake as the arms enfold me from behind.

"Why?" I manage to choke out.

But the fangs descend into my neck, and all dissolves into darkness.

Chapter 8 ━

A wild thumping and muffled shouts brought Vespa to the door. She unlocked the warding charm to find Truffler hovering over someone slumped against the doorframe. Someone in a gown and a hood.

"Athena's Girdle!" Bayne breathed behind her. "Get them in here!"

Together they dragged Olivia over the threshold until Bayne could lift her up and carry her. Vespa locked the door behind them, setting the strongest charm on it she knew, her fingers trembling as she did so.

She returned to the parlor, where Bayne had propped Olivia up on the couch. Truffler was shuddering over by the hearth, and Piskel, woken by the commotion, was patting his friend's hairy head with one hand and yawning behind the other.

"What happened?" Vespa asked.

Bayne peeled back the Empress's hooded cloak from her throat.

Vespa's hands flew to her mouth at the sight of Olivia's hair and clothes matted with blood. She wanted to swear by St. Darwin but knew it wouldn't help in the least. Air seemed impossible to breathe, as if she'd just been plunged underwater or punched in the stomach.

"Is she . . . ?" She couldn't finish the question.

Bayne was feeling Olivia's pulses, delicately examining the wound. "No," he said finally. "But she isn't conscious."

Vespa looked around. And then there was another punch. "Where is Syrus?" she asked.

Truffler was crying on the hearth, big, fat tears that sizzled with blue light when they fell on the hot stones.

"Truffler, what happened?"

In fits and starts he tried to tell them, but the words were nearly impossible to understand.

Finally, Bayne interrupted him. "Look, Truffler, is Syrus alive or dead?"

"Alive when we leave him," Truffler said. "Must be still alive. Would know in here"—he touched his chest—"if not."

"You would know if he died?"

Truffler nodded.

"Who did this?" Bayne asked. But Vespa was fairly certain she already knew the answer.

"*Xiren.*"

"By the Ineffable Watchmaker . . . ," Bayne began.

Vespa stared in shock.

"But how—" Now it was Bayne who couldn't force out the words.

"Many of them kill the faun guard. They take Syrus," Truffler said.

Olivia groaned and stirred a little, and they turned back to the task at hand.

"I'll get hot water and cloths," Bayne said. "We'll figure the rest out in a bit."

Vespa nodded, too numb to say more. She was thinking of the shriveled exoskeleton of the shadowspider back in the Museum, and Lucy Virulen's bridal gown, spun entirely of the finest scarlet shadowspider silk. She contrasted all that she had once known with the scarlet-robed figure silently watching them that morning. And there was the spider-figure who had lurked behind the webs of dark energy that had nearly ensnared them before they were dumped into the River. She shook her head. Nothing could be stranger than this.

She held Olivia's hand, and the Empress shuddered at her touch. Her eyes were rolling under their lids. Her skin was clammy and gray.

Bayne returned with a pan of water and clean cloths. Vespa dipped one in and wrung it out with shaking hands. "There must be something we can do against this," she said. "Some charm or spell." She couldn't bear to think of the potential repercussions of the bite. And she couldn't bear to think of Syrus, somewhere behind that dark field of energy, suffering the same.

"I know of a tonic for when people are bitten by other werebeasts," Bayne said. "But whether it will work on a shadowspider bite . . ." He shook his head.

Though the cloths came away bloody, it was soon apparent that Olivia hadn't lost as much blood as it had at first seemed. The bite, however, was disturbing—an angry purple knot with a red ring around it. It was hot to the touch and swelling quickly.

"This must be what Syrus saw on the kinnon," Vespa said.

"We should call Doctor Parnassus," Bayne said. "Truffler, Piskel, do either of you know how to find him in the Forest? He received a letter from me to call Council, so he should be aware that there are problems."

"Though I doubt he's expecting these kinds of problems," Vespa muttered.

Truffler nodded. "I find him," he said. Between one breath and the next, Truffler was gone. Piskel floated over to Olivia. He checked under her eyelids and looked up her nose. He listened to her breathing and cooed sadly as he fluttered near her. He looked at Vespa and shook his head.

"I know," she said. "I know."

"Piskel," Bayne said, "can you go alert the Imperial household? Let them know what's happened to the guard and that the Empress is safe here for the moment."

Piskel nodded, his eyes like lanterns in the low light. He fled up the chimney and out into the night.

"Let's get her somewhere more comfortable," Bayne said. He scooped Olivia up again and carried her upstairs.

Vespa looked around her before following him up. The house was quiet, almost too quiet. She realized she had no idea what the shadowspiders could actually do. Could they crawl down a chimney or under a door? Was their magic strong enough to break the wards? If so, the house could be overwhelmed with them before they knew it.

She shivered and prayed to the false saints under her breath that the wards would hold.

After they'd settled Olivia in as best they could, Bayne said, "I'll brew the tonic. It may not help and it may make her feel a bit worse, but it can't ultimately hurt."

"I don't see how it could get much worse," Vespa whispered. Now, as the lantern flickered over Olivia's pale hair and paler skin, Vespa allowed herself to fully feel the tenuousness of their situation. Unknown Elementals had wounded the Empress and taken Syrus. And someone in Scientia had sent them a secret message that she was sure had no better news than this.

She looked at Bayne, seeking solace. Tentatively he put an arm around her. Just this morning he had saved her life. Now Olivia's life hung in the balance, and possibly Syrus's, too.

"Do you think they hurt Syrus?" she asked.

He shook his head. "I don't know," he said. "But if they took him, as Truffler says, I'm guessing they may have other plans for him."

She wanted desperately to lean her head against his shoulder, but feared that he would pull away if she did. So she stood, feeling the warmth of his hand against her waist and trying to find some measure of comfort in that.

"He's a clever boy," he said. "He's escaped death many times before this."

Vespa looked up at him. "I know."

He looked as if he wanted to say something more, but he stepped back, glancing at Olivia. "I'll just go brew that tonic now."

She bowed her head as he closed the door behind him.

The world suddenly felt so cold.

Vespa didn't know how she had fallen asleep. She dimly remembered Bayne bringing the tonic. And he must have put a blanket over her as she nodded in the chair by Olivia's bedside, though she couldn't quite fathom it.

She had just woken from a strange dream. In it she had found herself in a chamber that she knew from the lack of windows and light to be deep underground. She held a lit candle, and its faint flicker tricked out gold bedframes, lanterns, baskets of what looked like loaves of bread and jars of oil, and elaborate carvings of Elemental creatures long lost to antiquity. There was a sense of great urgency. She needed to find something, and she needed to find it before many people died. She knew that. But she had no idea what she was seeking. She was deeply frustrated and utterly lost.

Restless, afraid she'd wake Olivia, Vespa floundered out of her blanket and stood. She longed momentarily for her old cozy slippers and wrap, both lost during the Rousing. She thought she had seen a book on dream interpretation somewhere and hoped that perhaps she could find it quickly and read it in the parlor undisturbed for a few moments. She didn't want to leave Olivia alone too long.

She opened the door as carefully as possible, whispering a silencing spell as she passed and trying to ignore the chill of the bare boards on her toes.

She was halfway down the stairs when she realized that the magic was working again. She'd set a strong charm on the door earlier and now had been able to keep the wood from creaking. Maybe she'd just needed something to help her focus.

She also realized she'd forgotten to light a lantern for herself. She tried to make a flame in her hand as she'd seen Bayne do, and was pleased when a little blue spark danced to life on her palm.

Just as she crossed the threshold into the library, the flame went out. Immediately she stubbed her toe on the table leg and swiped several books off the table in the process of keeping herself from falling. She hopped on one foot, cursing under her breath.

A light flared, and she startled. Bayne, who had seemed little more than the lumpish shape of a quilt in a chair, resolved into himself. He held a yew stake in one hand and an oil lamp in the other. His eyes were shadowed midnight blue. He looked almost leaner and more wolfish-looking than Syrus did these days. The harsh light aged him well beyond his nineteen years, and she could imagine how he would look, years hence. He was as beautiful by night as he was by day, old as well as young.

Vespa tried not to curse aloud again. She hated it when she couldn't ignore her attraction to him, and that seemed to be happening with greater frequency than usual.

"And to what does the library owe this visit?"

He'd seen her nearly naked this morning in her chemise and corset. Bare feet shouldn't matter so much, but she found herself trying to shake her gown around her ankles, as if the rumpled hem could somehow hide them.

"I might ask the same of you," she said, looking down at her toes.

"I'm keeping watch. But I gather that's not why you're here."

She shook her head. "I can't sleep anymore. I was looking for a book."

"About?"

After the Rousing, Bayne had collected all the books he could find and brought them here. She knew he'd be able to find what she wanted faster than if she just pretended she could find it on her own. But she was hesitant to tell him. It wasn't that she wanted to hide her dreams from him. She just didn't want to appear incapable of solving her own problems. She had been very careful to find her own solutions and learn in her own way, rather than relying on him to train her, even though she knew she probably made everything harder on herself by doing so.

He had found her obstinacy puzzling and infuriating—he had said as much—but had eventually given in to it, as he did with most everything these days. Except for the one thing she most wished he would give in to, of course.

She wasn't about to let him know that. And she didn't think he was about to give in.

"Dreams," she said at last.

To his credit, he didn't ask the nature of them. "Second bookcase to your left, seventh shelf."

She looked up. The ladder was on the other side of the room, and she wasn't quite tall enough to reach without it.

Bayne put the quilt aside and rose. "The ladder's too far, and you'd likely fall off it anyway."

She glared at him. He brushed past her, and she stepped out of his way before she could feel the etheric charge that always danced between them. Shaken as she still was by the dream and all that had happened today, she didn't want to deal with this now too.

He pulled the book off the shelf and handed it to her. She slid her fingers out of the way just before their hands would have touched. She had spent the past year adjusting to their relationship as business partners. They had gotten too close today, and she could feel that. She needed some distance. She couldn't endure having her heart shattered again.

Vespa had once believed being a Pedant would be more than enough.

Now it would have to do.

She looked down at the book. *Dreams and Their Interpretations: A Compendium of Magical Insights.*

"If you are having dreams, particularly a cycle that repeats, that could mean you are growing into the next phase of your power," Bayne said.

Vespa looked up at him. Words she couldn't say clutched her throat as his gaze swallowed her whole.

"You will need help if this is the case. Your power, repressed for so long, is likely to overwhelm you."

She frowned. "How's that? It's never done so before."

"But you had the Heart. Though it was powerful, I suspect it steadied you, helped channel your growing magic. Now there is nothing."

Somehow, though he obviously didn't intend it, his words were like a punch to the gut.

Because they were true.

She'd thought the same thing this morning. She'd only carried the Heart of All Matter briefly, just long enough to return it to its rightful owner. But she remembered how she'd felt—capable of nearly anything and more dangerous than she cared to admit. She remembered how the power had moved through her like blood. Like fire. She couldn't bring herself to say how much she missed having the Heart when it had never been hers to begin with, but sometimes that place in her chest where it had lived felt unutterably hollow.

She deflected all she felt by asking about him instead. "Was it like that for you? In the beginning, I mean. Unsteady and hard to manage?"

"Occasionally. But I was very good at hiding my power. It was never suppressed like yours was."

She clutched the book tighter, glad to talk about something besides herself or the ever-present dangers that plagued them. "No?"

"My parents had far too much else to worry about. I rarely saw them. It was easy for me to go off by myself in Scientia during the transition times when the power was growing and changing. Luckily, it only caused obvious problems twice. The first time, no one saw and I was able to put it to rights. The second, I was fortunate to be observed by an Architect who began my training shortly thereafter. I was ten. I've been in training ever since. Until now."

She nodded. There had always been secret encouragement of her Scientific learning from certain Pedants at the Museum, but that was as far as it went. She almost couldn't imagine not only being aware of her own power from the beginning but also being mentored by someone in the art from a young age.

"But weren't you afraid? Didn't you ever once feel you should give yourself up for heresy?"

"The thought occurred to me, but the Architect convinced me otherwise. He opened my eyes. I'm sure it was easier because of my youth."

Sorrow echoed in his voice. His mentor—and all the Architects—had been murdered by the Grue. Bayne was the last, the only, Architect remaining, as far as they both knew.

She had never seen him grieve once, though Syrus had said Bayne had wept as he closed the Architects' eyes.

Vespa didn't know what to say. "I'll just take this and study it, then. I'm sure something will turn up."

He nodded. Her heart sank as she turned toward the parlor. She wanted to say something that would ease the discomfort, something to bridge the chasm between them.

"Vee," he said. His voice was low and urgent. There was no fun in it as there had been this morning. Steady, she remembered thinking once, when he'd saved her from the Sphinx.

She closed her eyes for a moment and then turned, hugging the book to her chest.

"I can help you if you'll let me. It wasn't this way for me, but it was still frightening. Dealing with it alone must make it even worse. In the time that may come, we will need all the power you can muster."

For a second, a single second, she thought he'd forgiven her. She thought he had finally let go of his anger over being charmed into marrying Lucy Virulen. Maybe all her diligent work, her careful respect, would finally make him see that she meant him no harm.

He took a step toward her and then stopped, his brow furrowing. Concern transformed into uncertainty and mistrust. His eyes were shadowed again as he said, "But then, you do always seem to prefer doing everything on your own, don't you?"

He was still afraid that she would somehow snare him, still wounded that she'd charmed him, even when she'd had no idea she was doing so. Still. A year later, after her heartfelt apology, after all they had been through.

It was infuriating.

She lifted her chin. "Of course. I wouldn't want to put you to the trouble."

"It's not—" he began, then sighed.

His face hardened. The vulnerable moment was utterly gone. "I'd better get back to my post. Truffler says the *xiren* can be relentless, and we don't really know what they're capable of."

"What about Syrus?" she asked. "When are we going after him?" She was beginning to feel that every moment might be precious.

"We'll find him. Have no fear. We need to wait at least until the doctor gets here. I don't want to leave you alone with the Empress, and I certainly don't want you going off by yourself to try to handle this." It was as if he'd read her mind again.

She nodded, even though she wasn't entirely happy with the answer.

He returned to his chair and doused the oil lantern.

Vespa went slowly into the parlor, trying to pretend the moisture that fell on her hand was a stray droplet of water rather than a tear.

She couldn't go back to her room now. She knew she'd burst into sobbing if Olivia happened to wake and question what she was doing.

No, she'd sit here alone and read for a bit before checking on Olivia. Bayne had said earlier when they put her to bed that she'd probably succumb to night sweats and seem even more feverish for a bit. Vespa hoped that the discomfort Olivia was going through would help cleanse the poison from her body. She wished the doctor would get here, though she worried that somehow the shadow-spiders would make that impossible. And would they let Olivia be? Surely they knew where she was now. The shadowspiders might return and bring friends.

And poor Syrus. Even if, as Truffler said, he was still alive, she feared what might be happening to him. After a year of relative quiet it was all a bit much.

She turned the thick pages of the dream book slowly, reveling in their must. She wasn't sure what she was looking for. What was the room she'd dreamed herself in, exactly? The book smelled just like the Museum had—leather and paper, formaldehyde and ink. Only one odor was missing—that faint scent of burned bone that came from *myth* power. Vespa didn't miss that in the least.

A movement around the dying fire caught her eye. Piskel had returned. He floated over to her shoulder, clearly exhausted.

"Were you able to speak to the chamberlain? All is well there?"

He nodded, gesturing that all was well and there had been no further attacks.

It still surprised her that Piskel stayed with them. He had been angry at her for a long time for working in the Museum and for the fact that all his brethren had gotten dusted—quite literally—by the Grue. Only later had they learned that the Grue was actually eating the other Unnaturals in the Museum when he could to boost his power as much as possible.

Now Piskel was alone, the only sylph of his species in this part of the world. Somewhere across the sea beyond the jungles of Newtonia, there was a grassland where Piskel had said his people roamed. It had taken a while to figure all that out until one day they'd all been looking at a map together, and Piskel had marched across the Winedark Sea and thumped down on the unnamed savannah with such a disconsolate look that finally his origin dawned on Vespa. She'd known that Pedant Simian had gone somewhere beyond Newtonia on his expedition, but not precisely where. Piskel didn't particularly like the forest sylphs he'd encountered on his journeys with Syrus, so he stayed here most of the time, curled like a cat in his basket.

He looked over her shoulder at the book. Then he pointed to her head and made strange little gestures and noises.

"I had a dream, Piskel. About buried treasure."

She turned to the entry entitled "Treasure."

If the subject finds himself dreaming repeatedly of treasure,
buried or otherwise, he is about to enter a new phase of life.
He is seeking new power, buried within him, which will come
to fruition when the dream cycle finally ends.

Either that, or he is possessed.

"Perfect." Vespa sighed and snapped the book shut. Piskel looked between her and the book. The next thing she knew, he was inspecting her—looking in her ears, making her follow him with her eyes, looking up her nose.

"Stop it, Piskel," she said. "I am not possessed."

He stuck out his tongue and shook his head at her as if to say that possessed or no, she was still not right in the head. She rolled her eyes and yawned.

But when she put her head on the couch and curled up against the worn pillow, he nestled in the crook of her arm, his tiny warmth radiating against her side.

Chapter 9 ⬛━

When I wake, my head is throbbing and everything is upside down.

No. I'm upside down. Which is why my head is throbbing.

I can't really feel my toes. My hands are pressed to my side, and when I breathe, my chest is constricted. I look down—or up, I suppose. My body is wrapped tightly in scarlet thread. I'm hanging from the rocky ceiling like a shank of meat in a butcher's stall.

I suppose that's pretty much what I am.

The smell of meat, in fact, permeates the chilly air. Or something more like rendering fat. I remember what that smelled like in the autumn, when Uncle Gen would drive a pig or two down from the Virulen market for slaughter.

Uncle Gen.

The terror that grips me at least pushes my sluggish blood to my toes so that I can feel them tingle painfully for a few seconds before they recede again into numbness.

The last thing I remember is seeing Uncle Gen's face and realizing that he had become *xiren*. How has this happened?

I had searched for my kin. For months I had sought them in the Refineries and throughout the Forest as it grew anew. I listened for any whisper or rumor of them. They were nowhere to be found. The Refineries had been blasted open in the Rousing, and everything was gone. At last even I had to admit that they must all be dead. I had mourned them. I had performed the funerary rites at the proper intervals to ensure their souls were at peace.

But this is worse, so much worse, than discovering all of them dead. I have a bad feeling that more than Uncle Gen have been caught in Ximu's web.

My stomach rumbles, and there's an awful moment where I'm sure I'll vomit. Will I die if I vomit upside down?

The silk thread shields the parts of me that are wrapped from the cave's damp chill, but my face is freezing. (I'm sure my toes are too. I just can't feel them.) There's a strange glow on the walls, perhaps some sort of cave moss.

I look around. There are many others swinging here, some of them Elementals like Truffler. Possibly a few humans—the ones who have gone missing lately that no one has been able to find. Most of them are silent, but some make small moans or whimpers of pain. Beyond that, there is only the sound of water trickling here and there, and farther away, feet clicking and shuttling endlessly, as if the *xiren* are building something huge.

I don't know what I'll do about Uncle Gen and any other Tinkers who might be here, but one thing is clear. I need to get out of here.

I can't move my arms or legs even the slightest bit. I try expanding my chest with a big breath, but eventually have to let it out because the threads still don't budge. I try shrugging my shoulders up and down. There's a bit of give there but not much. And, of course, nothing's close enough for me to sink my teeth into.

This cannot mean anything good. Though my memory right now is fuzzy, I know that *Nainai* told us tales of the fierce battles between Ximu and Blackwolf, the Tinker King. He had fought the *xiren* after being betrayed by Ximu herself. He defied the Law when he felt justice required it. Blackwolf had been a great builder of things. *Nainai* had said that he'd built an army to chase the *xiren* across the sea, and he'd been the one to raise the wards against them.

But what had happened to him after that, I can't remember.

And then I remind myself that isn't the point anyway. I'm hanging upside down in a *xiren* meat locker, probably to be fed to their queen as a toothsome treat once they fill me full of their venom. If they haven't already.

Something clicks and hisses along the corridor outside. From my position it looks like something comes crawling in on the ceiling, even though I know it's the floor. It's about the size of a large dog or small pony. It walks on eight legs and looks mostly like a spider, except that it has a human face. Or what passes for it. I can see too that bits of it are welded together; hoses and soldered pipes connect the head to the spider body. They are making hybrids.

My stomach rumbles again, and a vile taste hits the back of my throat.

I shut my eyes, hoping it won't notice that I'm awake.

I feel it poke at me with a metallic foot. "I know you're awake, Tinker," it says. "You can't fool me."

Still I keep my eyes closed.

"Doesn't matter," the thing mutters. Its voice bubbles and hisses as if it can't quite get control of it. I hear it hack and spit out a gob of something on the floor. I swallow the bile in my mouth.

It pokes at me harder, and I can't help but twist, helpless in my cocoon. I can smell its poisonous breath.

"You aren't done yet," it says. "The Queen has special plans for you."

I crack open an eye. It's all I can do not to scream at the slobbering face pressed close to mine. "Special plans?" I choke. I feel like I could soil myself in terror, except the idea of what would happen if I did that upside down is just unpleasant enough to give me the control not to.

"Yes. Your uncle has spoken highly of you to Her Majesty. You will be fed only on her venom so that you may tell her whether the army she is raising has a chance of victory."

"Well, I don't really need her venom for that, thanks. The answer is yes."

The hybrid-thing cuffs me in the face with one of its whip-steel legs. I feel a slash open on my cheek.

"We are not talking of your puny Empress across the River. Ximu will take New London easily. We are talking of the army that sits in the north."

"Army in the north? What army in the north?"

The thing puts its face so close to mine that when it speaks, acidic spittle burns my face. "You will know soon enough. Or else you will be little more than meat for the Queen's brood."

There's a sharp pain in my neck, and I descend into nightmares—a flaming dirigible, white halls made of bone, a forlorn woman sweeping tombs under a dark sky.

But there is one dream. Olivia, sweet Olivia, in my arms.

• • •

My next visitor is even more unpleasant.

"Cut him down." It's my uncle, and at first I'm confused because he is dead. I remember him dying. And then I realize that I don't remember that at all, that my dreams have been so full of death that I don't know what's real anymore.

Then I'm being cut down, and thin spider arms are carrying me, sitting me upright against a wall. I'm still bound, so I can't really move much, but the relief of not being upside down almost makes me want to weep.

My neck aches terribly, and nausea rumbles through my stomach. I have no idea when I last ate, but I feel as though something has slowly been digesting me for days. A very unsettling thought.

"Syrus."

I open my eyes. I didn't realize I'd closed them.

"Listen to me, *waisheng*. I know how wrong this must seem to you, but believe me that I had no choice. We were taken from the Refinery during the chaos by *xiren* agents. The Manticore's death and the Heart's freedom lowered the wards and allowed them through."

"I don't understand." It's very hard to speak. My tongue is thick either with thirst or poison.

"Just know this—we had no choice. It was either do as the *xiren* bid or die."

I squint at him because everything has suddenly gone fuzzy. "Oh, I think you had a choice. And you made the wrong one."

"Queen Ximu has a plan for us. When the choice is offered and you see what you can become, I think you'll change your mind," Gen says.

"I already am what I want to be," I say.

"We shall see," he says. He turns to one of the hybrids waiting near him. "Truss him back up. He's not ready yet."

I hear his boots crunching on the cave floor as he walks away. "Gen!" I shout, but it comes out more like a croak. My throat is lined with cotton. "Gen! Don't leave me! Don't—"

The hybrids seal my mouth shut with their sticky threads.

Chapter 10 ━

It was close to morning when Doctor Parnassus arrived. The satyr came with dryads and servants and a heavily-armed escort; there was even a Minotaur among them who sported a wicked-looking axe.

Vespa ushered them in without preamble. Except the Minotaur, of course, who stationed himself outside the door.

Bayne came to greet the doctor, shaking his hairy hand.

"I received your letter, Pedant," the satyr said. "We have much to discuss."

"So it would seem."

The satyr looked around him, swinging his horned head as if trying to catch a scent. "I suspect the patient is upstairs?"

So the rumors were true, Vespa thought. Satyrs did indeed have an excellent sense of smell, which was probably why they'd once been used as poison tasters in the former court of the Emperor before they'd gotten so scarce.

"This way, sir," she said. She led them upstairs. The dryads and the doctor filed in, but before Vespa could join them, one of the dryads closed the door gently in her face.

Downstairs, Bayne was musing over tea in the parlor while Truffler warmed himself by the fire.

"I think it's time we went after Syrus," Bayne said.

"But what about Olivia?" Vespa asked.

"I doubt anything is getting through that Minotaur in broad daylight."

Vespa hesitated. "Shouldn't we seek Her Majesty's permission this time?" She didn't want to remind him what had almost happened last time they'd gone off on their own.

Then she heard the satyr's hooves on the stairs. One of his dryad attendants helped him on with his coat, and another handed him his cane.

"Doctor?" Vespa said, taking a step toward him.

He looked down his mulish nose at her. "Pedants," he said to her and Bayne, "I'm afraid there is nothing I can do."

"What do you mean?" Vespa said. A deep shudder began inside her. She was torn between being paralyzed by fear and wanting to run up the stairs.

"I cannot treat this. I think that perhaps you'd be better served to get yourself an Artificer."

"An Artificer?" Bayne asked, frowning as he rose from the settee. "Whatever do you mean?"

Doctor Parnassus looked around. "Haven't you got a Tinker about? I think he'd be far more help with your problem than I would be."

"He's been taken captive by the *xiren*," Vespa said.

"All the gods help us, then," the satyr said. He finished adjusting his coat and perched his little bowler hat between his horns.

"Doctor—" Bayne began.

The satyr held up a dark palm. "Now I must say no more, Pedant. Her Majesty asked for my confidence, and I've given you more information than I should have. Retrieve your Artificer. He will help more than I can."

He shook his head then, muttering about what had happened to education and etiquette in these dreadful times.

Vespa wished Syrus was here. Would the doctor have spoken more freely to him? Why had the doctor said Syrus would be of more help than he could?

"I shall see you both on the morrow at Council, I hope," Doctor Parnassus said. "Good morning." He nodded briskly and was out the door. His dryads followed, casting them embarrassed looks and dropping leaves over the threshold as they departed.

Bayne and Vespa looked at each other and both hurried up the stairs as quickly as they could.

Olivia was sitting upright in bed, drinking a cup of tea. The bite had been covered with a bandage. She looked pale and a bit feverish but otherwise fully herself.

"Pedants, good morning," she said, smiling.

Vespa and Bayne looked at each other. What in the world had the doctor meant?

"It is indeed a good morning, Your Majesty," Bayne said, bowing.

Olivia glanced at the maid who was hovering. The maid took the message and shut the door behind her as she went out on the landing.

"What's happened? Where is Syrus?" Olivia looked back and forth between them, fear creeping into her expression.

"What do you remember, Majesty?"

She touched the bandage at her throat before saying, "Something— spider-beings—fell upon my guard and slaughtered them. I was bitten, but Syrus and Truffler saved me. Is he . . . ?"

"We don't know," Vespa said. "Truffler believes him to still be alive. With your permission, we plan to find out." She carefully avoided looking at Bayne. They still hadn't mentioned their failed attempt at spying. She doubted now that there was any need.

"Granted." Olivia nodded and then winced at the pain. "But first, Syrus said there was a message hidden in the Phoenix. What was it? Did you find anything further?"

Bayne shook his head. "We can't yet read it. It's written in the sacred language of Saint Boole. We've done a few preliminary spells. We've examined the type of writing paper and the graphology. We need someone who is good at ciphers."

"I love ciphers!" Olivia said. "Let me see it. It will give me something to do while you're gone."

Bayne took the tiny scroll from his pocket and unfurled it for Olivia. She took it, spreading it on the coverlet between her hands.

"Interesting," Olivia said. "I suspected there was more to the envoy's visit than a simple invitation."

"We will happily do more to solve it when we return," Bayne said. "I think you will be well enough here; there are guards and servants aplenty, and we have put a heavy charm on the house to protect you."

"Yes, please go and find Syrus. And all of you return in one piece," Olivia said. She held out her hands to them. Vespa took the hand proffered her and squeezed it before letting go and bowing. Bayne did the same.

"Be well and bring Syrus home to us," Olivia said.

"Your Majesty," they both said.

Despite the danger, Bayne wanted to use the cover of night to sneak into the old City. "We've lost any advantage we already had.

They'll expect something. Night and the dark powers may hide us better than the tides of day will help. We can take glamours once we're inside."

Vespa frowned at this. "Are you certain?" They had never really tried anything like this before. The closest thing she could recall was when they'd discovered the secret entrance to the Tower Refinery and nearly gotten themselves captured by the Raven Guard. They'd had a better idea then of what they were walking into. This time, they knew nothing.

He smoothed the old map of New London on the table. "I've tested as well as I can where the field is weakest—"

"How?" Vespa interrupted.

"Very delicate, prodding magic," Bayne said. He continued, "I think if we go up along the River to the shallower parts near the Tower, we should be able to cross without incident. I want to use as little magic as possible until we need it most."

"Cross the River? We're going to swim it? In the dark?"

Bayne nodded. "It's risky, I'll admit. And if you don't want to go . . ."

Vespa rubbed her arms for warmth. The library was chilly with the memory of the freezing River. "No, I'll go. Just . . . don't get rid of my clothes again."

He smiled. "I'll try not to, so long as you aren't intent on drowning."

Bayne had lost the satchel of magical items in the River. All he had left were a few fireglobes and smoke mirrors, which he placed in his pockets. "These will have to do," he said.

Vespa sensed the trepidation in his voice. It mirrored her own, even if she wouldn't admit to it. She felt vastly underprepared without the Heart to steady her. Bayne's earlier offer of training smarted all the more because she knew she needed it, even though she was unwilling to say so. She had been trying to limp along with books and her own private practice sessions when she and Bayne were not out investigating some Unnatural event, but something was still missing. For all that she had been told of her potential, she didn't feel she was anywhere near meeting it.

"Well, that's that, then," Bayne said. Twilight had fallen outside. It was time.

Vespa could only nod. She didn't want to give voice to the thousand fears bubbling up in her chest.

Truffler was curled on the hearth when they approached him, but he sat up as he heard their footsteps. Piskel peeped out of his basket.

"We're going to try to find Syrus," Vespa said. "Do either of you want to come along? There's absolutely no shame if you don't."

Truffler came and took Vespa's hand. "Bring him back." It felt almost like a blessing; a little zing of magic went up her arm.

Piskel crawled from his basket and floated over to Vespa. He flew up to perch on her chignon, and she felt him nestle there. It reminded her of the way she'd nestled into the Heavenly Dragon's side after Syrus returned his Heart. And now, apparently, Syrus was the one who needed rescuing.

"Right," Bayne said.

He strongly warded the door as they left, Vespa lending him her energy to do so.

"There," he said. "Not even a Minotaur should be able to get through that now."

The Minotaur on guard looked down at him and snorted. "No offense," he said.

"Shall we, then?" Bayne asked. He put out his arm and Vespa took it.

Next she felt herself melting from the street. The relief at the dissolution of her body and all her worries was so great that for a timeless moment, she wished she could stay this way forever.

They came to form on the River bank, and her heart was just as heavy out in the moonless night as it had been in the candlelit room. Would they be able to free Syrus or were they just walking straight to their own deaths? What would happen to Olivia if they failed? And what had Doctor Parnassus meant about needing an Artificer to help her?

Vespa wrestled with the questions as Bayne went to the River's edge and stared across it. If possible, it looked even darker over there, as if a void had swallowed everything, even the stars from the sky.

"You still want us to swim this?" Vespa asked.

"We need to save all the power we can," Bayne said.

Vespa didn't relish being in the icy River again, nor was she happy about the prospect of slogging through the dark City in wet clothes. "Piskel, do you think you can carry our clothes across for us?" Piskel grumbled and sighed at such a menial task, but he nodded.

A long, uncomfortable silence stretched between them.

"Well, then," Vespa said. "Now or never, Pedant!"

She began unbuttoning her dress and slipped out of it in the chilly night air. She hoped Piskel could carry the weight of her corset and that he'd deign to carry her drawers and chemise. Relacing the corset might be a little difficult without the doorknob, but she'd figure that out if she made it across the River intact.

She heard Bayne sliding out of his shirt and jacket—the only one he possessed now—and saw the faint gleam of his skin under the stars. He muttered about how magicking up a boat would have been easier and quicker, but he made no other complaint.

The only sound besides the occasional *skezink* of autumn katydids was that of Vespa's laces being pulled from their eyelets.

Eventually they both stood in the dark, shivering. Piskel picked up one item at a time and slowly huffed and puffed it over to the other side.

"Now or never," Bayne said. His grin could be heard if not seen.

Then she saw the pale flash of him running toward the water and the splash as he dove in.

She followed a bit more gingerly. She wasn't keen on being in the River again after yesterday's adventure, especially not in the dark.

The icy water nearly stopped her heart as she stepped from the shallows into the current. She pushed as hard as she could against the rushing water, remembering to swim across it as Syrus had tried to show her. It carried her a little downstream, but at last she was bumping up against the steeper bank and pulling herself out by the edges of slick rocks she could see in the starlight.

Bayne gripped her wrists then and pulled her up. He was wearing his trousers and shirt, but the shirt was still unbuttoned. She felt the edges of it sweep against her and she shuddered, whether from the touch of fabric or the chill, she wasn't sure.

It took every ounce of strength she possessed not to let the force of it carry her body into him. Just the circling of his hands around her wrists made every hair stand on end with the energy of it. She could only imagine what would happen if she fell into him, if skin touched skin. A spell waited to ignite between them. It needed only the proper spark.

She lifted her head and caught the gleam of his gaze, the shadow of a wistful expression on his face.

"Your chemise, Pedant," he said, releasing her and thrusting the garment into her hands. His voice was as icy as the River they'd just crossed.

He turned his back, ostensibly to give her privacy. Vespa wriggled into the chemise, disliking the way it clung to her damp skin. She scrambled painfully across the rocks barefoot, feeling around in the dark for the items Piskel was still lugging across the stream.

The one good thing about this, as far as she could tell, was that she was wide awake.

Piskel collapsed on a nearby rock with the delivery of her second boot. He was nearly the same color as the rock and very hard to see.

"Thank you," she said. She tugged her damp stocking up over her knee and shoved her foot into the worn boot. She longed for the little dancing boots she'd had when she worked for Lucy Virulen, not that she'd gotten to use them much.

It was easier to think about boots than the whip-thin scars she'd seen crossing Bayne's abdomen and chest in the starlight.

Vespa struggled with her corset laces, cursing under her breath. Then Bayne's hands were at her back, pulling the laces with expert fingers.

"How do you . . . ?" she began, then stopped as he pulled so tightly, she gasped.

He finished up with a final tug. "I did have three sisters, you know." She could hear the smile in his voice, even if she couldn't see it.

"Ah."

When they were dressed, they stood in silence, looking up toward the City they'd once known. It was eerily quiet. Even the River made no sound. Piskel floated over and collapsed on Vespa's shoulder, and his wheezing was as loud as the old trolley that used to barrel down the hill on Industrial Way.

She wished she could feed him some energy or, at the very least, some jam cake. But she guessed that Bayne would frown on the former, and she had none of the latter.

"You will have all the cake you can stand when we bring Syrus home, I promise," she whispered to him.

Piskel squeaked in halfhearted anticipation.

"I definitely think we're going to need glamours," Bayne said.

"Can't say that I disagree," Vespa said. When they'd snuck into the vampire coven a few months ago, they'd used glamours to make certain the rumors were true. They'd never have gained access to the coven den otherwise.

One moment he was Bayne. The next he was a vampire, even down to the stench of the cold grave.

"Very nice," Vespa murmured.

It had taken her a while to learn to cast glamours, which were different entirely than shifting shape. A glamour was like throwing a skin over her own, rather than changing her entire being. Too thin and the mask would tear. Too much and it would be a rough approximation of the thing she was trying to cast.

But it was perhaps the one skill she'd managed to perfect, determined to show Bayne that she was capable of learning on her own.

After the incident yesterday she wasn't sure she could cast anything, but there was nothing for it but to try. One breath and she was herself. Another, and the thin tissue of a hag settled over her features. She was stooped and bent and hooknosed. And she hoped no one looked too closely because she guessed that the hair under her tattered hood might not be fully white.

"Well, then," she said to Bayne. "Where do you suggest we go?"

"Is Piskel well enough to lead us? I don't want to do anything that might alert whatever is here."

Piskel sighed heavily. He was about to lift himself from where he was sheltering under Vespa's hood, when she held him there and said, "Just tell me which direction, little man. Save your strength."

Piskel made a sound that seemed like north, if Vespa remembered her directions properly from Syrus's lessons. He'd been trying to teach her the old language, both written and spoken, but she admitted she wasn't very good at it.

"I think he wants us to go north," she said.

They oriented by the few stars they could still see. But when they climbed up to the street, they were plunged into a darkness so deep, it was like walking through ink. Piskel crawled under the damp strands of Vespa's hair that had come loose during the swim and shivered there.

"We may need to try something else," Vespa whispered. "I think Piskel isn't going to be much help." Her voice sounded like it was muffled by velvet, so thick was the darkness.

"I can give us night vision," Bayne said. "I'm loathe to do it, but it will be better than carrying a flame. Just be ready to shield yourself in case someone senses it."

Vespa nodded, then remembered he couldn't really see her in the dark. The next thing she knew, he had stepped in close to her and put his hand over her eyes. He whispered and there was a soft flare of magic.

His hand fell away, and she could see him. Not in color, but in shades of gray.

It occurred to her that he could have done this much earlier without her knowledge. "You . . . ah . . . didn't do this at the River, did you?"

He chuckled. "I could hardly call myself a gentleman if I had, now, could I?"

She gripped his wrist before she realized what she was doing. Under the false chill of vampire flesh she could feel his real pulse. "Bayne."

He looked at her, the blue of his eyes dimmed into gray by the spell.

"Do I have any chance of winning your regard ever again? Is there any chance that you might . . ." Her throat constricted, and she swallowed the last words she wanted to say. Her hag's voice made everything sound wrong. And yet the words still hung in the heavy air. *That you might love me.*

Now was not the time, she knew, but she couldn't help but ask. If they didn't come through this, she needed to carry the knowledge that there was still some possibility. She didn't want to die without knowing, and she knew that tonight there was a real chance she might.

She was surprised when he not only did not shake off her hand but took it between his own. His hands were cold as marble.

"There is nothing in my heart that is against you. But there are reasons why we must remain only business associates. Trust me in this. Let us leave it where it lies."

She swallowed again, wishing she hadn't said anything and feeling incredibly naive for thinking he might have changed his mind.

Finally, she nodded, and he released her gnarled hand.

She was grateful for the glamour, sure it hid her true expression.

Bayne cleared his throat softly and looked up toward the broken dome of the Museum.

"Let's find Syrus, then. Shall we start in the Museum?"

Vespa felt Piskel cling even more tightly to her nape, if that were possible. He moaned into her hair. "Judging by Piskel's reaction, I'd say that might be both the best and worst place to begin."

Business it was to be, then. Business she had done and could do. She was glad the sound of her heart breaking wasn't obvious.

She followed him as he made his way through the rubble. Things flitted at the corners of her vision, and she saw enough to once again wish that she was still blind. The dark magic here was heavy as the night. The last time she'd experienced malevolence of this weight and immensity had been in the Grue's presence, and it filled her with foreboding. What if the Grue hadn't been lost? What if he'd somehow returned to take his revenge?

She considered asking Bayne what he thought, but the closer they got, the quieter they both became. Soon it seemed she was even holding her breath for fear the darkness would hear her. And the hags and boggarts who passed them with gleaming eyes surely hadn't failed to notice them. She just hoped they accepted them as yet more dark Elementals drawn to this place.

The pounding of hooves from the hill made Bayne pull Vespa into an alley with him. A kelpie thundered by, its eyes white and wild. Vespa quelled the urge to follow it, to ride it straight into the River. She knew what waited for her if she did.

Once the twisted avenue was relatively quiet again, Bayne slipped out, and Vespa followed behind him.

She considered that it might be wiser to lead him to a side door into the Museum than through the front doors, and she plucked at his sleeve, tilting her head toward the University entrance. He looked toward the crushed main doors and took her meaning. Probably a bit too easy.

The old gates with Saint Bacon and Saint Newton had crumbled. The statues of the saints stood on either side of the entrance, their upraised hands holding nothing. The old boxwoods were skeletons of themselves. It looked like centuries had passed, though it had only been a year.

"Piskel," she whispered, "we need you to help us find Syrus now. Can you help? Is he here?"

The sylph floated out from underneath her hood. He was all gray, a ghost of himself. He nodded, his eyes big and solemn, and drifted toward the entrance Vespa had anticipated using.

The door was off its hinges like the front doors were, but there was no sign that anything had entered or left there for quite a while.

Vespa reached for the handle, but Bayne stopped her.

"I'll go first, just in case."

Vespa let him. If it came to it, he was more accurate with defensive magic than she was. And offensive magic, for that matter.

There was nothing in the hall but whispers. Piskel floated about for a bit, testing the dank air, deciding on the best course.

He made a dipping motion and flew closer to the floor.

"I think he wants us to find a way to go down."

"Where is the nearest staircase, if it even exists?" Bayne asked. Though he spoke as quietly as possible, his words seemed to take wing and flutter down the corridor.

"This way," Vespa said. She guessed that large portions of the floor had sunken or fallen away into the deep cave beneath the Museum when Tianlong had been freed. She wasn't sure, then, how they would get to the lower levels. She herself had never gone far into the depths of the Museum for fear of meeting the Grue in some dark hallway. She'd never realized he'd been hiding right beside her the entire time.

With Piskel nestling back in her hood, Vespa led them toward the nearest staircase to the lower storerooms. To do so, they had to pass across the Great Exhibition Hall, which was sagging and broken and festooned with cobwebs. It hurt her heart a bit to see the Museum in such ruin, even as she knew that her beloved place had caused such misery and suffering to so many. Piskel was obviously not enjoying being back. He kept making hissing noises, like an irritated kitten.

"We'll get Syrus and be out as soon as we can," she said to him.

Bayne gave her a look and put a single, corpse-thin finger over his lips. The heat that rushed to her face almost burned away her glamour.

Though the malice was even more palpable than it was out on the street, nothing stopped them, and they saw no one as they crossed the Hall. They descended the cracked stairs carefully, trying to make as little noise as possible.

It seemed ages ago that she had come here seeking a refiner, and even greater ages since Bayne had brought her down here and they had inadvertently kissed. That sweet golden country seemed so distant as to be almost imaginary.

They continued, skirting the gaping hole that had led them deep into the Well where Tianlong had slept for so very long. They went farther down the hallway than Vespa had ever gone, a corridor that tunneled and plunged through what she guessed was the

living rock above the Archives. Shattered glass and housings from everlanterns crunched under their feet. Sometimes Bayne wiped away cobwebs that came away red and sticky from his hands.

At last they pushed through a metal door that by all appearances had been neverlocked at one time. It gave with a vast clang.

They stepped out onto a giant ledge, the edge of a spiraling path cut into the living rock. It smelled of dirt and dark and death. What looked like thousands of caverns opened out onto this broad path. Far above, something Vespa couldn't quite make out sparkled and glowed. Dark lines stretched across it; the strands of a vast web, perhaps.

Clicking noises echoed and eyes gleamed as hundreds of spiderlike creatures emerged from various entryways.

"If they didn't know we're here, they know now," Bayne said.

"What should we do?" Vespa said. The nearest spider-creature was about one hundred yards away, but it had already turned toward them.

"Keep calm. Consider this an opportunity to gather more information while we search for Syrus."

Vespa swallowed. When she had faced the Grue or Olivia's predecessor, she had not been dealing with an entire army at once. Even the Raven Guard, as frightening as they'd been, had been few compared to the vast number of spider-creatures confronting them now. Something very wrong indeed was afoot.

"If they don't eat us for breakfast first."

"I don't think that's their intent. Not yet, anyway. For all they know, we're a vampire and a hag looking for a place to hide from the sun. Just pretend that we got lost. The less we say, the more we might learn."

"Hmph."

"Piskel," Bayne asked, "can you seek out Syrus? Find us when you can."

Vespa clenched her fists in the ratty hag sleeves and watched Piskel become a speck of ash in the vast darkness.

The nearest spider-creatures closed in on them. Bile rose in Vespa's throat as she saw that they were some sort of human-mechanical hybrid. Who was doing this and why?

"You must come with us," one creature said, its voice hissing and bubbling as though it was drowning in fluid.

They were escorted up the long path around the pit. Through open passages Vespa glimpsed things hanging from the ceiling, reminding her of visits to the butcher for special occasions when Aunt Minta wanted to be sure she got just the right cut of meat. The smell was almost the same. But Vespa had a bad feeling that the things hanging in the caves were not livestock, at least not as she defined it.

She wanted to ask Bayne if he thought Syrus was in one of these places, but she held her tongue. Surely the spider-things would be listening and reporting to whomever they were taking them to. And Piskel was doing his best to find him. He could probably find him more quickly than they could. All she could do was wait and hope there was another chance to get Syrus free.

The creatures herded them up to a great spiral staircase that seemed to have been blasted out of the living rock. Vespa couldn't remember it ever having been here before. Like the path, it was wide enough for several people to walk abreast. What creature or Elemental might need such a wide passage?

Up the stairs they went, the clicking shuffle of spider-feet going before and behind. Dread closed in from every side, wrap-

ping Vespa's lungs in its iron fist. There were so many. She hadn't imagined there would be so many.

At the top she finally realized where they were. They had just come up under the broken dome of the old observatory at the southern end, where the old orrery lay in skeletal shambles.

Where the Machine had been was a giant web stretched over the pit, the roof she'd seen from below.

In that web sat a spider of such immensity and darkness that Vespa stepped back at the sheer horror of it. One of the creatures behind her poked with its sharp metal appendage to get her moving again.

They were herded to the edge of the pit. A scarlet-wrapped sack hung from a shattered balcony nearby. Vespa could just make out the face of a faun. Olivia's envoy. Syrus had been right. She covered her mouth with her hand to keep from gagging.

Vespa realized that the back of the spider was to them, its heavy abdomen sagging on the web strands. Its head was under the shambles of the Machine and other fallen rubble that seemed to have been piled together to make what seemed a very uncomfortable nest. She could see the forelimbs moving, turning, and patting something. Or many somethings. For she also saw more of the spider-creatures emerging from the nest, carrying what looked like glowing balls—or eggs—very gingerly between their front appendages and taking them back down to the caves below.

Vespa bit back the curse on the tip of her tongue. This explained why there were hundreds, perhaps thousands of these things. The giant shadowspider was laying them, and her workers, like ants or bees, were taking care of them. How and why they hybridized with humans, she had no idea. She wasn't sure she wanted to know.

She looked up and saw that on the crumbled catwalk around the dome, scarlet-robed *xiren* like the one that had attacked Olivia stood in waiting. She could just make out the gold markings on their foreheads. They must be higher-ranking than these hybrid minions who tended the caves in the pits.

This was not simply some rogue Elemental they were dealing with. This was a queen. With a court and an army.

The false saints only knew where Syrus was now. Or if he was still even alive.

Bayne exhaled a little sharply, and Vespa could see he'd also noticed the *xiren* waiting above. But his vampire countenance remained impassive, except for the marbled veins running even darker through his white flesh.

Then the giant spider turned.

"On your knees," the spider-creature nearest them hissed. "On your knees before Ximu, Queen of the Shadowspiders."

The spider-creatures pushed them down, stabbing and poking, until both Vespa and Bayne knelt at the edge of the pit with heads bowed.

Nothing was said aloud or in the mind, but Vespa felt a wave of assurance from Bayne, as if he would say, "Calm and steady," if only he could. They had been in situations before that had been harrowing, but none quite so much as this since dealing with the Grue and restoring the Heart to Tianlong. She wanted to reach out to him and take his hand for some reason, but she knew that would be purest folly. She gripped the inside of her sleeve instead and kept her head bowed.

Though the air had seemed dank and stale and occasionally meat-scented since they'd entered the Museum, nothing compared to the stench that drifted over them as the great spider turned and faced them. It was the smell of venom and silk, droppings and death. It was the scent of a malice so ancient as to be nearly incomprehensible to the average mortal.

The stench rippled around them, tugging and warping and finally shredding their glamours like a pair of invisible scissors.

Vespa struggled to hold on to hers, but it turned to ash in her hands.

And then the thing was laughing. The laugh was so familiar that Vespa couldn't help but look up.

For all that she had changed, there was no question of who crouched on the web above them. It was the answer to what Vespa had often pondered.

Lucy Virulen had not been lost in the destruction of the Machine.

She was alive. Horribly, horribly alive.

Chapter 11 ▬

When next I wake, the cave moss seems to be moving, stretching, creeping up and down the wall. I squint. Maybe the venom is destroying my sight. After the dreams I've had, I can no longer tell if I'm seeing anything at all.

Or it could be something even more horrific than the hybrid.

I blink hard and swallow over my suddenly dry throat.

Something is definitely going on because the moss has split in two and is now creeping across the floor toward me.

Wode pengyou, a little voice whispers.

Friend? I think. And then I remember. Cave sprites. They helped us before, when the Grue nearly killed Bayne in the old Archive. Apparently, they've been here watching all along.

Last time, they made me promise that I would someday repay them the favor. But it seems I am about to be in their debt again, and I whisper as much.

"It doesn't seem I can repay my debt to you, my friends. What would you have me do?"

"Rid us of these vermin," one says. And then the chorus is taken up in whispers of *"hao"* all throughout the cavern.

"This is our home," one said. "We cannot leave it. Darkness is natural. But evil is not. Unkindness is not. We cannot harm our brethren, but they must go elsewhere."

I sigh. I suppose at least they didn't ask me for the moon, but this seems nearly as impossible. Ximu is making an army, after all.

"Well, get me down, will you please? And then we'll see."

The little ones scurry along the wall and ceiling, and soon I can feel them gnawing at the cords.

When the last tether snaps, I land like a sack of rice on the floor. They gnaw away the silk until my arms and legs are free. I ache all over, especially in the neck.

"*Xiexie.* I don't suppose you can get me some trousers?" I whisper to the nearest sprite. I chafe at my arms and legs.

His lantern-eyes shut as he solemnly shakes his head.

"Ah, well." Nothing the *xiren* probably haven't seen before.

"Can you free them?" I ask. I nod toward the others and immediately wish I hadn't.

"Some are too far gone," one sprite says.

I understand what the rendered fat odor means, and I vomit. Everywhere.

Then I hear a noise. Gen.

His eyes glow like fell moons. "Syrus—"

"I don't want to talk to you."

"You must understand, boy . . ."

"I understand that you are not of my clan." I stand to my full height and spit on the ground between us, the symbol of breaking bonds. "You are no longer my uncle. Do not speak to me as if you are."

"You're hurt, I understand that—"

The anger pulls me inside out. In houndshape I barrel out past him before he or any of the other monsters can stop me.

I nearly leap straight off the ledge that spirals around the pit, but only manage to turn in time. As I run, I hear a high clicking noise behind me that reverberates throughout the pit—a signal to the hybrids, I'd guess. Their eyes gleam at me as they emerge. There are dozens of caves like the one I was in; are they all filled with prisoners? How long have the *xiren* been secretly stashing their prey right under our noses?

Farther ahead I see a great contingent of the hybrids as they disappear to the upper level. Some of the rear guard, hearing the alert, turn in my direction.

I take the nearest open side corridor. There are more prisoners here, most of them suspended from the ceiling like I was. I see a few faces, many of them Tinker faces, and the sight enrages me further. I had thought they were all dead. That seemed the worst possible fate. But this and Uncle Gen's betrayal are far worse than death. I want to stop and free them, but I know if I do, I have no way of getting them out. If I can escape, the best thing will be to warn the Empress and return with whatever forces we can muster.

Which will be difficult considering how easily Olivia's guard was slain.

I put my head down and run until I am racing down one of the old Museum corridors, smelling the must of abandoned storerooms, the broken glass of everlanterns cutting my paws.

I'm creeping upstairs, my sides heaving with the effort of having run so much, when I hear the laughter.

It's a laugh I was glad to think I'd never hear again. That harsh music of a well-bred lady, that laugh that cuts you down even as you long to keep listening.

And against my better judgment, I go toward it. Because there are no reasons in this world why I would hear that laugh. I need to know why Lucy Virulen is here.

As silently as possible, I creep into the old observatory. I can just make out two figures kneeling and Ximu bending over them with her jaws wide.

I see her face and I understand. My cramping belly wants to turn my bowels to water at that moment, but I manage to control myself. Just as Charles allowed the Grue to inhabit him, Lucy has bonded with Ximu. For what reason, to what purpose, I have no idea.

And the two kneeling before her are none other than Vespa and Bayne. The fools.

I can't help but shake my head. Witch and warlock they may be, but they're none too bright. Surely they couldn't imagine that they could rescue me any better than I could rescue myself? I'm a Tinker. I know how to make anything and survive on nothing. Their magic wears out, but my skills never do.

Unless someone were to cut off my hand. And then, well . . . that might not work out so well.

Besides, all I have to do is get clear of this building. In hound-shape not even the swiftest *xiren* can catch me.

The only reason they caught me before was because they had the element of surprise.

I creep closer, keeping to the alcoves and broken archways. There are eyes watching from above. Something hangs near Ximu, a silken sack of what I'm guessing was once a faun, by the looks and smell of it. I'm guessing it's the one Olivia sent. Maybe now she'll listen to me, if I ever get to speak to my Empress again.

Ximu lowers her voice, whispering now. Venom drips from her jaws.

"You think you're so smart, waltzing in here under a glamour, thinking no one would be the wiser, eh?" she says. "You have no idea what I can do."

"I have no idea *what* you are," Bayne says. Ever the *hozide pigu*, that one.

I'm not glad that she cuffs him across the face. Because I'm guessing that hurts even more than when the minion thing below hit me with its metal leg.

She nearly knocks him down.

"You will be silent, bigamist."

"He is not a bigamist, Lucy," Vespa says while Bayne rights himself, cradling his jaw in one hand. "Your marriage was annulled properly when it was believed that you were dead and he was stripped of all his titles by his family. And, as for the two of us, we are business associates only."

I don't quite follow what either of them is saying, but Lucy/Ximu seems enraged by this.

"How dare you? Witch you may be, but I am a Queen. I am Ximu, and Ximu is me. We are one being now, as that bastard Charles is with the Grue. You are alive now only because it amuses me for you to be so. The moment you displease me enough, you are spiderling fodder. Do you understand?"

Vespa ignores all her blustering. She looks the Shadowspider Queen in the face and says, "What happened to you, Lucy? Why are you doing this?"

The gentleness in her voice gives Lucy pause. Then I notice that Vespa's fingers are glowing ever so faintly. She's trying to cast some kind of spell.

Lucy draws back, and the scarlet fangs that had been protruding from her horribly stretched mouth retract.

When she speaks, sobs catch on her words. "He let go of my hand," she says. "He promised to take me to Old London, where I would be loved and adored. He promised me power beyond imagining. And then . . . he let go of my hand."

There is a terrible silence. We are all imagining the same thing. Caught up in the whirlwind of the Waste and the pull of the open portal, who knows where a person might end up if she wasn't ripped apart altogether. I know that's what Bayne and Vespa assumed. They had been sure that the force of so much wild, deadly magic had either ripped Lucy and Charles apart or sent them hurtling into Old London, never to be seen again. They'd discussed it many times, mostly, I think, to reassure themselves that all was well and that the battle was over.

Then Lucy smiles. "But the power he promised came. Not in the way I'd imagined but perhaps even better. Ximu and I are one now. And I will take back what was lost to both of us, you may be sure of it. And then I shall have my revenge on him for his lies and his inconstancy."

What she says freezes me to the bone. She is sure that Charles is still alive. She keeps speaking of him as if he's alive somewhere, somewhere close by. How can that be? We all saw the portal swallow them and snap shut. I fight the urge to shout at her or at Vespa. *Ask her! Find out what she knows!*

For all the good it will do. We are in the black pits of the tenth level of the Hell That Eats People Alive and Spits Them Out in a Million Pieces, as *Nainai* would say. And there is no Heart of All Matter or Heavenly Dragon to save us this time.

"Lucy . . . ," Vespa begins.

"Silence! That name no longer has any meaning for me. You will address me properly as Queen or not at all."

"What does Your Majesty want, then?" Bayne asks. "You have us now and may do what you please. Surely that is enough?"

Bait her. Get the answers.

"First, I am going to finish taking New London. Shouldn't be hard now that your Empress has succumbed to my little poison gift, should it? I will collect her next. And then I will march north to the ancestral home of the *xiren*, Scientia."

I bristle at the mention of the poison gift and think again about Olivia. Was she hurt? Has she not recovered?

The last bit of news startles Bayne enough that Ximu laughs.

"You didn't know that, eh? We were driven out by the Tinker King, but the palace your family usurped centuries later was mine, built for me. Now I will go and take back what is mine. And I have you to thank for that."

"What do you mean?" Vespa says. She's still not being properly respectful, so I'm not surprised when Ximu cuffs her. It's almost a light, playful blow, but it sends her to the floor.

"Obstinate and uppity as ever, aren't you?" the Queen asks, bending closer to her. "'Twas your little trick that allowed me to escape. The Heart didn't just free Tianlong. It freed *all* of us."

Vespa straightens slowly but keeps her head bowed.

I've snuck steadily closer, and now I can see Bayne's face. It's drained of all color. "What do you mean *all*, Majesty?"

"I mean every Elemental who had been trapped or exiled in the last Great War, Architect. Are you so ignorant of the history of this world that you know nothing of what I speak?"

"Apparently I am, Majesty. Pray enlighten me," Bayne says through gritted teeth.

"Very well. But I should think that the Architects would have schooled you better. Unless they too were ignorant, which would not surprise me."

She settles in for the tale before them, like nothing so much as a mother gathering her children to her at bedtime. A giant, hairy mother with poison fangs.

"Once we all lived here together in great chaos. There was constant fighting. Empires rose and fell with regularity. Alliances were forged, betrayed, broken. But eventually it seemed that most Elementals aligned either with the darkness—the Umbrals, they were called—or with light and air—the Empyreans. It was decided that for the good of our world, we would all agree to the Great Law, which said that Elemental must not kill Elemental. We agreed in good faith. But it was not enough for the Empyreans. They were ever looking for a way to subdue and trap us Umbrals.

"When humans came, they provided the perfect opportunity. They were not necessarily bound by the Law, and they were malleable. Both sides manipulated them ruthlessly.

"I built my palace in the far north from the bones of a Titan I had slain before I bound myself by the Law. I lived there quite contentedly until the Tinker King came with his tinkering and his magic and drove me out with the help of the Empyreans. He made an army of automatons that could not be swayed by my poison, and when we fled across the sea, he set wards along all the cliffs and shores to keep me and mine from returning to our home. Then he took our palace for himself."

Her voice is harsh and deep with the anger of centuries. I don't wonder that she is so gleeful now to be free.

"But he also fell, and his people were scattered all over in little, sad pockets, their magic used and abused by those who settled here after them. And so I have risen, and I will restore my realm in the north despite the Tinker King's deception."

I think again of *Nainai's* tales of the old kingdom in the north. I knew better than to question her outright, but sometimes on bitterly cold nights, I wondered if such stories were true. Were they just supposed to make us feel better, to make us feel that we had once been more than a people who pieced a life together out of broken things?

And now the greatest enemy of our people, who I had also come to believe was nothing more than a shadow, is before me, telling those stories as truth. What will she do with all my people that she has stored in this cavern? What are the plans that Gen keeps alluding to? I half wish I would have listened.

All I know is that we have gone from frying pan to fire.

Ximu leans over Vespa and Bayne. "And now you understand. Your Empress is but a minor encumbrance. It is the north and Scientia that I go to claim. And I have you to thank for all that. Ironic, isn't it?"

"Empress Olivia is perfectly willing to allow you to live here, you know," Bayne says. "She has no use for this part of the City anymore. She will happily cede it to you in exchange for peace. And your fealty, naturally."

Ximu chuckles. She pokes at the remains of the poor faun envoy with a foreleg, so that the scarlet sack swings back and forth like a pendulum. "I have heard this offer somewhere before." She leans so close that she could easily bite the head off either of them. "And the answer is still NO."

Neither Vespa nor Bayne speaks.

She withdraws a bit, contemplating. Even though I never liked her, it is still hard to see Lucy's face erupting from the body of a spider, horribly stretched and warped by the foul magic joining the two of them.

"I should very much like to eat you now, but I do not forget those who have served me, even if inadvertently. I should offer you something for your service," Ximu says. The wicked tone of her voice suggests she is about to do the exact opposite. "That little Tinker we caught was to be my Prognosticator, but I'm sure I can find better uses for him. How would one of you like to be my Prognosticator and Court Magician? The other can be Captain of my *xiren*. It would amuse me greatly and make use of all your talents. What do you say?"

She is not really giving them a choice. I can see Vespa's shoulders tensing, readying herself for a fight. She is not very good at all with offensive magic; I nearly choked on my own laughter when Bayne tried to teach her one day and she missed every target. But the field here is pretty wide. All she'd really have to do is set fire to that web under Ximu, and Ximu would take a nasty plunge down into the pit.

Just then something large—a bat, a bird, a pixie?—dances in front of my muzzle and zigzags around, blinding me with golden glitter and squeaks of joy. I stumble backward, pawing and snapping, falling on my side while Piskel covers my eyes and cheeks with brilliant kisses and warbles ecstatically that he's found me.

I melt back into human form, naked on freezing stone.

"Piskel!" I hiss.

But it's no use. I can hear the *xiren* above me come to attention. I hear Ximu screaming. Feet come toward me, and at first I'm sure I'm doomed, that the horrible hybrids will have me in their metal pincers soon enough.

But they're human feet.

I'm trying to wipe Piskel from my face and stand, when Vespa and Bayne are both suddenly there. Vespa barely has time to say my name before she and Bayne get hold of me.

"Will it work?" Vespa asks.

"We can only try," Bayne says.

The magic stretches and tears me from this place into another. Ximu's laughter follows us through the void.

CHAPTER 12

W ell, you do know how to make an entrance," Olivia said from Vespa's narrow bed. She was propped against the pillows, almost as pale as the sheets. Her hair streamed across her shoulders in waterfalls of gold. Her eyes widened as her gaze fell on Syrus, and Vespa followed it to realize that Syrus was still quite naked.

"Here," Vespa said, grabbing an old opera cape from a chair and throwing it around his shoulders. She tried not to see the horrible wounds at his throat and the thread marks still imprinted across his ribs before the cape covered them.

Syrus turned red as fire as he clasped the fabric around him.

Olivia inclined her head, wincing a bit. "Pedants, Artificer. I am glad to see you safe."

"Majesty, we have grave news," Bayne said.

"I reckoned as much. Especially since some of you came sans clothes." She smiled, but it was a faltering one. "Tell me."

Bayne told her of Ximu, of the strange melding of Lucy Virulen and the Shadowspider Queen. He explained how the Heart had freed all the magic in the world, both dark and light. And how Ximu had sworn to retake Scientia.

"But not before she takes you, Your Majesty. She expects to come collect you soon and overrun New London on her way north."

"She does, does she?" Olivia said. "What of our envoy? Does she not also wish for peace? Surely she will see reason. Surely there is still some humanity left in her."

"Majesty," Bayne began. His voice was very tired. Olivia frowned at him. "Your envoy is dead. Ximu does not wish to have peace with you. You are but a small obstacle in her plans to take Scientia."

Syrus added, "She has my people, Majesty. She is turning them into *xiren*. My uncle is the one who captured us, and he is helping her do all this. I've seen the caverns where she keeps her prisoners trussed up like sacks of meat. There is no humanity in that."

Olivia lowered her eyes for a moment, and her hands moved restlessly on Vespa's worn quilt.

Vespa said, "Your Majesty, it has been our experience that once this type of melding occurs between human and Elemental, they become an entirely different creature. Reason and appeal to human decency never worked with Charles after he accepted the Grue. Lucy seems to show the same condition."

"Is there no magic that can separate them?" Olivia asked.

Vespa looked at Bayne.

"That has not been tried, Majesty," he said. "Perhaps some Elemental magic might separate them, but we would not even know how to begin. There is the danger of killing them both, which is against the Great Law. No Elemental would aid in that."

"That Law may need to be changed," Syrus said darkly.

"Then what are you both suggesting we do?" Olivia said at last.

Bayne said, "Flee, Your Majesty. My family's airship can take you to Scientia, where there are powerful fortifications and defenses. You can at least buy yourself some time and decide what to do there. And we should warn them of what is coming."

"But might something also be wrong in Scientia? I have not yet been able to fully decipher the message, but it is most certainly a code. What if there is danger there, too?" Olivia said.

"That is very possible, Your Majesty. But it seems to be our only option. There is no way we could make the harbor and commission a ship elsewhere before Ximu's army overtook us," Bayne said.

"But what of my people? What of this City we have worked so hard to rebuild?"

Bayne shook his head. "We must warn them and take whomever we can with us. The *Sullen Harpy* is a large airship, but she cannot accommodate everyone. The sooner the better, so the choices they need to make can be made in time. Ximu will not wait long to cross the water, I promise you that. We've called Council for this afternoon. You can make your decree on what should be done then."

Olivia's face was ashen, and she cradled the bandage on her neck as if it pained her all the more for the news she'd just heard. Vespa understood how difficult it must be for her. Olivia had been trapped in the Tower all her life. Like all of them, she'd believed the story was simple and easy—that once the Elementals were freed, all would be right again with the world.

They'd all been wrong.

"Is there nothing else that can be done?" Olivia asked.

"I would advise sending your guard, and anyone who is willing to stand with them, to the River, but they will only buy us a little time," Bayne said. "Without a standing army, there is no way we can turn back the tide."

Olivia nodded. Her jaw was stiff as she said, "Escort me back to the warehouse."

• • •

Council was called in Olivia's receiving room. The faded elegance of the room's furnishing seemed a palpable reminder of all they were about to lose. It was chilly, and Vespa rubbed her arms, wishing for a coat. They'd left Syrus at home, presumably to pack but mostly to rest and allow Truffler to minister to him and his wounds.

A contingent of the Empress's guard had been dispatched to watch the River bank. "At the first sign of trouble, send a messenger to let us know," Olivia had said to them. "Do not try to be brave. You are meant only to give us information. Do whatever you must to protect yourselves."

The fauns had bowed, and their new Captain had said, "We will do what we must to keep your realm safe, Majesty."

Vespa had struggled to hide her tears as she watched them go.

That had been several hours ago, and now the last of the Councilors were finally straggling in. Half of them were elected from the surrounding Forest and the River—the most powerful of the Elemental denizens. Doctor Parnassus took his place next to a naiad who huddled uncomfortably in a tub of water that had been brought for her. There was also a hamadryad—hemlock, by the looks of his dark pointed leaves and even darker eyes—who was already snoring at the table. The rest had been elected from the human population that resided in New London. There was some restlessness and shuffling, but Vespa could see that none of them had any idea what news was about to be thrown at their feet.

Olivia came through the door near the dais. She was still very pale. Her hair had been put up, and she wore a high-collared gown to hide the bandage over the *xiren* bite. Vespa noticed that the skin looked raw just above the collar, and Olivia pulled it higher as if to avoid scrutiny.

Still, she stood on her own, and her gaze was serene as she looked at everyone. "Please be seated," Olivia said.

Chairs scraped as people sat. The naiad leaned closer to the table.

"Some of you may have heard that our Imperial Unnaturalists have brought us grave news. Pedants Lumin and Nyx, would you care to share your findings with us?" she asked.

Vespa deferred to Bayne, and he reported. The mere mention of Ximu, her joining with Lucy Virulen, her history and plans, made the air above the table thicker and darker. Many Elementals shook their heads, but others had grim looks that made Vespa wonder if they'd known more than she'd thought.

Everyone was silent at the end. The weight of all of Bayne's warnings hung heavy in the air. There had been many a Council meeting that had gone awry because he'd insisted there should be a standing army, a Wall, magical protection—all things Olivia had refused to allow because she believed in peace.

Murmurs began around the table.

Bayne raised his hand for silence. "I have one question for our Elemental brethren before we move on."

All of them looked at him warily.

"How many of you knew that the Umbrals had been released? And, if you knew, why did you not tell us?"

They looked at one another, and then someone elbowed the hamadryad, their spokesman. He cleared his throat with a sound like leaves being swept from stone, and said, "We suspected that perhaps the freeing of Tianlong had also freed those who had been

bound in the Great War. We were gathering evidence to place
before this Council in hopes of persuading Her Majesty to pursue
greater fortifications. We were apparently too late."

"Apparently," Bayne said.

"What should we do?" a human woman asked. Her name was
Verity, and she was the head of the newly formed baker's guild.
Piskel especially liked her because she often brought pastries to
Council meetings. She had not done so today, and Piskel was sulk-
ing on the table next to Vespa's elbow because of it.

Olivia spoke, her words cracking with emotion. "I believe we
must evacuate our fair City. It has been made clear to me that we
will not be able to treat with the enemy in any reasonable fashion."

The chorus of voices rose beyond a murmur this time.

Bayne stood and held his hand up for silence again. "There are
several things we can do to help us prepare. Vespa and I can work to
craft some sort of shield. It will be weak, but it may buy us some time.
We can help people decide where they will go and by what method.
Some can be escorted to the harbor and take ship for Newtonia and
Babbageburg. Others may wish to take their chances and shelter with
the Elementals in the Forest, though I'd not advise that. Depending
on the capacity of the airship, we will certainly take as many as we
can that way. The Grimgorn Ambassador has been alerted and is
even now drawing up his recommendations for us."

Bayne had to shout his final words. "But all this must be done in
an orderly fashion! If we allow panic to overtake us, then we will
certainly doom more people than we will save."

Orderly fashion? Vespa resisted the urge to shake her head. The
panic had already begun. Everyone would be running over top of
one another to get out as soon as they left this room.

Then shouting came at the door. A faun sentry burst through it, his eyes white with fear and his jacket smeared with blood. He was one of those who had been sent to the River.

Vespa hoped he wasn't the only one remaining, but her worst fears were confirmed when he shouted, "The *xiren* have crossed the River! We held back what we could, but they're invading the City!"

Bayne's eyes took on a feverish glow. He turned to Vespa. "Take the Empress and get her ready. Pack only the most necessary things. I'll get the Ambassador and the Captain."

Vespa nodded.

"Piskel," she said, "warn Syrus and Truffler, if you please. Tell them to meet us at the airship landing stage."

His sulking completely forgotten, Piskel nodded and zipped out through the open door.

Vespa hurried to Olivia's side, fighting the teeth-clenching fear that seized her. "Let's get you to the airship, Your Majesty."

CHAPTER 13 ━━

I'm woken by Piskel barreling into me and pulling my eyelids open to make sure I'm fully awake. He's squeaking and so brilliant that I bat him out of my face in protest, covering my eyes from the blue spots that swirl behind my eyelids.

I sit up on my pallet, wiping the cobwebs of nightmares from my eyes. I have no idea how I could sleep at a time like this, but I'm sure I'm still feeling the effects from Ximu's poison. My entire body aches, but I'm comforted by the sight of my workshop rather than the horror of the caverns under the Museum.

"Piskel, you melonhead, what in the Seven Hells is wrong with you?"

I understand all too quickly when he begins marching back and forth in the air.

"The army is on the move, then."

He blows himself up like one of those dried puffer fish I used to see in the market and makes hurrying gestures.

"Meet them at the airship, eh?"

He deflates and nods.

I stand up and start gathering things into a pile, looking for my satchel, but it's out of restless habit rather than focused intention.

"What about my people? What will be done?" I am thinking of all of them in the cavern, wrapped in scarlet silk, poisoned and ill. It makes me sick to think that I didn't save them, that I left them to their fates because I was too concerned about my own.

But what can I do now? If I stay, I will certainly be captured, and I obviously am not very good at rescue missions on my own. If I go, perhaps there will be another opportunity. Perhaps. I grit my teeth.

Then I hear the weeping.

I follow the sound into the parlor. Truffler is there by the hearth, weeping over cold ashes. It occurs to me that if I stay, these two may not live to regret it.

"Old man," I say against the pain in my heart, "you'd better save your tears for when the water runs out." Though I, too, could weep thinking about my uncle Gen. I pray he did not choose his fate. I pray that Ximu has somehow enthralled him and that I can break him free. I cannot bear, no matter what I've said, to think of him as a willing traitor.

Truffler turns then and rushes to me, hugging me hard around the leg. Piskel floats down to pat him on his hairy head.

"Worried," Truffler sniffs.

"Well, that makes three of us. And now we really have to get out of here."

He nods and holds up the satchel I was looking for. "Already started packing."

We grin at each other then, and to the sounds of shouts outside, we tear around the house picking up whatever we can find that seems of use.

I gather up my pile of tools. Piskel comes to me mournfully clasping his little knit blanket and muttering about how he supposes he'll have to leave the basket behind.

I take the blanket and put it in the satchel. Piskel drifts around looking at other things he's collected and eyeing me every now and then to see if I've taken the hint.

"Look, whatever we can carry, we'll take. *Hao ma?*"

He turns practically plaid with pleasure and starts picking up everything he can carry in his tiny arms. Bits of shell, thimbles, curls of ribbons—who knew sylphs were such awful pack rats?

I sigh and turn to my workbench. So many things I was working on—all now pointless. I take the few tools I think might be of most use and are lightest. I spy the golden egg, the gift bearing the strange message that was given to Olivia, and scoop that up. And of course I pack the dartpipe and darts. There's no way to be fully prepared—I can't imagine what lies in wait in Scientia.

I run upstairs to see if there's anything in Bayne's or Vespa's rooms. But in Vespa's room I'm immediately confounded by the stockings hanging everywhere, the drawers over the warped dressing screen, the scattered books.

Manticore save us, but she's a messy girl!

I pick up the closest book I see lying by her cot—something about dreams—and shove it in the bag.

Bayne's room is austere and gentlemanly. Everything is neatly put away, which surprises me, considering how pampered he must have been by servants in his former life. I don't see anything I can take. Hanging from one of the doors of the battered wardrobe is his family sword, snapped in half by the Raven Guard. He'd found it in the rubble and hung it here, I guess, as a reminder of what he'd lost.

I hurry down to the library. All these books they'd collected and I'd started translating about to be lost. That burns me more than anything. I half wish we'd left them where we'd found them or made some other safe Archive elsewhere. Bayne planned to do that against such a time as this, but that time has come sooner than any of us imagined.

I swipe a few instruments that are lying about—a retrofitted tattler, some old null-goggles—and that's all I can manage. Truffler lumbers in from the kitchen bringing what's left of the cheese, bread, and sausage I'd gotten last at market.

Piskel whimpers a bit about there being no cake.

"Let's hope there's some where we're going, my friend."

I unlock the door to absolute chaos. "Stay close," I say to both of them. Truffler looks back into the house where we've lived. He wasn't keen on living here, but he did so. Now I feel I should give him the choice to go back to the Forest if he wants.

I kneel quickly before him. "Look, old man, if you don't want to go with us, you don't have to." Piskel has obviously done better than one could expect, being parted from his home in the high grasslands, but Truffler? I don't know.

He shakes his head. "Let you go before. Not going to again."

"All right, then. Follow as best you can. I won't leave you behind."

The black tide rises over the edge of the City, reminding me of nothing so much as the Creeping Waste. To think we thought ourselves so very free, only to have gotten trapped in an even bigger mire!

I have heard that there is little to no magic in the Old World. I'm beginning to think it would be an excellent place to live.

The news spreads through the streets like fire. I witness some of the first lootings as the madness spreads. My heart burns in my chest. In so many seconds a year's worth of careful work is undone by fear.

I never want to be driven by fear like this again.

The way back to the airship is not the straight line I hoped. I can hear rallying cries coming from the way I planned to go. Some valiant fools have chosen to stand and fight the *xiren*, and though their attempts are largely in vain, still I can see the line shifting through smoke and fire. Great sections of the new City have burst into flame.

A terrified cart horse that's torn free of most of its harness careens down the road.

"Now's our chance," I say. I run out, heedless of thrashing hooves, and grab what remains of the bridle. I lift Truffler up and then swing up behind him. I honestly haven't ridden more than a pony or donkey in my time and never faster than a trot, but interesting times make for interesting adventures, so *Nainai* once said.

Maddened by fear, the horse is easily motivated to keep going. The only problem is keeping him going in the direction I want him to go. I lean low over Truffler, gripping the horse's heaving sides with my knees. Piskel holds on to me, and I'd swear he's almost chirping with joy. Melonhead.

I get the horse pointed in the right direction, and he runs through fire and smoke, bullets sometimes whizzing past us. I see my first *xiren* just as a clear space opens to the airship. A great dome of clear air shimmers around the airship. Vespa and Bayne are shielding it as best they can.

The *xiren*'s golden facial markings gleam in the roiling smoke. I see them right before I see the long-handled sword that slices my horse's legs out from under me. I'm only just able to clasp Truffler to me and roll across the pavement away from the foe. Weak and dizzy, I stumble up, trying to see him again through the smoke before he cuts us both in half.

I fumble for my dartpipe but come up with a sausage. I cannot believe I am going to die with a sausage in my hand against the most ancient enemy of my people when the way to my escape is only a few yards away.

He advances on me, scarlet fangs erupting. And then his torso is crashing to the ground, and his legs are following it in a spurt of black blood.

Bayne steps through the smoke, holding the magical blade I've seen him summon up before when times demanded it.

"I was beginning to wonder if you were coming," he says. He looks down at the sausage. "Most impressive weapon I've seen in quite a while."

"I thought Architects followed the Great Law?" I say.

"We bend the Law when it suits our purpose. And that wasn't fully an Elemental anyway, correct?"

He's right about that. At least part of the *xiren* is human, albeit a very small part.

We grin at each other, and then he nods toward the ship. "Come on. We can't hold this much longer. They say the main force is only a few streets over. We'll soon be engulfed."

I stuff the sausage back in the bag and take Truffler's hand. We follow Bayne down the alley toward the only hope we have left.

Chapter 14 ▬

Vespa had refused to go on board when she'd first been told to, arguing that she could protect the ship better if she was outside it. That was only partially true. In reality, she just couldn't stand being closed in not knowing what was happening.

The ship billowed and pulsed next to her like an unhomed sea creature. Its silver sides expanded and contracted as if it were breathing. She could hear people speaking through its skin. For a moment she almost wondered if the Grimgorns had magicked some poor Elemental into serving as a vessel, but she wasn't sure how that was possible.

She was trying to think of anything that would distract her from the truth. New London had fallen. All their work and effort to rebuild had been in vain. And all because, above all things, they had hoped for and believed in peace. It hurt her soul to think of how all the people who had survived the Emperor and the Rousing and who had stayed to rebuild would now be sacrificed to Ximu's need for vengeance.

There was nothing she could do to help them now, though. There was nothing she could change. She could only focus on the very small hope that somehow Bayne could find Syrus, and they could all leave for Scientia before the *xiren* overran the airship.

She stared back toward the fall of the City. She'd been furious at herself and Bayne for not forcing Syrus and Truffler to come with them to the Council meeting after they'd rescued him. But when she saw them all plunge through the smoke and back under the shield, she was able to swallow her heart back down to its normal position.

The ship's Captain was worried that he wouldn't be able to get the kind of lift he needed. The winds weren't at all favorable; everything was far too still. Vespa frankly wasn't sure how the thing was flying at all. As far as she knew, all such conveyances had been powered by *myth*gas. Olivia had banned the use of *myth* throughout the Empire after the Rousing, so Vespa was left to wonder. It disturbed her to think that she might be using the very thing she'd fought to stop, but there was no choice now. She just hoped the thing could get off the ground before the *xiren* managed to tear it to shreds.

Bayne and Syrus rushed up to her, looking quite the worse for wear. Truffler nodded at her.

"Vespa, take Truffler up the ramp. Syrus and I will help get the remaining guy ropes unhitched."

"But how will you get in the ship?" she asked.

"Just . . . do as I ask," Bayne said. He was covered in bloody slime, and his coat was singed around the edges. He was stretched close to snapping, she could tell.

Vespa couldn't help but ask one more thing. "Have we gotten everyone on board we possibly can?"

She could still see people weaving frantically through the smoke, and the dark *xiren* forming ranks as they converged on the airship.

Bayne looked at her for a long moment. "We have done all we can. And if we don't leave now, everything will be in vain. Everything."

Vespa swallowed the words of denial. She longed for the power of the Heart again. She would have swept through the army of shadowspiders as if they were bowling pins on the green lawn of Virulen. But she didn't have the Heart, and she couldn't control her own power. It was quite possibly the most frustrating moment she'd ever encountered. She was a witch with more power than any born in generations, and yet she couldn't use it when she needed it most, to save those she loved.

Bayne seemed to know what she was thinking. There was something in his gaze that said he wanted to offer comfort, but there was no time.

"Go now," he said, his voice harsh and low.

Vespa did as he asked, helping Truffler up the ramp. The poor hob was crying, and she could imagine how his heart hurt to think of his beloved Forest under threat again.

"We'll do all we can once we're safe," she said to him. "You know we will."

He nodded, but she didn't know whether he believed her.

They climbed up the gangplank and into the holding bay where crewmen, guards, and others were frantically shifting cargo around to make way for people, their trunks, and whatever else they could fit inside. Vespa tried not to see the wide-eyed children clinging to their mothers, or the elders who'd stayed in New London because they'd had nowhere else to go after the Rousing.

Many of them looked at her with hard eyes—their savior fallen from her pedestal. She thought she heard a whispered curse or

two before she turned with Truffler to climb toward the passenger decks.

The ship's purser was directing people to accommodations. This was one of the luxury airships that had often traveled between Scientia and New London filled with passengers on a southern jaunt, so it had many rooms and levels. Vespa had heard of such airliners but had never had the occasion to travel on one.

"Room 313! Up the stairs and then down the corridor to the left," the purser yelled at her before she could even ask. After she and Truffler climbed the stairs, Vespa saw that the corridor was lit by everlanterns. She leaned forward to inspect one while Truffler shied away. He felt the magic too.

"They're using *myth*, aren't they?" Vespa asked him.

He nodded, his eyes narrowing in anger.

She stared at her own greenish reflection in the lamp-glass, almost in disbelief. She knew what they were running from, but could what they were running *toward* be just as bad? She remembered the Phoenix as it had unfurled its message, and she wished she knew what it had said.

Still, there was no choice. She led him down to Room 313.

"Will you be all right here?" she asked the hob as they entered. She knew the Elementals didn't much like iron or steel. There was plenty of it here, but she thought she could probably make a little nest for him on the floor that would be more comfortable than resting in the iron bunk.

"Fine," he said, though he hardly sounded like it. "How many days?"

"Five, I think," Vespa said, though she wasn't entirely certain. As a girl bent on exploration, she'd always looked toward the sea and

Newtonia. She'd calculated every possible route that way but never had much looked north. There had been the Waste to consider, after all.

It had been adventure she'd been after back then, anyway. She smiled bitterly to think at how a year had changed things. Today she was sure that adventure was far more trouble than it was worth, and she'd trade all of it for a warm cup of tea and intelligent conversation by the hearth. How foolish she'd been to think otherwise!

The ship rocked against its moorings, and she gripped the bed railing. Truffler sat down on the floor, put his arms over his head, and curled into a moaning ball.

"It'll be all right, Truffler, I promise," she found herself saying over and over.

She felt the shield go down outside the ship so that it could fly free. Now were the crucial moments, and she was stuck alone in a room with a terrified hob.

Vespa went and put her arms around him, resting her cheek against the coarse hair of his head. It was as much to comfort herself as him. He smelled of mushrooms and lichen and leaf mold.

"You must love Syrus very much to come on this journey," she whispered. "I know he appreciates your bravery."

Truffler uncovered part of his face and peered at her with one dark eye.

"He's going to need you more than ever soon, I imagine," she said. "Can you keep being brave?"

"Will try," the hob grunted. "Want to sleep now." Hobs tended to be nocturnal, so it was no wonder he was exhausted now.

"Good fellow. Yes, of course." Vespa got up again, and the ship

rocked her back toward the bed. She scooped up some blankets and dumped them on the floor near the hob. "I assume you'll want to avoid the bed."

He nodded and crept into the pile of blankets, huddling down in them until he couldn't be seen.

"I'll bring Syrus to you as soon as he's aboard and we're aloft."

All she heard from Truffler was another grunt before he was snoring assiduously.

She closed the door carefully behind her, frowning again at the line of everlanterns that led her down the corridor. She heard shouts as she got closer to the hold. There was a vast discharge of air, and cries of "Aloft!"

Vespa searched for the Empress's quarters but was told by her pale-faced maid that the Empress had gone to the observation deck. Vespa made her way down winding steel stairs, bracing herself against the railing as the ship lifted itself into the morning.

She found Olivia peering out through a window, gazing at the burning City below.

Olivia did not look at her as she joined her at the glass. Her knuckles were white on the brass railing. "All that remains of the heart of my Empire," she said. She smiled bitterly.

"But your realm isn't lost," Vespa said. Her voice sounded tinny and ridiculous to her. "We are traveling to the strongest city in your Empire even now. All will be well."

She reached for Olivia's hand, but Olivia withdrew from her.

"Don't try to comfort me, Vee. I was a fool. We are gazing upon the cost of my tremendous foolishness."

"Olivia, don't."

"How can I not?" Olivia said, resting her forehead against the glass. Tears slid down her pale cheeks and dropped on her fingers like diamonds. "You and Bayne were right."

"I never—" Vespa began, but Olivia silenced her with a look.

"You didn't have to. It was clear you thought as he did. You were just too polite to say so."

Vespa grimaced. Were her thoughts that obvious to everyone?

Olivia tilted her head. "What?"

Vespa waved it away. "Nothing, just . . . Look, the difference here is that I wanted to believe as you did. I wanted peace. I wanted us to build a city of learning and knowledge and art, a place where Elementals and humans could live together in harmony."

She took Olivia's hands, and this time the Empress didn't withdraw. Vespa looked into her eyes, trying to ignore the raw red streaks she could see rising above the bandage on Olivia's skin. "I still believe in this, Your Majesty. I still believe we can build what we dreamed together. And you must believe it too. It just may be harder than we thought."

A sad, little smile crossed Olivia's face as she looked below again. "Much harder now," she said.

"Just promise you won't lose hope," Vespa said. "It's all we have now. And your people must see that you carry enough hope for all of them."

"My people . . . ," Olivia said slowly. "Will they ever trust me again?"

"I don't know," Vespa admitted. "There are many angry, confused people in the hold. It may comfort them if you appeared and spoke."

Olivia nodded. "That is a good thought." She rested her head against Vespa's shoulder. "I am so grateful for you, Vee. I think so often of that night when I saw you across the ballroom in the Tower. I knew in that moment you were the only person in the world who could save me. The only person who would bother."

"Really? How did you know that?"

"Your courage shines like a light, dear one. And we are all drawn to it like moths, even the most reluctant."

Vespa snorted. Before she could stop herself, she said, "I can think of one who is the most reluctant of all."

"Still no change, then?" On occasion the two of them talked of the Matter of the Reluctant Pedant, as Olivia sometimes alluded to it. For herself, Olivia was circumspect about her own romantic life, having sworn that she would not marry until her City had been restored to a workable semblance of its former glory. Her parallels to the Great Elizabeth of Old London rose in Vespa's mind. She had just recently been reading about Elizabeth and how she had foresworn marriage the better to rule her country.

Vespa shook her head. "Before we went into the old City, I asked again if there could be anything between us. He said there could not. That we must remain business associates only."

"But that is preposterous!" Olivia said. "After all this time, surely he's not still holding that charm against you?"

"I'm afraid so," Vespa said. "I can think of no other reason, though he claims that is not it."

"Well, I suppose there will be many more eligible bachelors in Scientia than there were in New London."

Vespa shook her head, half-amused and half-horrified they were talking of such things at a time like this. But they were both exhausted, terrified, and deeply saddened. Vespa supposed she preferred this sort of false banter to thinking about whether or not the *xiren* had more weapons she didn't know about.

"For your sake, Olivia, I hope so."

Olivia was about to answer when they both saw two familiar images in the glass.

"Speaking of reluctant moths . . . ," Olivia whispered.

They turned. Bayne and Syrus came up to them. Piskel peeked out of Syrus's wild hair, then blushed when he saw Olivia and dove back behind the Artificer's ear.

"Majesty," Bayne said, bowing. He tried to wipe his hands along his coat and came away with soot.

Vespa tried to keep her expression neutral, though it was hard to hide her relief.

"Pedant," Olivia said. "Or shall I call you Knight?"

Bayne had the grace to blush. "Majesty, really there is no need . . . ," he began.

Olivia smiled. "I fear that it would have to wait anyway, since there is not much to a title without land. And all the land around our City seems to be occupied now." She frowned and looked again out the window.

They were just over the edge of the Euclidean Plain now and could only see the tinges of smoke disappearing behind them. Vespa clutched the rail, trying to promise herself again that this was real, that the ship would not dissolve beneath them.

"Don't trouble yourself over it now, Majesty," Bayne said. "Let us hope that we can regroup in Scientia and think of happier things then."

Olivia nodded.

"I just pray the *xiren* don't have airships or cannons," Vespa said. "They don't, do they?"

"Even if they did, we are in luck," Bayne said. He gestured off to starboard, and Vespa's eyes widened in wonder.

By their side was a phalanx of flying Elementals—young Dragons, Griffins, a Harpy—and at the head of their formation flew the Phoenix.

"They arrived at the last minute and helped get us aloft safely. They will escort us to Scientia and shield us from anything harmful."

For the first time since Olivia had entered their townhouse door the other night, Vespa saw the hope she'd been seeking cross the young Empress's face.

Olivia watched the Phoenix for long moments before she said, "I will go speak to the people now."

"Very wise, Your Majesty," Bayne said. "Shall we escort you down?"

Vespa found herself wanting to stay on deck, to watch the colors of the Phoenix shift with the oncoming night. But she knew she'd probably better go along and see if Olivia could turn the tide of resentment that was sure to be building in the ship's hold.

The Captain came to address them as they crossed to the door. Vespa watched him as she had watched the arrogant envoy during his introduction, trying to deduce any anti-Imperial sentiment. But the Captain was respectful, bowing with his hat in his hand.

"Majesty," he said. "It is our very great pleasure to have you aboard. We expect to land in Scientia with good weather and with the services of our escorts five days hence."

"Thank you, Captain. We appreciate your aid during this journey."

"Ma'am." He bowed smartly again and returned to the control

room. He barely spared Bayne a glance, but Bayne had a strange look on his face.

"What?" Vespa asked as they fell into line behind Olivia. "Did you know him?"

"He was once Captain of my parents' ship, the *Gay Cockatrice*. He didn't even seem to recognize me."

"I suspect you're going to get a lot of that where we're going, unfortunately," Vespa said.

"I'm most certain you're right," he said.

CHAPTER 15

I follow them all back down to the hold, lost in my own thoughts, suddenly exhausted. I wonder how Olivia will accomplish this; she still seems frail to me. For all that, I'm not really feeling well, either.

I grip the railing as the ship seems to lurch away beneath me. I have the sinking feeling that the ship will plunge out of the sky. Not now, perhaps not even days from now, but at some point the *Sullen Harpy* will fall like a great burning star.

I want to return to the observation deck. I want to see the Phoenix flying again in the twilight and believe that all will be well.

Vespa looks at me. "Syrus?"

I hold the railing with both hands. I can't seem to stop shaking all of a sudden.

Piskel is buzzing around me like a bee. "Stop it," I say through gritted teeth.

Vespa's hand is on my arm, then on my forehead.

"Is something wrong?" Olivia's voice pours over me like water.

"He's burning up," Vespa says. "He was bitten more severely than you, Majesty. Perhaps I should get him to his room, if you can excuse him."

"Of course," she says. That voice, so cool, so soft. I wish she was taking me instead. I manage to bite back the words I want to say. Everything is blurring, all the edges running together. Even thoughts.

"Yes," I hear myself saying.

Then Vespa's arm slides under my shoulder, and I feel her holding me up. Piskel is twittering in my ear. Some nonsense about not giving in, about how some special flower high up in the mountains beyond his home could fight the poison. No idea what he's going on about, except that I just really want to sleep.

I think about how nice it would be if I could sleep in Olivia's arms, and I feel a warm drowsiness rushing over me.

Vespa pinches me on the arm. "Not yet, young man," she says. "We've at least got to make it to your bunk before you drift off."

I blink away every strange vision and dream just so I can get myself down the hall.

"Are those everlanterns?" I hear myself ask.

Piskel stares at his reflection in the glass, stretching his mouth wide and making ugly faces.

"Yes," Vespa says. "And hush. We'll figure all that out later."

Then we're in the room. There's a giant mound of blankets on the floor, and I nearly sink into them, confused but grateful.

"No, no, that's Truffler. Over here," Vespa says. She helps me get into an iron bunk. She gets the satchel off me.

"I'm not fooling with your clothes right now," I hear her say somewhere far above me. "Just rest. We're all safe. I'll bring you food when you wake."

I try to agree, to say something. Nothing comes out of my mouth except a long sigh.

• • •

I'm back in the cave, listening to the water drip. I feel as though the cave sprites are somewhere nearby, conferring about what to do with me, but I can't actually see them.

"Now," a dreaded voice says. "You will tell me what you see."

The words tumble out of my mouth. I tell her about how I'm certain the ship I'm on will explode. I tell her where we're going. I tell her even that I tried to fight one of her people with a sausage.

"You are a ridiculous fool," Ximu says. I have to smile a little at that, because it's true. "But perhaps you may be useful after all. Tell me how the ship will fall. And where. And when."

The burning star is in my mind's eye, but I have no idea. I know nothing. I tell her as much.

She taps me on the cheek; the hairy spines of her feet hurt. "Not good enough. You must get much better. Or else."

"Or else what?" I'm cheeky, but I don't care. Our mutual dislike has already been well established.

"I can make things much worse for you, even though your body is not here with me. I can torment your mind in such ways as you cannot imagine. You must look more deeply, Prognosticator. I have spent much power on you to place you where you are. I let you escape. I need you to be my eyes and ears. I need you to find things. See you do not fail me."

I start to shudder all over at this realization. Somehow she has buried a seed of her filthy magic in my mind, and now it's sprouting poisonous vines all through me. How will I ever get free?

I struggle then, like a fish on a hook. "What? What thing am I supposed to find?"

"I need you to find a key. And many other things besides. And you will tell no one, do you understand? I will kill all of your people with a word. You, dear Tinker, are my secret weapon."

"And if I refuse?"

"No one can refuse me!" She is so very confident.

"Vespa and Bayne did." It's a simple fact.

And she punishes me for it. So hard, I fall into a deeper blackness, an ugly torment of reliving the past and trying to figure out if it's also the future.

A white city rising through flames, a palace hewn of bone before the world began, a Tinker King in his patched robes filling the air with magical delights, a silver army waiting far below the earth . . . and a box, an ancient, sealed box . . .

"No!" I shout. I don't want her to see. I don't want her to know.

"Yes," she says.

She's still there, squatting inside my mind, sifting through my visions and plucking them with her spider feet into the vast web she spins. It's beyond anything any of us have imagined—what she plans. I can only see it in bits and pieces. Much she is still hiding from me. And yet I must know. I must hold on because if I can know what she plans, I can warn the others.

"You will not tell a soul."

I can't help it. I ask. "Why?"

"Because if you do, you will never see your people again."

And cruel-hearted evil thing that she is, she shows me their faces. The faces of the long departed, the faces of those I never truly knew. Uncle Gen. My cousins. All the other clans.

"You have seen them here. Just like you, they are a piece of my Great Design. And if you want to ever see them again, you will do as I say. See what you're meant to see, send your dreams to me in the night, and you will be reunited with them."

I am silent, hunkered down in the cold, endless dark with her. But she answers the unspoken question anyway.

"And if you do not, all shall be slain."

When I wake, I feel as if I've been thrashed from one end of the cabin to the other. I remember some strange nightmare about being back in the cave again, but when I reach for more, everything falls apart into dark tatters. I suspect it's near dawn, but there's no real way to tell without windows. Truffler is still huddled in his blankets, snoring. He'll be asleep for most of this trip. The iron and the forced separation from his land will make him unwell. I hope he will recover as Piskel has. Some Elementals never recover from being removed from their places of origin. Others are more mobile than we'd like them to be, apparently.

I notice that I've managed to throw what few blankets were remaining to me on the floor, and Truffler has accumulated them into his nest. Piskel uncurls from beside me and yawns, rubbing his eyes.

"Hungry?" I ask.

He looks at me, and long lashes sprout around his eyes. He bats them at me.

"I'll take that as a yes. But I don't have any cake."

I instantly regret saying so because his face falls. He droops over to my shoulder.

I dig in the satchel, looking for the sausage, cheese, anything. It's all gone.

"Piskel!"

He avoids my gaze sheepishly. '

"You ate it all, didn't you?"

He nods, still without looking at me.

"Well," I say, "I hope there's food aboard, or we're all going to be much thinner by the time we reach Scientia."

I follow the corridor back down to the cargo hold. People are milling around, sitting and talking, or curled against the curved walls, sleeping. It's quite hot down here, and I can smell the faint, all-too-familiar odor of burned bone. *Myth.* They're definitely burning *myth* to fly this ship. Surely they know that's illegal? Maybe they don't care.

The few Elementals that I gather were at court when the attack happened are huddled together uncomfortably as far from everything else as they can be. Many of them look terribly ill, and I'd guess it's the presence of the *myth* and the disconnection from their home. I'm wishing I'd brought some dirt, water, anything to offer them that might be of comfort. But I wasn't exactly thinking of all that when we were racing through the burning alleys.

I watch some children playing jacks as unconcerned as if they were not fleeing all they'd ever known. It reminds me so much of home that I'm a bit startled when I notice that the people are looking at me without warmth. There's still a prejudice against my people, even though I was singlehandedly trying to teach the New Londoners how to live without the destructive magic they'd used unknowingly for centuries.

New tragedies bring up old habits, I suppose.

Piskel prods at me. He wants me to stop gawping and find us some food.

I stop near a crewman checking a manifest list against some boxes. I'm surprised they even had time to get together a list.

"Excuse me, sir, where might I find food for me and my companion here?"

Piskel grins hugely at him.

The man looks as though he's about to have a heart attack. He backs against the stack of crates as if I've just thrust a venomous snake in his face and points with a quivering pencil up another winding stair without speaking.

Still not too comfortable with the Elementals, either, I see.

I follow the winding stair until I smell something promising. They've set up a makeshift mess and are slinging gruel into bowls. There's evidently not much to go round because each person only gets one ladleful.

Piskel sticks out his tongue at the slop, but nevertheless pulls out a tiny spoon from some invisible place and slurps it up from my bowl. People stare and turn away when they see us.

I curl up against a window with my bowl and spoon and look out. We're far over the green Euclidean Plain. We're indeed nearing dawn, based on the thin line of light on the horizon. There's not a cloud in the sky. One would never guess we left New London burning behind us.

As I watch, a herd of unicorns below surges over a grassy knoll, their manes and tails like silver currents in the green. It has been centuries since they were able to run here. For the longest time this was all black desert, part of the Creeping Waste. A year on, and the grasslands have fully recovered. As far as we know, all their old inhabitants have been restored. Even if we're unsure about what we've done or what the future holds, at least we can know that in some small corners of this world, we changed things for good.

I just wish it didn't make my heart sink so much to know my people are behind me instead of ahead.

"Syrus!"

Vespa calls from the door. Heads turn for a moment, and then she gets the same sullen stares and cold shoulders that I did. Even if she doesn't want to recognize it, I think everyone else sees what I see in her—her Tinker heritage. She's paler than many of us but only because of her father, I'd guess. The cheekbones and eyes are there, the way she smiles. But unlike the rest of us, she's held on to the magic that we tend to lose as we grow older.

We've never really talked about it much. I don't know how to bring up the conversation, remembering how the Cityfolk used to feel about those with Tinker blood. I doubt she feels the same as them, but I'd imagine her mother is a rather sore subject. She doesn't talk about her, so I assume she'd rather not.

She crosses to me. Piskel stops eating with his spoon halfway to his mouth, looking at her with hope bright in his little face.

"I've been looking for you everywhere." Vespa looks around and lowers her voice. "Come upstairs."

I return my bowl to the mess kitchen, feeling somewhat ashamed. But Piskel is ecstatic, sure that this means we're about to be served tasty treats.

We follow her down a corridor, up several flights of stairs, through another observation deck that doubles as a library and gaming parlor, apparently. On the last level we pass faun sentries, who look faintly green from the flight and the smell of *myth*, most likely.

"Does the Empress know they're using *myth*gas?" I ask.

Vespa shushes me. "I don't know—I don't really see how she

could miss the smell—but it's not something we think should be brought up just yet. Olivia has had a lot to deal with in the last few hours. We need to figure out the lay of the land first. Things in Scientia are likely to be difficult."

"Did you decipher the message yet?"

Vespa shakes her head. "Olivia is working on it, actually. She has a fondness for ciphers, so she says."

"What will happen to the Elementals on board? Will they be given homes?"

"I'm not sure. I hope they'll be able to adjust. Some of those in the hold look quite pitiful, don't they? I'm trying to work with Bayne and Olivia to see if we can give them better accommodations or feed them magic, anything that might comfort them. Maybe you can help me with that."

"Of course."

"And the Captain mentioned that when you're feeling well again, they might be able to use your talents in the control room. The Engineer apparently never made it on board, so if something breaks . . ."

When she says that, fear settles in the pit of my stomach, almost as if what she's said is more a prediction than a possibility.

I suppose a look crosses my face.

"What?" Vespa says.

"I don't know. I guess this just feels too easy."

"You thought that was easy? I'd hate to think what you'd find hard."

A flare of anger blossoms in my heart. "You don't want to know," I say.

We enter a warm audience chamber, lushly fitted with brass and carved wood fixtures. As I run my hand along a bookcase, it shivers under my hand, and I realize that this is living wood. The dryad is still huddled inside, forced into making the wood gleam and change its shape to the occupant's desire. Even the Virulens did not have such horrors. Piskel shrinks back against me, spitting and hissing.

It strangely makes my neck ache at the place where the hybrid spiderlings had been injecting me with their poison. I put my hand over it. The wound is still very tender.

"Is something wrong, Artificer?"

I turn and find Olivia near my elbow. She holds out a fluted glass filled with a pale yellow liquid.

"A tonic to ease you," she says. "We have both, it seems, been through much travail of late."

Her words and manner are so very pretty, but I'm still repulsed by the touch of the poor wood under my hands.

"How can you bear to be in here?" I ask.

Her eyes fly open wide. "What do you mean?"

I realize that it's not just Bayne, Vespa, and me alone with Olivia. There are others here—the Captain, courtiers, hangers-on—the sorts I despise.

I shake my head. "Sorry, nothing. I just meant . . . the closeness, you know."

She frowns slightly.

"It feels a bit stuffy," I say lamely, and take the glass she offers.

"Perhaps you still have a bit of the fever?" Olivia looks as though she wants to put her hand on my forehead, but she wouldn't dare to here. I wish we could walk alone under the eaves of the Forest. It would be so much more natural than all this posing.

"Perhaps."

"I find it comes and goes. Just when I think I'm well . . ." Olivia glances aside at the others to see how much they're paying attention. Then her eyes are searching mine. "Have you had strange dreams, Syrus?"

"Strange dreams?" Somehow the question makes me nervous, as if I've been caught thinking things I shouldn't.

She looks down, suddenly vulnerable. Suddenly not an Empress, just a girl. "Strange dreams of fire and armies . . . armies of machines . . ."

It's as if our minds are connected by some invisible tether. It feels dangerous, like a wire of live *myth*. I step back a little.

"I'm sorry, have I said something wrong?"

I drown in the gray seas of her eyes, wanting to tell her, wanting to say how much I know. *And if you tell anyone, I will kill them.* I can't say anything. My tongue can't make the words. Even as I try, my memory loses its grasp on what I want to say.

"I . . ." Finally I'm able to shake my head and just say, "No, nothing wrong. It's the fever and all that."

"Bayne has been telling us what he was able to find out about the shadowspiders. The venom of the Queen is said to give the gift of prophecy. I keep hoping maybe I'll be able to forecast some good luck." Olivia smiles then.

It takes me a moment to catch up because the words seem to drop into a vast space that's trying to open in my mind.

"Syrus?" Olivia prods.

My attention snaps back, and I realize she's made a joke. "Ah ha, yes." I force a laugh.

My heart is fluttering. Piskel can feel it because he laughs at me and starts casting significant looks in Olivia's direction. I

glance aside and notice a checkerboard on a nearby table, spe-
cially designed with high sides so the pieces can't slide off. There
are two chairs.

"Would you care to play, Majesty?" I ask. A game at least will
take our minds off these things and perhaps stop the strange looks
of the others around us.

I sip at the yellow drink she's given me. It tastes frothy and lem-
ony at once and I have to wonder what's in it, whether it will do
anything to close the dark wound I feel inside.

"Of course," she says.

We take our places opposite each other. Vespa looks over from
her conversation with the Captain and smiles at me as she sees us
settling ourselves.

Piskel is strategizing almost before I've assembled my pieces.
The sylph loves games. He'd be a fierce poker player, I'm quite certain. He points emphatically at my pieces, motioning and gesturing
as to which way they should go.

"You're giving our game away, *didi*," I say out of the corner of
my mouth.

Chagrined, Piskel thumps down on my shoulder with his chin
in his fist.

Olivia looks up briefly from the board. "That word you just
said—*didi*—what does it mean?"

I correct her tone with a smile. The tones of the old language
are hard to understand for people not used to them. "It just means
little brother. I call him that sometimes. I don't think he minds."

Piskel makes a small *bmph* noise, as if to say, *So you'd like to think.*

"And what are the other words for family members?" she says,
sliding her first piece out.

The pieces seem to be magnetized in some way because they stay right where we put them. I want to take the table apart to see how it works. It doesn't quite feel like this is made with *myth*, but then there's so much of it in the room because of the *myth*gas and living wood that I can't really tell.

I tell her all the names—*nainai, gege, waipo, mama, baba.* How we have names for the maternal and paternal sides of the family.

"So many different words! How do you keep them all straight?"

A servant comes to take our glasses and offers us some other refreshment on a silver tray. I hesitate, thinking of all the people and Elementals in the hold.

"Is there enough?" I ask. My stomach growls as if to protest the merest thought of refusal.

And there are cakes.

Piskel's eyes bulge out of his face. Afraid he'll start zigzagging plaid streaks around the room, I contain him gently with a hand, and he squeaks at me with indignation.

Olivia watches us with a bemused expression. "Of course. Have some."

"But the people below . . ."

"Are also being cared for. We don't have much—I doubt this will happen every day, but for right now the Grimgorn envoy is being gracious with his master's stores. We shouldn't trouble ourselves over accepting that generosity." She leans closer to me so that no one else can hear. "I'm aware of what's going on here, Syrus. Have no fear. It will be addressed when we reach Scientia."

I nod and slowly lift my hand away from Piskel.

He makes a triumphant dive toward the tray and begins gnoshing on a bit of crumb cake right then and there, much to the servant's dismay. I scoop him up, cake and all, and hold him while he gorges himself.

The servant offers me a piece, but I shake my head. "I think Piskel needs it more than me."

"You're generous to a fault," Olivia says.

"I like to think so."

Piskel is rolling around in the crumbs in my hand, clutching them to himself with abandon.

"Your move," I say to Olivia.

"I know." She smiles.

Three days out, and I've become used to the daily climb up toward the Imperial suite.

But today for some reason I don't go there directly. What I said to Vespa was true. This was far too easy. And though I can't really understand quite why, I'm fairly certain that even now as we glide over the Euclidean Plain, we're being watched.

I haven't explored the ship much, but today I take the long gangway beyond the hold toward the engines. I want to see how they work, if the rumor about the *myth*gas is true. Piskel is warning me away and wanting me to go back to what's familiar.

I look him straight in the eye as he floats in front of my face. "Little brother, in the pocket or lock it." I try not to be rude, but he can be so irritating! He pouts for a moment, then swan-dives into my pocket as I hold it open.

The burned-bone smell gets stronger the closer I get.

A dark shape moves over near the hatch that leads to the engine compartment.

Trying not to be overly suspicious, I call out to who I assume is a crew member.

"Good morning . . ." I choke on my greeting, though, when gold facial markings flash in the dim everlanterns.

Uncle Gen. Or what was Uncle Gen once upon a time.

"What are you doing here?" I say.

"I might ask the same of you." There is a hiss to his speech that was never there before, reminding me that he is truly not my kin anymore.

I wish my heart wouldn't break every time I see him.

He climbs slowly from the rigging and comes to face me.

Piskel briefly sticks his head out of my pocket, sees who it is, and dives back in.

I grit my teeth and ask again. "What are you doing?"

"I thought you said you would never speak to me."

"I'd hoped I wouldn't have to."

He puts back his hood, and I immediately wish he hadn't. He no longer has hair, just gleaming gold markings over black skin. There is what looks like a metal port at the base of his neck in the same place where I was bitten. I do not want to know what it's for.

"Why?" I say.

"I have told you. This was the better choice. Ximu made me see that this is a better fate for our people."

"How? How is this possibly better?"

It seems for a moment that he might lose his temper, as sometimes the old Gen would. Especially when *Nainai* was nagging him. But he doesn't.

"She will return our ancestral home to us. She will make us kings . . ."

"When? After she stops treating us like meat sacks to feed her spiderlings?"

"Only those who defy her are treated so. The rest of us will become more than you can possibly imagine."

"As warrior slaves? I doubt it."

"No," he says with the first trace of eagerness I've heard in his voice. "No. An army is already waiting . . ." Then he stops himself, as if perhaps he told me a secret he wasn't supposed to. "We just need the key," he says.

I shake my head. Those words sound so familiar. *Find me the key.* The key to what? And where?

"She has sent me to ensure that she gets it," he finishes.

"And so you're doing that by sabotaging the engines?" I ask, looking aside at the engine hatch.

"Just dumping fuel," he says. "If you don't have enough fuel, then you'll be forced to land. The Queen is very near Euclidea. I will meet her there, and you and your Empress will go with me."

Clan mothers help me, but I already know I can't kill him.

Uncle Gen has always been an excellent wrestler. The only way this is going to work is if I'm faster than him. So I don't answer. I just put my head down and barrel into him with my shoulder, trying to knock him down. I wish I had the ability to cast some magical sleeping spell on him or to make him disappear.

But he opens his arms and takes me down with him. He seizes my hair until my eyes water. I kick and jab, and we roll across the gangway and down between the struts while Piskel squeaks and vacates my pocket.

Bless that sylph, for he's in Uncle Gen's face, blinding him and stinging him with curses like a mad wasp until my uncle lets go of me to deal with him.

I sit on his chest and draw my knife. Piskel buzzes close, threatening him.

Uncle Gen laughs. "You wouldn't dare, boy."

"I've done it before," I say, thinking of cousin Raine with a twist in my heart. "I'll do it again if I have to."

"Not this time," he says.

In one great heave he throws me off. The next thing I know, he's out through the hatch.

Breathless, I follow him and look out. He's floating down and away clutching a crimson sail, presumably spun of spidersilk. He manages to get close enough to the ground before one of the dragons swoops from its position at the fore to investigate. I don't see whether they come into conflict or not. The humming engine soon obscures my view.

But now, even though I don't quite understand it, I realize what he wants. Not just me, but Olivia. And it seems to me more, much more, than just the attempt of one sovereign to overcome another. He wants Olivia *alive*.

I climb wearily upstairs. When I enter the Imperial suite, it's obvious to everyone that something's wrong. They stop what they're doing and stare at me.

I find it hard to tell them the truth. I don't want to tell them that one of my own clan is leading the *xiren* against us. Or that he got away from me.

"What's happened?" Bayne asks.

"*Xiren*. Trying to tamper with the engines. I stopped him, but he got away."

Piskel looks between me and them, and then seems to decide it's in his better interest to let this go. The basic facts are correct. I just didn't elaborate.

"You said you thought this was too easy," Vespa said, coming to me and handing me a bit of cordial from the suite's cabinet of spirits. "I guess you were right. Sorry I doubted your judgment."

I nod. "Hopefully there are no more of them on board."

"We must be vigilant," Bayne says. "If we can just make it to Scientia . . ." He doesn't finish. There's really nothing more to be said. With each passing day we're that much closer to Scientia and the uncertainty that waits for us there.

Olivia writes a quick message to the Captain and sends it off with her maid. "At least he'll be aware of the situation. Let us hope the crew finds no more of them on board."

There's a long silence as the room settles around me, and I relax under the welcome influence of the cordial.

Olivia goes back to studying the cipher. It looks as though she's trying to correlate numbers and letters. I see that she's written out several possibilities on a pad but hasn't quite solved it yet. She flips her pen for several seconds before she says, "Bayne, may I have your advice?"

He turns. I'm not sure she's ever willingly asked for this, though he's often given it.

"Majesty?"

"Have you any notion of how your family might react once we land? I can gauge nothing from the envoy, the Captain, or any of your family's servants."

Bayne sighs. "I think of this nearly every moment, Majesty. The truth is, I really have no answer."

"Have none of them given you any sign?"

"It has all been very quiet, Majesty. Almost eerily so. If I didn't know better, it feels as if they were expecting just this sort of thing to happen, so that they could place themselves in the proper position to aid you. But that all seems like far too much conspiracy and would require foresight I doubt my father has."

"Hmm."

"Why, if I may ask?" Bayne says. "Are you close to translating the cipher?"

"Possibly," Olivia says. She clutches at her neck, as if the pain keeps her from thinking. "But it could read a few different ways, unless I'm misunderstanding. I think it's how the numbers are broken in sequence and what they symbolize."

Vespa has returned to her cozy chair and is knitting with some yarn and needles she found in a basket in her room. Piskel assists by counting stitches. Or trying to. We are all doing our best to cover up the *xiren* with other problems.

I examine the patterns of numbers over Olivia's shoulder, but inside I'm worrying at the problem of Gen, the fact that I cannot bring myself to betray him though he has certainly betrayed me and all our clan by siding with Ximu. And I wonder, as I stare down at the rows of ones and zeros, whether he can ever be restored to what he was once before. We restored those wights and wraiths we could match up after the Rousing; surely we can reverse the Queen's dark magic as well.

Vespa clears her throat as if to get my attention and says, "Well, what do we actually know?"

"About?" Bayne asks.

"The Grimgorns. The Ambassador said they had a new Artificer, yes? And that they wished to swear fealty to Olivia personally. It seems that they are still using *myth*, if the things in this ship are any indication. What can be deduced from that?"

"It feels a bit hostile to me," Olivia says, gazing down at the cipher. "As if I'm under house arrest."

"My parents have always been manipulative and self-interested, it's true," Bayne says slowly. "But I can't imagine they'd actively seek to hurt anyone."

"Bayne, they disinherited you!" Vespa says.

Bayne's lightning gaze flicks out at her. "Thank you for the reminder."

"I just mean—they do hurt people. They hurt you!"

"That's . . . private," he says. "They could have had me killed or locked away in an asylum any number of times. Even when they knew what I was, they didn't ever really threaten me."

"Except with a marriage you didn't want . . . ," Vespa retorts.

Olivia and I look at each other, and I suspect our faces mirror our thoughts.

"We are not talking about me," Bayne says, exasperation leaking into his voice. "We're, as you so rightly pointed out, trying to deduce what we know, so that we can move forward with any plans for the future. The problem is that we never really had a choice as to whether we wanted to come here. We had to leave. The ship was our only way out. We took it."

It amazes me how much like an old married couple these two sound with their sniping and bickering. And yet neither of them will give in to the other. I find it strange.

Olivia is humming to herself. It's almost as though she's not listening, even though she's the one who started this conversation. I watch her as she pores over the numbers. She scratches absently at the bandage, and I can see that the skin all around it is red and raw.

"What do we do, then?" Vespa asks.

"My feeling is that we test the waters when we arrive in Scientia. I don't doubt that my parents are trying to manipulate things to suit their own ends. But I can't believe they quite expected anything like this. I believe they'll be as surprised and taken aback as we were. The news that we've awoken potentially more Umbrals besides Ximu should be spread far and wide. Perhaps even the Lords of the other Cities will want to convene to decide what course of action might be taken. Precisely because my parents are manipulative and self-serving sorts, I'm quite certain they'll do whatever they can to protect Scientia's interests."

"But am I part of that interest, I wonder?" Olivia says softly.

"They would be foolish indeed, Majesty, to do away with you openly. And I doubt it would be to their advantage to do so, not now. But it's true we shouldn't rule out that you may be in danger. You have been since we freed you from your predecessor. This situation, albeit complex, is nothing new."

"I'm not sure that's entirely comforting."

When I see Olivia's running low on ink, I find another bottle, uncap it, and hand it to her. It's startling to me that she was never trained in statecraft. She certainly was never intended to rule.

I feel I must try to reassure her if I can. "I think Bayne's just saying that we've gone through much to get here. We may go through more, but we're building our strength. We know more than we would have otherwise if we'd not all gone into the spider's web." I shudder to think about it, remembering Uncle Gen's surety that we would all be kings. Olivia looks at me as if she feels the same awful sensation I do in the pit of my stomach.

"True."

"We will just have to be careful," Bayne says. "I don't trust my parents, but I'll take this situation over being stuck in the caves of that demon any day."

Vespa nods and Piskel trumpets his agreement.

"Besides," Bayne says with the ghost of a smile, "there may yet be those loyal to me there. There are many favors I can call upon to be repaid, if necessary."

"All may yet be restored?" Olivia asks. The hope in her voice is almost painful.

"All may indeed be restored," Bayne says.

I want to see it—Olivia crowned and in some beautiful palace, ruling us all with just peace. But nothing of the sort enters my vision.

All I see is a white palace aflame and a silver army marching to some uncertain end.

CHAPTER 16

On the fifth day approaching dawn, the *Sullen Harpy* was beginning its long, careful descent toward Scientia. Vespa had heard Syrus mutter off and on about how the ship was going to crash horribly throughout the voyage, but when questioned, he would never answer directly as to what he was talking about. He had stopped mentioning it after the *xiren* had been discovered. Perhaps he felt he'd averted disaster.

But what if the poison had indeed given him the gift of sight, as it was reputed to do?

If such a thing was going to happen, it would have to happen in a hurry, she thought. They were very nearly there.

This dawn she watched the sun spread seeking fingers over the mountains that loomed to the north and east. Far away a white jewel floated on the bosom of a raised hill—Scientia, she guessed.

Bayne came to stand beside her.

"Did you ever think you would see it again?" she asked.

"No. No, I did not." As ever, it seemed there was so much under the surface of his words that she could barely trace all the emotions there.

She wanted to ask him how it felt. It wasn't hard for her to imagine. Being in the Museum and seeing the destruction had been difficult, even as she owned that the Museum's very existence had been founded on dubious principles.

"Are you happy?" She regretted it as soon as she'd said it.

The blue fire of his gaze lashed her before he said, "I don't know what that means."

"I wish you did."

"I do too," he admitted with a sigh.

She decided to leave that one alone and said instead, pointing toward the distant white walls, "That's where you grew up, then?"

"Yes," he said.

The hill was densely packed with tiers of buildings and walls. "Where are we supposed to land?"

He pointed to a spit of land that thrust out into the scarlet waves of the Winedark Sea.

"There."

Vespa blanched. "Why?" was all she could say.

"Because it would be a long walk to the palace otherwise." He shrugged. "It can get a bit blustery, but it should be fine."

She could already feel the sea wind buffeting them as the *Sullen Harpy* nosed into it.

"Landing one of these is definitely not for the fainthearted," he said.

"I can see that," she said.

"Sir, madam," the purser called to them. "Best go prepare for landing. It can get a bit rough. We should be fully down in an hour at most."

"Thank you," Vespa said.

Bayne helped her back up to her cabin and then returned to the one he shared with Syrus. She could already feel the ship bucking and being buffeted by the sea wind. Though she'd wanted to see how by all the false saints they were going to get the ship properly moored, in some ways she would be just as happy not to know.

Vespa wished she had the dream book to study while she waited. She'd left it in the Imperial suite where they spent the evenings trying to understand the cipher, while ignoring the growling of their stomachs. Supplies were so low that only the children had been fed this morning.

She hesitated, but it was an hour of waiting with nothing to do. Might as well go seek out the book Syrus had brought her and see if it yielded any answers. In the latest dream, she'd been in the chamber filled with gold, looking for something she couldn't find.

Vespa went out into the corridor and, as she turned the corner, the airship tilted, and someone fetched up hard against her.

"Excuse me," she said.

Then the person looked up, and the golden shadowspider markings shimmered on his forehead.

"*Xiren*," she whispered. Another one.

He looked just as surprised as she was. He hesitated, and then there were voices of crewmen coming upstairs. He dashed down the corridor away from her.

Vespa considered trying to stop him with a blast of etheric energy, but she knew how poor her targeting skills still were. Add that to the fact that they were on a ship full of volatile *myth*gas, and so she shouted instead.

Bayne came out of his room just as she was weaving as best she could toward it.

She told him what she'd seen and which way the *xiren* had gone.

"All right, then. Get back in your room and lock it tight."

Part of her wanted to heed his advice, but she just couldn't.

"Business associates, remember?" She smiled. "I can help you."

He nodded then, and they stumbled as best they could in the direction she'd indicated.

Vespa realized as she ran that she didn't really know much about what the *xiren* were capable of, despite the few things Bayne and Syrus had been able to find out about them. If they could change into spiders, would they be so small that they could easily hide? And if that were true, could the ship literally be crawling with *xiren* agents?

The thought definitely made her flesh creep.

When they came to the end of the corridor, the *xiren* was nowhere to be found.

"Which way?" Bayne asked. "We must find it!"

They looked at each other with the same thought. Syrus had told them that the other *xiren* had wanted the Empress. "Olivia!"

Bayne lunged up the stairs, taking as many at a time as he could. Vespa followed, hating the encumbrance of her skirts and the way it felt as if she might trip over her own pounding heart.

When they entered the solarium, they were relieved to find Syrus and Olivia hunched over the cipher while her maid sat nearby darning a stocking. It was a deceptively tranquil scene of domesticity.

Syrus and Olivia looked up. "I've figured it out!" Olivia said. "I know what it says!"

Then she saw Bayne's face. "Is something wrong?" Olivia asked. "The Captain had told us to prepare for landing. This seemed much the best way."

"There is another shadowspider aboard," Bayne said.

Syrus looked at them in alarm. "And you can't find him?"

Bayne shook his head.

Syrus rose and was rocked back on his heels as the ship plunged against the sea wind. "If I can wake Truffler, he might be able to sniff him out."

He looked toward Olivia for permission.

"Please," she said. "If you find him, retain him for questioning." She said this with a hard set to her mouth that Vespa almost hated to see, even as she knew it was necessary. "We'll talk about the note when you return. The news it brings is not much better, I fear."

"Your Majesty."

All of them bowed, and then they were racing down again to Syrus and Bayne's room. Syrus woke Truffler with great effort and not a little bribery involving certain things the hob loved—the promise of mushrooms, for example.

"Can you find this *xiren* for us, Truffler?" Vespa asked when the hob finally crawled out of his blankets. "We would be most grateful to you; you will have done something very important if you can help us catch it."

Truffler grunted and sniffed the air. Without bothering to even answer, he was out of the door and down the hallway, sniffing and swinging his head this way and that like nothing so much as a dog hot on the trail of a pheasant.

They followed him and were about halfway down the stairs toward the hold when they heard shouting from the control room they'd just passed.

"Syrus," Bayne said, "go fetch the Empress! I want her closer to the escape gliders, just in case."

Syrus nodded and hurried back the way they'd come.

Bayne and Vespa hurled themselves back up the stairs and through the control room door. The *xiren* was fighting the navigator to get control of the ship's wheel. While there were several officers with sidearms, none of them would fire for obvious reasons. A sidearm was usually a last resort or used to keep pirates from taking the ship from the outside. The navigator gave a good fight, but he was no match for an expert assassin with poison at his disposal. The others, unable to get round the struts and other support instruments, slunk out of the way.

The navigator soon slumped to the deck, and the *xiren* gripped the wheel, turning the airship so abruptly that it tilted quite dangerously.

Vespa watched, frozen with horror.

Bayne crept toward the *xiren*. It was too close on the navigation deck for Bayne to use the magical sword Vespa had seen him use in the past, so he attempted to cast a sleeping charm.

The *xiren* shook it off with ease. Bayne tried something stronger, but it rebounded. Evidently, the *xiren* were capable of producing shields when the situation warranted it.

The etheric energy bounced around the room, and Vespa prayed it would just go out, against all the Laws of Magic. She thought for a moment her prayers had been answered until she saw smoke pouring out of the control panel, and the smells of melting wire and metal drifted across the cabin. The officers started screaming.

Vespa looked around for any sort of extinguishing equipment, but it was all up closer to the control area, not on the observation part of the deck where she stood.

"Put it out!" she yelled to the people who were still on the control deck. But they were too terrified to act, and getting around

Bayne and the struggling *xiren* wouldn't have been easy.

Vespa closed her eyes and concentrated. She tried sending dampening power out to the fire. But it seemed to have the opposite effect. Whether it was the presence of the *myth*gas or something else, the fire, which had previously been smoldering, burst into full flame.

Finally, the *xiren* must have realized he wasn't going to get out of the situation. He disengaged from Bayne and stepped back, all the way into the burning control panel.

Vespa watched in horror as he allowed himself to catch fire. She wondered why at first, but then she understood when he vaulted off the control bridge and barreled past her out the door.

"He's going for the *myth*gas!" Bayne yelled.

The flaming *xiren* dove for the wall of one of the ballonets that lifted and lowered the airship. Bayne came after him, only just managing to tackle him before he went through the wall, which breathed over them like the gullet of some giant Unnatural.

While Vespa watched, gripping the railing until she thought her knuckles would crack, the two rolled over and over. The flaming *xiren* was bent on getting to the ballonet, and Bayne was just as bent on keeping the ship from exploding. They fought on the small landing until the flames were smothered. For good measure Bayne delivered a strong blow to the *xiren*'s head. He went limp.

"That should hold him for a while," Bayne said.

Vespa had just sighed in relief when a small explosion rocked the control room.

She and Bayne looked at each other in terror.

"Damn!" Bayne said. "We should go below and secure a glider. We shouldn't be that far from the ground, but getting everyone there will still be treacherous."

Truffler had come down the stairs from the upper deck, but he was mesmerized, watching fire blooming from the control room door.

"Come, old man," Vespa said, climbing up to him and taking his hand. She led him past the unconscious *xiren* and down the stairs.

The hold was chaos. People screamed and cried as crewmembers tried to herd them away from the oncoming flames. They wrestled one another for access to the little pods of escape gliders that were attached to the bottom of the airship, while the poor Elementals huddled together—the dryads going leafless in terror.

It was the attack on New London all over again. Except this time they were one thousand feet in the air above rock and sea. And there was no one to fight.

Vespa wrestled with her own terror. She didn't think she'd ever been this afraid in her life, even when it looked as though Charles was going to win. Even when it had been hopeless, she'd kept her head down and tried to solve the problem.

But this time she didn't have the same surety. She wasn't certain how to deal with creatures who could blend into the shadows and were so ruthless and single-minded about achieving their agenda. Charles had certainly been ruthless, but she had had the Heart to stop him. She didn't know how to stop a fire from spreading to the bubble of *myth*gas over them when she couldn't rely on her own magic. Without proper control of her magic, she didn't think she could stop even a sylph.

"Bayne, what can we do?" she shouted. "There aren't enough gliders for everyone. We must do something else!"

Truffler held Vespa's hand, but he was moaning in utter terror.

Bayne cast about, searching the smoke-choked hold for anything that might be of use. "There's likely to be a big explosion soon; we're minutes away from it. We just need something—a sail, a canvas—that can catch the wind and float us free of the blast, like the other *xiren* evidently used to escape. We'll use magic to keep it steady, like a flying carpet in the forbidden tales."

"That doesn't sound all that promising!" Vespa said, looking around. She didn't really see anything that might be of use.

"Staying here doesn't look so promising either!" Bayne yelled.

"Let's ask the Elementals—maybe they can help!"

She dragged Truffler over just as another explosion rocked the ship and more rescue gliders detached from the underbelly of the cargo hold.

Vespa raced over to the huddled Forest Elementals. The fauns stared at her with sullen eyes, and the dryads were nearly naked, having shivered off all their leaves in the smoke.

"We're trying to find a way to get us all safely to ground. Will you lend us your magic so that we can all do so?" Vespa asked.

They all looked at her without saying anything. Truffler said a few strong-sounding words that she didn't understand.

"Vespa!" Bayne cried.

She heard the detonation of the *myth*gas just as a great jet of green flame burst through one of the ballonet walls. In front of it ran Syrus hand in hand with Olivia and Piskel buzzing around them in mad terror. Olivia's maid was a few paces behind them, and Vespa watched helplessly as she was swallowed in gouts of *myth*fire.

There was no more time to think or plan. Vespa enclosed everyone nearby in a giant protective shield. Luckily, this time it worked.

Bayne was nearest her, and she took his hand. She could only force out three words: "I need you."

To keep a protective shield of such size viable in a cauldron of fire, especially after not having done such work in a long while, nearly drained Vespa dry. Then she felt Bayne.

He was there in her mind again as he had been long ago in that golden country where sylphs had floated around them. Everything danced in a whirl of *myth*fire, golden leaves, bits of burning things following them on their journey through the sky above Scientia. Vespa was dimly aware of the wounded airship limping away from the City before the final blast sent the remains careening down into the scarlet waves. The escape gliders circled, some crashing into the sea, some into the walls, some very few landing on the strip before Scientia's gates. The magic pressure eased as a griffin and a young dragon who had been escorting the airship took the sphere and nudged it between them toward safe ground. She felt the Elementals within lending their strength too, holding them up, keeping the shield impermeable to the flames.

Bayne was looking at her in that way he'd said he never would again on the road to Ximu's lair.

Bayne, Vespa said, deep within the country of their magic. *Does this mean . . .*

His eyes were blue, so blue and full of things that she knew if only she could just find the key, she could unlock all he wanted to say. She knew also in that moment that she could compel him to tell her, but she knew the price of that.

What is it? Vespa asked.

He looked down at their joined hands. The green and gold fire swirled around them in patterns she could barely track.

I swore, Bayne said at last, looking up. The pain there, the absolute regret, nearly stopped Vespa's heart.

And then everything unraveled around them. For a moment Vespa thought they were still falling through the air, until she realized that they were actually safe on the ground. The dragon and griffin stood near them, and the other Elementals huddled between them, still slightly stunned and likely sick from giving over so much magic. Syrus and Olivia were nearby, and Vespa saw their fingers slide apart while they both blushed and pretended not to look at each other.

Here and there, people were climbing from the few battered gliders. Guards and other crewmen raced across the cracked red earth toward them.

Vespa turned to Bayne. "You swore what?" she said. Her throat burned as if she'd swallowed the ship's fire.

She was exhausted, so exhausted that her very bones vibrated with it. She took a trembling step toward him, not sure he'd heard her. "What did you swear, Bayne?"

But he would not look at her, nor would he answer. He turned away and faced the burning dawn.

CHAPTER 17 ━━

I can't breathe without an inner trembling nearly shaking the skin from my bones. What I saw came true. I watched the ship fall in green fire from the sky. Watched it *in the sky* while I floated in a magic bubble.

I feel like I'll be breathing that fire and smoke forever. That terrible realization that what I had seen came true. The vast darkness opens inside me and laughs.

"Syrus," Olivia says. She's coughing and looking ill again, and I wonder if the poison made her see the same things.

"Did you see it?" I ask. "The ship?"

She frowns. "Yes, of course."

"I mean, in your mind. Did you see it in your mind? Did you know that it was going to happen before it did?"

"Well, no. At least, I don't think so. Did you?" she asks.

I'm afraid to tell her. I don't want her to ask me questions that I won't or can't answer. I bite my lip against the truth. Piskel, of course, gives everything away by stepping out from behind my ear and nodding emphatically.

"Syrus, what did you see?"

I don't want to tell her. I don't understand it myself, why the visions fill me with such terrible foreboding. I'm not even sure what they mean. Well, obviously I know what the airship one meant now. I suppose the white city is the one on the hill above us, hidden by tiers of walls. But the army?

I shake my head. "It's all really too fuzzy to try to explain."

But she figures it out anyway. "So you knew about the airship?"

"Yes." I feel deeply chagrined, wishing I'd put more stock in something I didn't want to believe.

"When things become clearer, tell me," she says. She knows I'm hiding things; it must be plain on my face. "I want to know. You may be able to prevent disaster."

I can't help but wonder: Even if we know something, can we still prevent it?

Guards, crewmen, and several dray carts are finally making their way to us across the landing area. We are hemmed in by the wall of the city rising on one side and sea cliffs on all the others.

Someone yells, "'Ware! Kraken!"

And we're all suddenly racing to the cliff's edge, those of us who can. The wind becomes not just an insistent tug but a slap, stinging my eyes with its salt and fish. I adjust my satchel so that it doesn't chafe my neck. In the near distance, looping tentacles break the scarlet surface of the Winedark Sea and close around the wreckage of the *Sullen Harpy*. A great eye rolls up out of the foam, and a giant beak devours the broken airship. I am just really, really glad I did not go down with the ship at this moment.

"A Kraken!" Olivia says. The wind has put color in her cheeks and shine in her eyes. "Can you believe it?"

I think of the Kraken we helped rescue from beneath the Tower a year ago, just before Tianlong was released. I smile and say, "Yes."

The murmurs of everyone around us are carried away by the wind. We all turn as a carriage approaches from the landing area. It reminds me strongly of the carriages of New London, and as it gets even closer, I'm quite certain that the horses that pull it are *myth*work.

Olivia stiffens beside me. She's noticed the same thing.

A thin man emerges from the carriage. He's dressed in the manner of servants before the Rousing—powdered wig, frock coat, embroidered waistcoat, and heeled shoes. The man looks positively antique.

Olivia casts a frown upon him. "What is the meaning of this? Surely your masters realize that all such carriages of this nature have been forbidden throughout the Empire?"

He barely inclines his head. "Your Majesty will forgive this breach of your edict, but we have no other conveyances at present that afford you the royal luxury to which you are no doubt accustomed."

A strained look comes across Bayne's face.

"I am accustomed to the luxury of having my edicts followed, Mr. . . . ?"

"Sir Reynard, Majesty." He signals to the footman to open the door.

Olivia peers inside at the crushed velvet and silver fittings, the gleaming everlantern, and the sumptuous food hamper that appears in the center of one of the seats at a touch from the footman. "My, my," she says in an aside to Bayne, "your family does not believe in doing anything halfway, do they?"

Bayne's eyes lock with Reynard's. "No, Your Majesty, they do not."

Olivia lifts her chin. "Sir Reynard, we would be most obliged if you would send word to your lord that while we appreciate this hospitality, we cannot accept it. We endured the airship because it was our only means of transport, but now that we have a choice, we would prefer a conveyance that does not offend our Elemental subjects. If no such conveyance is available, then we will ride on the dray cart."

I feel as though my heart will burst with pride at this, though everyone who is within earshot mutters in surprise. The Elementals who survived with us look relieved, and Piskel thumbs his nose at Sir Reynard.

The man is a slick diplomat. Whatever surprise or mirth he may feel at the Empress's decree is hidden in the flourish of his deep bow. "I shall relay the message, Your Majesty," he says.

He disappears back into the carriage, hardly sparing us another glance.

Olivia doesn't hesitate. "Come," she says, waving all toward the dray cart with her.

Bayne tries to speak, but no one is paying attention. I see him close his mouth as Olivia calls to an old man, "Driver!"

He is busily loading the few battered trunks that made it to the ground onto his cart.

"I am afraid we must burden you with more cargo," Olivia says.

"Eh?" the old man says, holding a brass tube to his ear.

Olivia yells into it. "Pray forgive us, but we must ride on your cart to the palace!" she shouts.

The driver understands this time. Startled, he blushes and says, "Why of course, lady. Me and Morlock and Porlock here would be honored." He nods toward his charges—two oxen that turn their heads at the sound of their names. They look well cared for, which is more than could often be said of some of the dray animals in New London.

"Good enough, then," Olivia says.

She turns to me and smiles. "Might you help me up?"

If she is determined to do this, I'll certainly not stop her. I circle her waist with my hands and lift her up to the cart. Slender as she is, she's oddly heavy. My face heats at her closeness.

"Thank you," Olivia says. She hitches up her skirts and climbs toward the back of the cart as if she were stepping onto a ballroom floor. I help Truffler and Vespa, and then Bayne and I are scrambling up as well. The rest of the Elementals and the humans who managed to land safely take other carts or walk.

Bayne removes his jacket and spreads it for the women to sit upon. "I fear there is little other comfort I can offer at present."

"It's enough comfort now to know that we are alive," Olivia says. Vespa takes her hand. I think we're all trying hard to pretend the danger's over, even though we know it's just beginning.

The ride is long and painful. Each time the cart goes over a rut or hillock, it feels as if the cart jumps six feet. My bottom feels every jolt in the road.

Luckily, the view makes up for it.

In the distance a ring of mountains poke their heads into the clouds. The sea cliffs rush toward them, and their meeting has spawned a broad hill crowned by a city that glows eerily white. The city rambles down the hill in tiers, and the palace disappears from view as we come under the gates. Bayne spreads his hands as we enter. "Scientia, the City of Knowledge."

My eyes bug out of my head. I'd glimpsed it from the sky, of course, but I mostly was keeping my eyes closed then and hoping I wasn't about to die. Piskel peeks out of my collar and whistles long and low.

We enter under a giant clock tower, its face lit by *myth* and flanked by the wings of the Ineffable Watchmaker. Enclosed within it is a station, and now I understand some of the tracks and lines I couldn't make sense of from the air. "This is the speed trolley," Bayne says. "I was going to suggest we take one of these if it's still in operation, but no matter."

Despite the fact that *myth* is likely still the source for their energy, I admire the trolleys as they pull soundlessly out of the stations and climb through the steep streets to their various destinations across the city. I think again about how I wanted to convert the boiler in the warehouse to something other than coal. If only the same could be true here. What could we create if we could find the proper source of energy?

There are, in fact, levels of streets, and our oxcart naturally descends to the lowest (and slowest) level. Above us on raised tracks I can see things that look like individual train cars whizzing by, many of them brightly colored or sporting wings.

"Another luxury of Scientia that New London never got around to having," Bayne says when he notices me looking up open-mouthed. "Probably a good thing too. Air-cars are quite dangerous, especially when . . . well, there you have it."

I watch in amazement as a car departs from the track and leaps the spaces between buildings for several seconds, its beetlelike wings outspread, before being joined with a track going the opposite direction.

"They're trying to make them completely free-flying, but they haven't figured that out yet," Bayne says. "It's a system of powerful magnets and *myth*current that makes it work. But sometimes," he says, bringing my attention back down to the street and the rusted hull of an air-car nearby, "it doesn't work so well."

I keep watching the air-cars, wishing I could ride one and at the same time feeling guilty for wanting to. I can't imagine the enormous amount of energy those tracks must need to propel, release, and receive the cars.

"Can be very good for shipping, though," Bayne says.

I nod. I can imagine a system of these coming up from the docks at Vaunting Harbor all the way up to New London.

People are lining the streets, but they do not throw flowers or shout greetings. They're likely more interested in what we have in our pockets than who we are. It reminds me very much of Lowtown in the olden days, with its hexshops and gin palaces, rag-and-bones dens and dollhouses (as *Nainai* would sometimes call the brothels). Their glances at us are furtive and their voices low. There is none of the boisterous joy that had risen up in the New London we'd rebuilt. These people are either cowed and afraid or up to no good.

Olivia seems to notice because her expression is grim. She pulls her collar closer over the bandage just after I spot a bit of blood seeping through. I want to say something but decide it would be best not to call attention to it here.

"The oldest bit," Bayne says above the din of the streets, "is the white palace you saw on the crown of the hill. That's where I grew up. When my family came here before the destruction of Euclidea, they renovated some of it. The rest is haunted, and we never go in there. The livelier districts are here in the lower rings anyway, which were built after my family came to live in the palace."

"Have you been visited by any of the ghosts?" Vespa asks.

"I've often thought I saw a black wolf walking the halls deep in the night. Once I think he even looked at me with amber eyes, but that could also have been the New Year wine talking," Bayne says.

I'm glad of the sunshine; at the mention of the black wolf, it's as if a deadly chill reaches down from the crown of the hill to seize me. "That's where the Tinker King lived, isn't it?"

"The Architects believed so, though the research was admittedly thin," Bayne says.

"We always told stories that when we first came into this world, our leader, Blackwolf, who became known as the Tinker King, reigned here, long before the scattering of the clans and the coming of New London," I say. "Most of us just thought they were bedtime stories meant to make us feel better about our plight. It's hard to believe that they're true."

I don't mention *Nainai*'s fondest dream—the clans reigning here again. I loved her stories, but her daydreams made me uncomfortable. Why was the Forest not enough? And what did I have to do with it? She always told me I was destined for greatness. I see very little greatness in my circumstances now.

I always thought when *Nainai* said such things that she meant I would save my people from the Refineries or find a new place for us to live. I suppose I did help free the Elementals, but that has become more of a curse than a blessing these last few days. As for my people, I know where they are now. Far behind me with Ximu's army.

Everyone falls silent, as if they pick up on my mood.

At last the massive white gates of the Bone Palace block out the sun, and the oxcart pulls into the shadowed recesses of the palace's inner court. Bayne and I leap off the cart and help the others down.

Despite the austere ivory of the palace exterior, the courtyard glimmers with a multitude of tiles from palest blue to rich
navy. Interspersed here and there are wider, broader tiles with the
Wyvern emblem of the Grimgorns. Fresh water splashes from a
basin, quiet and refreshing after our long, harrowing journey. This
is the newer part of the palace; I have the distinct feeling that the
old has been thoroughly covered by the new where it has been
allowed to do so.

No one is there to greet us—not Sir Reynard or any other servant. After a few moments Bayne says to the driver: "If you would
be so kind as to wait here, I'll send someone to help unload the rest
of your cargo. Meanwhile, refresh yourself and your charges."

The driver nods and hunkers down next to the cart.

Bayne turns toward us, and the expression on his face is carefully neutral. "This way."

But Olivia puts her hand on his arm. "I want to tell you something before we go farther."

"Your Majesty?"

She takes the note from the Phoenix from her pocket. "I think
I understand the code. Whoever built the Phoenix wanted us to
know that things are not as they seem, and that we may be in grave
danger."

"From whom?" Bayne says. His words are clipped.

She shakes her head. "It doesn't say. And it's only signed 'NT.'
Does anyone in your household bear those initials?"

"Not when I was here, anyway," Bayne says

"What should we do?" Vespa asks. She's got Truffler by the hand,
and Piskel is floating around her. She looks as lost and vulnerable
as we all feel.

Bayne runs a hand through his hair and shakes out ash. "There's not much we can do," he says. "We must just go forward and take the adventure that comes to us." He looks around at all of us, and then finally Olivia nods.

"All right, then," she says. "Onward." That one word is quite possibly the bravest I've ever heard.

Bayne leads us. I try to pay close attention to the route, but I have to give up after what seems like half an hour of wandering through courtyards and long halls. I'm generally good at this sort of thing, so it annoys me that the Bone Palace is already getting the better of me.

We're about to pass through yet another elaborate courtyard when a young man extricates himself from a group of well-dressed people standing under a tangle of vines.

"Bayne!"

The family resemblance is obvious, though the boy's coloring is different—light brown hair instead of dark, hazel eyes instead of blue—but the nose and chin are the same.

Bayne's face twists as if he wants to speak, but he doesn't. Yet when the boy embraces him, his arms go round him.

"Arlen, you should not," Bayne whispers.

The boy holds him all the more tightly before stepping away.

I'm just beginning to wonder if the note is mistaken when a shadow separates itself from the others under the arbor.

The young man who walks toward us is so familiar, he makes my stomach twist. And yet he is so unfamiliar that I can't be sure of what I'm seeing. I watch all the blood drain out of Vespa's face as the man gathers his brocaded coat about him and smiles uncertainly at us.

He walks right up to Vespa, as natural as if they were just passing on the street. He holds out a gloved hand on which rests a giant ring carved with the Wyvern crest of Grimgorn. Vespa recoils like a spitting cat, refusing to take his hand.

He says in a calm, remarkably kind voice, "Charles Waddingly-Grimgorn, ducal Regent, at your service."

CHAPTER 18

I know who you are," Vespa said. She did not give him her hand; instead, she looked like she might strike him. "I know *what* you are."

Bayne was white with fury, too flabbergasted to speak.

Syrus put himself between Charles and Olivia.

Charles regarded all of them with a rueful smile. "I expected this. And I am very sorry for the shock. But I am not at all what you think, Miss Nyx."

Piskel started toward him with armfuls of curses, but Bayne clapped a hand around him in the air. He buzzed inside Bayne's palm, shrieking.

Vespa said, "If you are not the Grue, then what are you?"

"Myself again, thankfully."

"Explain yourself," Bayne said. "How came you to wear the ducal seal of Grimgorn?" He was still white as a sheet, his eyes glittering. One hand trembled as he held Piskel, as if he would incinerate Charles on the spot.

Charles answered Vespa. "I went to Old London, as you witnessed. There is precious little magic there, so the Grue was starving for want of it. But there are pockets of it here and there, I suppose. An old country doctor, of all people, helped purge him from me at last."

"But . . . I saw it eat your heart that night outside the Manticore's prison," Vespa said. "I saw you become it." Her voice was still barely above a whisper of horror.

Charles nodded. "Truthfully, Miss Nyx, I had only been in your father's employ a few short months before the Grue found me in the basement and offered me power or death. I am ashamed to say I wasn't man enough to die. There was so much I wanted to know and do; I so desperately wanted to live!

"As to how I came to be Regent, that is an even sadder tale, which I shall relate over supper. I am glad you accepted my invitation, Majesty, so that I might explain these things to you in person."

He bowed to Olivia, but she stood still as stone, glancing between Bayne and him.

"Sir Reynard," Charles called. The seneschal detached himself from where he had been waiting under the arbor and came to Charles's side.

Again the rueful, almost sheepish smile overtook Charles's expression. And then the smile faded, and a look of true sorrow crossed his face. "I am very sorry for the pain I must have caused you. All of you," he said, locking eyes with each of them in turn. "I don't expect that we can be friends right away, but I shall endeavor to do better by you hereafter. Especially you, Miss Nyx. Especially you." He tried to hold her gaze, but she wouldn't allow it. She stared hard at the floor.

Bayne opened his mouth to speak, but Sir Reynard interrupted before he could say a word. "My Lord Regent will tell the rest of his tale after you've had a chance to rest. For now, please, let me lead you to your quarters. And if you have need of anything, we will be happy to accommodate you. Welcome to Grimgorn."

Charles bowed to them. None of them returned it.

"This way, please," Reynard said, smiling an unctuous smile.

Arlen looked like he wanted to say something to Bayne before Sir Reynard led them off, but Charles held him still. Bayne shook his head ever so slightly.

Vespa found it hard to walk or breathe, so stunned was she by the sight of Charles.

"Did you see him?" she asked Bayne. "Did you hear what he said?"

Bayne looked aside at her. "Yes and yes."

"Do you believe him?"

Bayne was silent. Their shoes echoed on the marble floors.

"What should we do? How can we possibly stay here?" She clutched at his sleeve.

He nodded toward Reynard, whose ear was tilted toward them. "Wait," he mouthed.

Vespa managed to keep silent, though everything she wanted to say nearly choked her. How could any of this be? How could they believe a word Charles said? How had he gotten here, and how by all the false saints had he become Regent of Grimgorn? And what could they do about any of it? She was absolutely incredulous. He could no more be telling the truth than . . . than the Grue could.

And yet she'd sensed no magic about him. She hadn't even had the faintest wrong feeling whatsoever except her own very horrified feelings at seeing him walk up to her wearing the trappings of a Duke. She had sensed no duplicity in his eyes, which she had noticed, rather oddly, were similar to the color of her own. Perhaps a bit more hazel. She had always thought his eyes like cesspools. And his hair had funny golden curls that she'd not noticed before either.

She made her hands into fists and marched alongside the others, trying not to think about it. But it was nearly impossible not to. What in the name of Darwin and all his Apes was going on here?

The expressions on the faces of the servants they passed were difficult to read, but wherever they went, whispers followed. Vespa glanced at Bayne and saw a muscle in his jaw twitch at the latest group of whispering courtiers.

Olivia dropped back and took Vespa's arm. "Penny," Olivia said. She smiled at her, and Vespa returned it as best she could.

"It seems a rather grim place," Vespa said, looking aside at a mosaic of a wolf engaged in a battle to the death with a spider that resembled Ximu. "Who knows what we've walked into?"

"We must have strength and courage, my friend. That is what you've taught me," Olivia whispered. She squeezed Vespa's arm. "Strength and courage."

Reynard led them each to quarters in very different wings of the palace. Vespa didn't miss the fact that this was a way of keeping them isolated from one another, an easier way of keeping abreast of them all separately. She didn't like it. Something was very wrong here, and she was certainly starting to suspect why someone had sent the note via the golden Phoenix! She especially worried about Olivia. It was obvious how terribly vulnerable she was now. What would keep Charles from taking advantage?

Vespa shook her head and looked around the room she'd been given. It was beautifully appointed, with a carved bed draped in swathes of peach and teal silk. The pillows were embroidered with fine designs of fish and shells. There were statues of well-endowed mermaids and leaping dolphins in raised frescoes all along the walls. There was a basin with cool, clear water over by a colonnaded window and a tray filled with cherries and apricots from the orchards of Scientia.

And in a cut glass and mirror-encrusted chest was a bottle of what looked like some ruby cordial and a tray of delicate cardamom and nutmeg–scented cakes. Vespa didn't hesitate. She poured herself a glass of cordial and stuffed herself with cakes and cherries until she thought she might be sick.

She considered that it probably wouldn't take much to poison her, if that was the route Charles chose to rid himself of her at some point, and she laughed aloud.

Add it to the list, she thought. With everything that had happened in the past week—rescuing Syrus, the discovery of Lucy ruling the shadowspiders, the destruction of New London, the explosion of the airship just as they arrived in Scientia, Charles—she found herself sobbing. She had never thought when she had dreamed as a child of being the first female Pedant that it would be so terribly lonely.

She dashed the last few tears away and inwardly scolded herself for being self-indulgent. Syrus had risked much to get her the dream interpretation book, despite all he had been through. She needed to figure out what it meant. If, as the interpretation book had said, the dream meant that she was about to enter into a new level of magic, she really wished that said new level would hurry and arrive.

Then and again, she'd never expected to have to carry twenty people and Elementals to the ground safely after an airship exploded all around her. She hoped the Elementals were being settled in whatever accommodations were best for them; the dryads would need to be taken to the orchards or gardens as soon as they'd had an opportunity to put their feet in a tub of water and drink. She would have to find them as soon as she could.

She pushed through twisting curtains onto a balcony that looked out over the city and beyond to the Winedark Sea. She half smiled to think she'd always wanted to find adventure on it. After witnessing the Kraken devouring the rest of the ship, she doubted her interest in discovery would survive such a vision.

But the sea in all its vast scarlet tossing was beautiful and wild. She couldn't imagine what it must have been like for Bayne to grow up with this sound in his ears all day, with the sharp salt winds. There was a great power in this wind. She felt it singing all around her, but she had no idea how to use it.

She leaned her elbows on the hewn balustrade and looked far out to where she imagined Newtonia waited. And Piskel's grasslands. And who knew what else.

For a second, despite her earlier misgivings, she longed to cross that ocean and escape whatever fate surely awaited them in Grimgorn. Even if by some miracle Charles was just as he said, there were still Ximu and her armies to contend with. The spies on the *Sullen Harpy* were a clear sign that the *xiren* had followed them, and who knew how many might have been on board that they'd missed? She shivered.

There had to be a way to prevail against Ximu. Just as there had to be a way with Charles. She still found his tale nearly incomprehensible. But, through it all with the Manticore and the Heart, she had always believed that there was a path she couldn't see. And now was no different. She just had to find it.

Her thoughts unreeled until at last exhaustion forced her into the bed. Her final morbid thought: if the cordial *had* been poisoned, at least she would die in luxury.

Water splashed, and Vespa opened her eyes. At first she couldn't recall where she was, and then the memory settled over her like a stifling blanket. The airship. Scientia. *Charles.*

She threw off the coverlet and sat up. A maid was refreshing the water in the washbasin and refilling the fruit bowl. Her gold-flecked glance took Vespa in and held her there.

"You might want to get up," the girl said. "You're expected at dinner in an hour and Kraken only knows what the Regent will do if you're late."

The notion of a formal dinner with Charles sounded less than appetizing, but she swung out of bed. Her own smell followed her. It had been a while since she'd bathed. She looked at the dirt and ashes in the creases of the sheets in embarrassment, and realized that all she owned was on her back. Not that she'd had much in New London, but she'd at least had a change of clothes.

She followed the maid to the bathing room, where it seemed a legion of maids waited beside tubs of magically warm water beneath a domed ceiling. Under the dome it looked as if the old tiles had been ripped out and replaced with a mosaic of a Wyvern rampant. They bathed and scented her and dressed her hair and brought an elegant green gown with matching green-dyed deerskin slippers for her to wear. The fabric under her fingers was very fine, certainly evered in the seams and pleats.

Vespa had put up with this long enough. She crossed her arms over her chest. "I can't wear this," she said. "You must find something that isn't evered. You do realize this is against the edicts of our Empress?"

The maids said nothing, but they whisked the garments away. What they brought back was much plainer—an ill-fitting, gray daydress surely meant to shame her—but Vespa wore it with pride. At least she knew with certainty that none of her friends had died to make this garment. She sadly couldn't say the same for the *myth*-heated baths. She'd ask for unheated water next time, though she shivered at the prospect.

When all was done, the maids led her back through the twisting, arched halls and broad stairs of Grimgorn to a small but sumptuously appointed room. No attempt at conversing with any of them brought more than a smile or a whispered answer. When she asked if any of them knew where the Elementals had been housed, they simpered at her and would say nothing. She was concerned, deeply concerned.

The maids left her at the entrance. She went in a little uncertainly, all her defenses at the ready. All the luxury and beauty here put her on guard, especially since she knew much of it was illegal. There was a forbidden Refinery here somewhere. The room was draped with tapestries of the old conquests of House Grimgorn and filled with display cases of antiques that the Grimgorns must have collected over centuries. Everlanterns made their all-too-familiar circuits around the room, lighting everything with a soft, steady glow. It reminded her of nothing so much as the Emperor's Cabinet of Curiosities into which she'd followed Bayne what seemed ages ago.

Under a pillared dome, long, low tables and couches with intricate, eversilk-embroidered cushions had been set up. The tables were crammed with arrangements of flowers and food, a veritable jungle of feasting from sugared dates and figs to vast fish cooked whole, their scales gilded for the table.

Bayne lounged in the same coat he had been wearing earlier, though it looked as though it had at least been brushed. He was talking to his brother and Olivia, and Vespa noticed Olivia's gown was as plain as her own. Apparently, they'd all forsworn the evered garments. Nevertheless, the sight of Bayne made Vespa's breath catch, especially when he looked up from the plate of figs the three of them were sharing and smiled at her.

Charles came to her side then, and Vespa stepped as far away as was humanly possible. "You do not seem to be wearing the gown I sent for you, Pedant Nyx."

"Eversilk is illegal. As is all this," she said, waving her hand at the trappings of the room.

Charles nodded. "A regrettable necessity for which I beg your forgiveness. I shall explain all of that soon enough."

His reactions confused her. She had never known him to regret anything.

"I . . ."

Luckily, Olivia came to her aid.

"Vespa darling, come sit with us, if you please. Excuse me," she said. Olivia pulled her away while Charles bowed.

"I could see you were in want of rescue," Olivia said.

Vespa smiled tightly, glancing at Charles, who seemed to be pacing the room. "Yes."

Olivia looked at her with concern. "You don't seem well, dear."

Vespa thought that the Empress didn't look entirely well herself. She still was very frail, and her skin seemed to have a permanent gray tinge to it. There was a slight hum as Vespa leaned in close to her, like a mechanical whirring. She had thought often about what Doctor Parnassus had said, and it still made no sense to her. What could an Artificer do to help her? She realized she'd not yet mentioned it to Syrus, so intent had they all been on getting to Scientia. She would have to speak to him about it as soon as she could.

"I doubt any of us are entirely well at present," Vespa said.

"Indeed," Olivia conceded.

Bayne and Arlen looked up as Olivia and Vespa settled near them. They were playing some sort of peg game, and Bayne was clearly losing. It was the illusion of perfect family tranquility, belied by the unspoken tension in every gesture and glance. Finding out the truth was uppermost on all their minds, but none of them dared ask their questions aloud.

Then she heard Olivia's indrawn breath. She followed Olivia's gaze to Syrus.

"Darwin and all his Apes!" Vespa said before she thought about it.

"My, my," Bayne said. "Our Tinker boy cleans up well."

"Yes," Olivia said. She was clearly unable to look away.

Syrus stood rather stiffly at the entrance to the room. Vespa would not have recognized him if Olivia hadn't first. He wore an old-fashioned black frock coat and a scarlet cravat. His hair had been carefully sectioned and braided in rows that fell around his shoulders. It was a sight better than the patched clothes he normally wore, but Vespa wasn't surprised that he had also refused the evered garments the servants of Grimgorn had no doubt tried to give him.

He came toward them, walking a bit unsteadily in stiff boots.

"Your Majesty." He bowed to Olivia. Piskel peeked out from

behind one of his braids. Vespa was glad to know that some things didn't change. Truffler slipped out from behind Syrus and climbed up on the divan next to Vespa.

Olivia seemed to have recovered herself sufficiently to incline her head. "Artificer."

"Very nice," Bayne said.

"They took my clothes," Syrus said, speaking through gritted teeth. "This was all they could manage that wasn't evered."

"I think it suits you very well," Olivia said, smiling shyly.

Syrus said no more at that.

Bayne made room for him, and they all seated themselves. Vespa noticed that though there was food on the table and more coming out by the moment, no one seemed to be doing more than picking at bits of fruit and cheese or sipping wine.

"Are we waiting on something?" she asked Bayne.

He made a move on the pegboard against Arlen. The boy was pale and withdrawn, and had the same pinched expression the people of Scientia had shown when they'd ridden through the gates.

"I think there is one more guest," he said, "though I'm not entirely certain. Arlen mentioned we were waiting on someone special."

"Hm." Vespa felt if there were any further surprises today, she didn't think she wouldn't be able to handle them. She had never considered herself overburdened with delicate sensibilities, but she admitted she would not have minded retiring to her bed for the foreseeable future over everything that had happened.

Charles stopped pacing and cleared his throat. "Well, then, while we're waiting, I hope you'll allow me to welcome Your Majesty to Grimgorn. We shall have a more formal welcome with the rest of the court tomorrow, but I thought perhaps this more intimate venue where we could chat would be more appropriate."

Olivia inclined her head slightly.

Charles avoided looking at them but stared at some distant point beyond them, as if it had opened a portal into his past. "You all despise me. I understand this, but before you pass judgment, please hear my tale."

Glances flew around the table, with no one knowing quite where to rest their gaze. Bayne had that guarded expression that made Vespa wonder if he was calculating what would happen if he sent Charles up in a puff of smoke. She wondered if she needed to remind him that now that the Grue was out of Charles, he was fair game. She was sure Bayne had thought of it. She was also sure that Bayne would never do such a thing.

"I returned here from Old London worn and weary from my struggles with the Grue. The Grimgorns remembered me from the ill-fated events in New London"—Syrus coughed at that—"and took me in. I fell in love with the eldest daughter of Lord Grimgorn, Lady Artemisia. I was deeply honored when the Duke allowed me to take her hand in marriage."

Bayne nearly leaped over the table. Only Olivia's cool hand on his arm kept him in place.

Charles glanced at him, twisting the ring on his finger. Then he continued.

"It was not long after that word came of the Empress's edict banning all *myth*. Like dutiful citizens, we tried to enact this, but at a terrible price for Scientia. Not long after, a plague swept through the City, caused no doubt by the lack of *myth*-powered sanitation and exacerbated by a lack of reliable medicines."

He met Bayne's eyes. "Many, many died. Nearly all of the noble family, including my beloved Artemisia. Only Arlen survived because we sent him away to the country house before the worst of it hit."

"Liar!" Bayne shouted. This time he rose from the table. He slammed his fists on it, and Vespa could see them glowing with magic.

"Bayne." She tried to calm him, but he shook off her hands. She tried to speak inside his mind, but it was such a maelstrom of anger that she couldn't break through.

"Pedant," Olivia said, her tone like ice. "Please be seated."

Even that strong admonition didn't faze him, until Arlen said, "It's true . . . what he says."

Bayne glared at him, his face so griefstricken, Vespa had to look aside. She had often wondered how he'd felt about his family and whether they had been close before the wedding fiasco with the Virulens. He had never spoken of them after his disinheritance, and she'd been afraid to say anything that might give offense. She saw Charles watching him in that moment. Though his expression seemed nearly as careworn as Bayne's, there was still a calculating gleam in his eyes that Vespa didn't like.

"How can it be true?" Bayne asked. "How? Why did no one alert us in New London?"

"We tried. Evidently, our messages never reached you. And regardless, it was wise of you not to come to our aid; it's likely you would have spread the sickness to your City, which has enough of its own problems."

Syrus sat back against a pillar, arms folded across his chest. "And so how did you stop it?"

"When the Duke passed the signet to me on his deathbed and

asked me to be Regent for Arlen, I had to make a critical decision. There was stored *myth* in the warehouses. We used it to provide medicines, heat, and sanitation. People recovered. We are using the last of that store of *myth* going through winter, and we will create no more. And while I regret the need, in many ways there was no choice. Ruling is difficult."

"I'm sure," Syrus said.

Bayne didn't say anything. He was simmering, and Vespa was just waiting for him to fully explode.

"Ruling is indeed difficult," Olivia said. "But our edict stands. You must find another way, stored *myth* or no. The use of this source is offensive to those in our realm who have lost their kin to its production."

"I feel the same, Majesty," Charles said. "We already have plans to that effect. Plans I will reveal in the demonstration tomorrow."

He turned back toward Bayne. "Rise, please," Charles said.

Vespa thought Bayne might tackle him at that moment. He rose slowly, fury lining every muscle of his body.

"I won't make you kneel, though that's typical for this sort of thing," Charles said. "I'm guessing you would incinerate me if I tried."

"I still might anyway," Bayne said.

"You may want to wait until I've at least given you this." Charles slipped the signet off his finger and held it out toward Bayne. "I'm passing on the Regency to you. Whether Arlen wants to reinstate you to the fold and allow you to be Duke, I leave that up to the two of you to decide."

Vespa tried to suppress a gasp. She had been sure that Charles would do everything to retain power over Bayne, including using the seal as a goad.

The ring glimmered as Charles held it out for a long moment before Bayne finally took it, bowing slowly.

Charles bowed, but it was to Vespa that his gaze went as he said, "I hope you can see by this gesture of goodwill that I mean you no harm."

Syrus snorted and was abruptly shushed by Olivia.

Then there was absolute silence except for the click of Bayne's boots on the floor as he returned to his seat.

He slid the ring onto his finger as Arlen curled close to him.

Vespa thought she heard the boy whisper, "I want you to be Duke again, brother."

Bayne bowed his head over Arlen's. "Later, dear boy. Later."

There was a knock at the door.

"I believe our other guest of honor has arrived. Enter!" Charles said.

Everyone looked toward the door, and a man entered who was the most well dressed of them all. He sported wavy, black hair cut short at the back and sides in a peculiar way. His snapping black eyes surveyed all of them without emotion. He wore a smartly cut coat and embroidered waistcoat with a contrasting gray silk ascot.

Charles moved to greet him.

Vespa knew who he was long before Charles announced him.

Tesla, patron saint of New London.

Olivia had said the note they'd found was signed "NT.'"

Nikola Tesla.

Saint Tesla.

Vespa suppressed a gasp behind her hand.

The room was echoingly silent.

Saint Tesla had returned.

CHAPTER 19 ⟶

S aint Tesla," Vespa breathes beside me.

I've seen his face on some of the old books and church pamphlets from New London. There was a statue of him outside the Church of Science and Technology chapel in Lowtown, though it had gotten knocked from its pedestal during the Rousing. Still, I remember that face, and I know how the Cityfolk had once revered him.

Bayne and Olivia are also staring at him in wonder.

"Ladies, gentlemen," he says, bowing to all of us. Truffler makes a sound of approval. Piskel sneaks cautiously out from behind one of my braids to peek at him.

Charles makes hasty introductions, ending with Olivia, whom he introduces as the Empress of the Known Lands. "She has just joined us from the capital, New London, which is apparently under siege even as we speak. Isn't that so, Your Majesty?"

"It is." High color comes into her pale cheeks at the hidden slight.

"This New London," Tesla says. "They say an experiment of mine brought it here by accident. But I have no recollection of such an experiment, nor any recollection of the man they say is responsible for funding and aiding me in it."

"That would be John Vaunt," Charles says, "our previous sovereign, who was tragically killed last year."

Vespa glares at him, and Piskel buzzes angrily beside my ear until I whisper at him to stop.

"Yes, that one," Tesla says. "Perhaps I shall meet him in the future, then. Funny thing, Time."

"Maybe you should drop a boulder on his head when you do meet him and save us all the trouble," Vespa mutters next to me. I cover my mouth with my hand to keep from laughing out loud.

"So," Bayne says, "tell us how you came to be here, sir. I should very much like to hear this. I presume Charles here has told you that we are on the brink of war. He brought you at a most inopportune time, I should think."

Tesla's gaze darts between Bayne and Charles, and he swallows. "Well, I . . . have heard something to that effect. But hopefully my demonstration tomorrow will render your worries obsolete."

Tesla's accent interests me. There's a lilt there that I don't recognize.

I look around the table. From their expressions I can guess that they are remembering a similar demonstration that took place a year ago and how that turned out apparently none too well for anyone.

"You do realize that an army of unstoppable demonic spiders is coming toward us as fast as it possibly can?" Bayne asks. "I sincerely hope your demonstration contains something that will deal with that!"

Tesla looks over at Charles, gauging how much he should say. "We shall see tomorrow."

"I believe the Saint was about to tell us how he came to be here," Olivia says.

Tesla smiles briefly. "I am certainly no Saint, Majesty. I am, in fact, the humblest of sinners. But the reasons I came here are simple. Charles sought me out and told me of this world with its vast resources and untold wealth. He assured me that I would have freedom such as I have never known to create the visions that have entered my head since I was a child. All I had to do was find a way to bring us here—"

"And so you did," Bayne interrupts. "And now you are here."

Tesla seems bewildered at the acidity of Bayne's tone.

"Lord Duke," Olivia murmurs at him. It is an odd thing to hear her say.

"My apologies, sir," Bayne says. "I feel fairly certain you are a victim in this elaborate game Charles is playing. Have you any notion of what he did in order to bring you here? How he nearly destroyed this world for his own selfish gain before he arrived in yours?"

Charles's expression is an interesting mixture of resentment and contrition. It's rather like watching a snake turning itself inside out as it tries to shed its skin. I can't help but be reminded of when Bayne baited Ximu to find out her plans, and it seems he is now intent on doing the same with Charles. I wonder if Charles can hold out better than she did.

"I have told him of what happened to me, yes. Of how I was enslaved by the Grue and the consequences of that," Charles says slowly.

"So, I am deeply curious, if Old London was the balm to cure all ills, why return, Charles? There must have been some reason," Bayne says.

Charles runs a hand through his hair. Somehow he looks much

less threatening without the signet ring. "Well," he says, "because this is home."

"Ah yes. Home." Bayne's gaze could boil the air.

"I understand that you don't believe me, my Lord. I hardly believe it myself. But I ask you to consider: What would you have done had you been in my position? Truly we come from entirely different worlds. I was born a tanner's son in the worst part of Lowtown. You were heir to the second-most-powerful family in all the realm. You had more power than you fathomed until it was taken away. I had never had any but was offered it beyond my wildest imaginings. I think you would have done exactly as I had if you'd been born in my circumstances."

Bayne stands. "I would never have done as you did, Charles. Never."

Charles's smile is so sharp, it could cut. "Then let us hope you never meet anyone who offers you such power, lest you be proven wrong." He looks at the ring on Bayne's finger, and Bayne's face goes a deep shade of red.

Bayne turns to Olivia. "If I may have your leave, Majesty."

"Granted, my Lord. Albeit with a bit of displeasure."

Bayne bows. "My apologies, Majesty, but thank you."

He storms from the room. I want to follow him, but I don't want to leave Olivia and Vespa alone with Charles.

Tesla settles in next to me. It's going to be a long evening.

When at last we're released, I make sure Olivia and Vespa are returned to their rooms safely.

"I must speak with you," Vespa says.

She brings me into her room and shuts the door. It feels odd being here in this vaulting room, rather than in our old parlor with its threadbare settee.

"I'm listening," I say.

"Are you feeling better?" she asks. "You look well." I can tell she's admiring the uncomfortable suit, and it makes me blush.

I feel that things aren't entirely right with me, but I have no idea how to describe it. Physically I'm well. But inside there's something dark, a hole I'm desperate to shut away. "I'm fine, I suppose," I say.

"You're sure nothing's wrong? No lasting effects from Ximu's venom?"

Her scrutiny is making me nervous. "No," I say, even though I feel like I'm lying. "Why are you asking?"

"Well, I think something's still wrong with Olivia, and I was worried that you might still be feeling ill as well. Have you noticed anything strange?"

"Not with me. What do you mean about Olivia?"

"When you were captured, Doctor Parnassus came to see Olivia. He told us something odd. He said that we should find you as quickly as possible because only an Artificer could save her. Have you any idea what that means?"

I've been standing against a pillar, but I feel I need more support. I slump into a nearby chair. "Only an Artificer can save her? That's all he said?"

"Yes. He said he couldn't say more; it would violate the sacred trust he has with his patients. I've thought about it ever since. I wondered if you had any ideas as to what he means."

A vision rises behind my eyes, that same vision of a silver army marching through Scientia. "No," I say. "I truly don't know." I look at her. "Why didn't you tell me before?"

Her face falls. "I just . . . I didn't know what the Doctor meant. I was trying to figure it out for myself."

I cross my arms over my chest. "You seem to do that far too often." Anger is boiling inside me, but I know it does no good. There is far too much to worry over to waste time quibbling.

She opens her mouth as if to defend herself, and then seems to have the same realization. She spreads her hands apologetically. "I'm sorry. I just don't want anyone to think I'm weak. I want to be able to do things for myself."

"Even when someone tells you that perhaps you can't?"

She nods, looking me in the eye. "Even so."

I sigh. "Perhaps this will teach you to let go of that notion. I could have been trying to help you long before now."

She smiles, but it's bitter and unsure. "I will take that under advisement." She pauses for a bit, and then says, "You said that your people believe Ximu's poison gives visions. I remember you saying before that the airship was going down, and it did. And I wondered if you'd seen anything, anything at all, that might help Olivia."

I shake my head. I can't say anything for the fear growing in my chest. Something is very, very wrong.

Vespa pats me on the shoulder. "Get some rest. I'm sure you're as exhausted as any of us. Maybe the answers will come tomorrow." She smiles wearily, and I try to smile back.

But the foreboding will not leave my heart. Something is wrong with Olivia.

I ask Truffler and Piskel to keep watch over Vespa and Olivia. I still have my misgivings about Charles's intentions.

And I admit I'd like to wander on my own for a little while. The sense of foreboding is lodged firmly in that dark place in my soul.

I do not want to go to sleep for fear of what will be waiting when I close my eyes.

I distract myself with the Bone Palace. There is much to learn about this ivory maze and its broad halls. The fact that Charles allows us to roam it relatively freely surprises me, but then again as I see the servants watching me, I suppose his spies are everywhere. And I am not hard to spot.

It will be good to explore and try to do something useful to stop thinking about the dinner. While I think perhaps I could ultimately like Tesla, perhaps even learn from him, I'm not sure I can trust him with his obvious allegiance to Charles. And Charles . . . who knows what that snake is planning? He's slipperier than an enchanted eel.

Bayne mentioned the palace is haunted, and it may very well be, but I'm more interested in knowing how its history is inscribed in its bones. To me, it's a place of legend; I scarcely believed it could be real. And yet here it is—the Bone Palace of *Nainai's* tales.

The deeper I pass within, the more I get the feeling that I'm traveling back through time. Eventually, I can see where the new additions of Wyvern motifs end and old Tinker architecture begins. Ximu had said she'd built this place at the foundation of the world, and I could believe it. But my people had made it not just a spider's den but a palace of wonders.

Finally, I pass to where there are no everlanterns. It is nearly pitch-dark, except where the corridor opens out on terraces that overlook vacant courtyards. The moon is sailing overhead, and that naturally calls to the hound in me. For once, rather than shifting in anger or fear, I simply slide out of my human skin and into my fur and leap down the steps into the light. I chase at shadows, trying to pretend overcoming every darkness is this easy, when I feel something watching me. I catch a scent on the night breeze and turn.

A black wolf is sitting on the stairs. I stop and stare back at him, unsure as to whether he's friend or foe.

He leaps down, and my hackles rise at his approach. He comes to me, ears erect, tail stiff. Closer and his scent washes over me. He is not entirely wolf. I have never met another of my kind before while I've been in houndshape. Certainly I've known that some must be out there, but I've never sought them out, afraid of a confrontation I didn't want to have. This wolf seems merely curious.

And then he nips at my shoulder and takes off. I yelp, mostly in surprise rather than pain. When I look around, he's waiting on me, tongue lolling. He bows, clearly inviting me to play, and dashes off.

I stare. Of all the things that have been strange these last few days, this is perhaps the strangest. And yet I can't resist. I dart toward him, and together we run back and forth across the courtyard, our barks and growls echoing against the stone as we nip and leap and give chase, dancing between urns and statues, skipping through moonshadow.

At last we fall together into a heap of heaving sides and twitching paws. I rise up, desperate to ask who he is and how he came here.

He looks at me with one last amber gaze before he melts into darkness.

The hound slides away from me, and I'm left standing naked and cold on the courtyard stones.

"Who are you?" I say to the silence, though I'm sure I already know.

Nothing answers.

CHAPTER 20 ━

After she said good-night to Syrus, Vespa turned to Truffler.
"Truffler, do you think you could find something for me?"
Truffler nodded slowly with a definite look of trepidation.
"Let's see if we can find a library."

Truffler looked at her quizzically, but he didn't ask. He'd learned not to.

She opened the door and peeked out, half expecting a guard or something equally unpleasant. But the halls echoed with the whispered silence of servants going about their work and the hum of everlanterns circulating above.

Truffler took a deep whiff. "This way," he said, gesturing off to the right.

Vespa followed him through corridors, up and down stairs, past courtyards, beyond all recognition or sense. She had no idea how anyone found their way through it, much less out of it.

She had been deeply worried tonight when she'd seen Olivia. The Empress had tried to hide her throat with a shawl, but as she'd shifted, Vespa had seen the ugly, raw wound that slipped along her collarbone. She was even more worried at Syrus's reaction to her questions. Though she didn't necessarily think he was lying to her, she had a feeling that he knew something he wasn't telling. She'd try again with him, but for now she wanted to see if she could find some help on her own.

Doctor Parnassus had said they needed an Artificer to heal Olivia, but Vespa wondered if perhaps there wasn't some stronger magic they hadn't tried that she could call upon. There must be something that could be done. Perhaps here in Ximu's ancestral home some ancient cure might be found.

At last Truffler led her to a set of wooden double doors between ivory pillars. She could smell the books already. She touched the door handles and brought her stinging fingers up to her mouth. Neverlocked.

"I figured as much," she said. "Stand back."

Truffler did so, putting his fingers over his eyes.

She disabled the lock with a zap of energy that made her feel better than she had in a while.

"Maybe things aren't so bad after . . ." She stopped.

The library's vastness was the first thing that took her breath. Row upon row upon row of books disappeared into the gloom, lit occasionally by the circulating everlanterns. Tall ladders disappeared up toward the rafters. A great dome vaulted over the ivory-and-jet parquet floor, filled almost to its curve with books. Whatever the original design had been on the dome ceiling had been tiled over with yet another Wyvern, of course, this one frolicking in a field of flowers. Busts and globes and even a tiny orrery that reminded her of the old observatory in the Museum were scattered in alcoves and on tables throughout the stacks.

But what made her wish she could turn and tiptoe out was the single oil lantern burning in the center of the table next to Bayne as he looked up from the book he was studying.

"Oh dear." She should have guessed as much. The magic on the lock had seemed rather familiar, now that she thought about it.

She looked down at Truffler. "Did you know he was in here?"

Truffler shrugged.

"You could have warned me," she hissed at the hob out of the side of her mouth.

"Did you need something?" Bayne asked.

"Hmmm . . . yes," she said, drifting toward him. "I was hoping for a book about magical healing, if such a thing exists."

He put a forefinger between the pages of the book he was reading and closed it as she approached. She saw the words *Great Plague* illumined on the spine.

"I doubt you'll find that here," he said. "You're more likely to find something about how best to cook a Kraken hatchling or Scientian geography or . . . the history of my illustrious forebears."

"Oh."

"Are you trying to heal Olivia?"

"I thought I might. It seems to me that her bite is getting worse, even though she tries to hide it."

"I've tried healing her myself, you know," he said. "It didn't work."

"Oh," she said again. She hadn't known that, either. "Well, what are we to do?"

He sighed. "I've been searching for the answers. As well as any histories regarding Ximu."

"And?"

He looked very much as if he wanted her to leave, but she couldn't bring herself to. She was restless with the fear of all that was still unknown. She had to do something, find some knowledge that might be useful. And she could scarcely admit to herself, but she didn't want to go back to her room and be in its vast darkness, even though Truffler had agreed to stay with her.

"Right now I am looking at something else."

She waited to see if he would tell her. Sometimes if she remained silent, she found that he would eventually confide in her.

He cleared his throat and flipped the book back open. The new ducal signet glinted on his forefinger. "I'm reading the public accounts of the last year, trying to verify if anything Charles said was true."

She made a sympathetic noise, remembering how angry Bayne had been.

"Everything he said is recorded as truth. His and Tesla's arrival. His marriage to my sister Artemisia. The plague and the subsequent deaths of my family and hundreds more. The decision to go back to using stockpiled *myth* until another solution could be found. It's all here. And there is no magical tampering that I can tell." He slammed the book shut. "And I completely do not understand it."

"Well . . ." Vespa hesitated to say what she was thinking but then decided to press forward anyway. It was something that had been growing in her mind ever since the dinner. "Have you considered that maybe he's telling the truth?"

He stared at her.

"No, not you, too," he said. He put his head in his hands for a brief moment and then looked up at her. "First my only surviving brother, and now you? He wants something. I know he does," Bayne said. "He was a scheming snake even in his Architect days. He tries to pretend that it was circumstance that made him a slave of the Grue, but you know it wasn't. You of all people should know."

Vespa had been thinking about that too. "I never knew him before he was possessed, Bayne. He could have been just as he says—a poor fool who was offered a bargain he couldn't refuse."

"Are you sincerely saying that perhaps Charles is just what he claims to be? Has he enspelled you, too?"

"You know better than that," she said. "Do you sense any magic beyond the use of *myth* here? And yes, that is bad, but his explanation does seem plausible. We know from experience how many have suffered for lack of the medicines and other things we once used thoughtlessly."

"It's true I don't sense any magic. Or at least, not very much. But then tell me this . . . what happened to all the Elementals who lent us their aid and escaped with us? Where are they now? And what about the note Tesla sent us?"

"No one will answer me about that," Vespa said in a small voice. "And we still should try to ask Tesla what he knows. More than he's telling, I'm fairly certain."

She turned to Truffler. "Do you know what happened to the other Elementals, Truffler? What do you think is going on?"

"Not good," the hob said, shaking his head. "Not good."

"We avoided the hard questions before," Bayne said. "We all turned a blind eye to everything that went on in the Empire. The Architects moved too slowly because they were afraid. Had it not been for my inadvertent discovery of you, who knows what would have happened with that blasted Machine and the Waste?"

"Then what do you propose we do?"

"We need to find out what he's holding back. While all of this may be true, I believe there's something else beneath the surface. I am not convinced that he's not in league with Ximu, for example. He may be holding us here for her. He and Lucy always did have a camaraderie." His mouth curved down with distaste.

"But she said she was seeking vengeance on him, remember?" Vespa said. "Somehow the way she boasted so freely made me feel she wasn't lying."

"Oh, she wasn't telling us everything. We got out of her lair far too easily, especially if Syrus's uncle was trying to sway him to her service, as Syrus said."

Vespa frowned. "Are you sure? I don't think—"

"We couldn't have left without her allowing it. Remember how hard it was just to get in there? She was laughing when we left, Vee. Laughing. I don't think she would laugh if we hadn't stepped straight into her web by leaving."

Vespa remembered that terrible laugh echoing behind them in the void. "Well, what do you propose we do?"

"Be vigilant. Conserve our strength. Learn all we can. Charles is making a big show of how accommodating he is. Let us take advantage of that."

It was true that Charles was definitely trying to win them to his side. Vespa considered that it might be profitable to let him think he was winning her over. Perhaps he'd reveal more of his plans that way. What had Syrus's granny said? You caught more flies with honey than vinegar?

She considered telling Bayne but knew that he'd never agree to it. If she was going to try this, she'd have to do it on her own.

"All right, then," she heard herself saying. "But when you have more information, you will tell me, won't you?"

"Count on it." He smiled, but the smile was forced. He had other things on his mind right now.

"I'll leave you to it, then," she said.

She looked down at the stack of books near him. One was about the history of the old palace, and she picked it up. "May I take this one if you're through?"

He nodded.

"Good night, Pedant."

"Good night, my Lord," she said. He glanced at her so that she blushed and dropped her gaze.

She went out with Truffler into the hall, carefully closing the doors. She felt the neverlock snick back into place behind her.

Truffler helped her find her room again. She opened the door and then stopped.

"Moving on to the next plan," she said.

She flopped down into a cozy chair by the writing desk and put her head in her hands. "Whatever that is."

Chapter 21

Ximu comes for me in the morning, just as I'm on the verge of waking.

"I see you survived the airship accident. Well done." She has me again, so tightly bound in her silk, I can barely breathe.

"Ill done," I say. "That was ill done of you."

"You always were a saucy little lad." Lucy's face looms out of the dark—all her once-praised features distorted by her union with Ximu. "Though I hadn't planned on it happening, it was ultimately a good test. I needed to see how Vespa's power is progressing, since I really didn't get enough chance to test it in the Museum."

"What if it hadn't been as good as you'd hoped?"

She smiles and pats me on the cheek. The stiff hairs on her spider-feet hurt. "Then I suppose our conversations would have been cut really short."

"Seems like an awful risk to take, considering."

"Well," Ximu snaps, "it would have been easier if you all hadn't run away with the one thing I need."

"Vespa?"

"No, nitwit. Not Vespa. Though I will use her power if it comes to it, and thus I must know if she's capable of the challenge. It's Olivia I want."

"Olivia? Why?"

"Because she is the key."

"To what?"

"My army."

I think I stop breathing. Gen had said something about an army, but I'd been unable to get more out of him. "I thought you already had an army."

"What, those minions? It takes nearly all of them to farm our food and take care of the youngling replacements. Even the *xiren* are kept busy with their duties. No, many, many more are needed. And I know just where to find them." She is almost gleeful; there's a lilt to the normal harshness of her voice that I don't understand.

"Where?"

"Under the hill. Beneath the graves and bones of Scientia. Far beneath the haunted halls of my beautiful palace there waits an army of clockwork. The very same army that drove us out, immune to our poisons or magic. We will awake them and use them against the humans just as the Tinker King did against us. I find the irony of that poetic."

I'm sure she does. "But what does that have to do with Olivia?"

Her face is so close, I can smell her spidery breath. "You're concerned for her, are you?"

I can't think of anything clever to say, so I keep silent.

Her grin grows wider until I see her fangs. "Ah. I thought so. You'd best let go those feelings, my little spy. They will not serve you."

Still I say nothing. I fear I know all too well what she's speaking of, and I fear to know even more. I wish there were a way to free my arms and plug my ears. I wish even more there were a way to wake up.

"How does she fare, your Empress?"

I don't want to tell that, either, but I find myself offering the truth. "Not well. She has some sort of illness left from the *xiren* bite."

"That is because she is not what you suppose her to be."

"What do you mean?" The words are dragged out of me with reluctance. I have dreamed of her so often. I held her cool hand after the destruction of the *Harpy*. I wanted . . . the clan mothers only know what I must have wanted, but it makes my face flame, even here in this nightmare.

"Shall I give you a history lesson?" Ximu asks. "It's a tale perhaps no one in the world knows these days, except for me. I hear all."

I'm filled with dread as a scene opens in my mind. A room forms, a dark laboratory with surgical tables and restraints, bubbling beakers, and a tall cylinder filled with glowing blue liquid that must be magic. It reminds me of Vespa and Bayne's workroom back in New London, a place I definitely did not enter without invitation.

"In the Tower," Ximu says. "This was John Vaunt's workshop."

John Vaunt. We call him the Two-Faced Emperor now because he fooled everyone into thinking he was both man and woman over the centuries in order to extend his reign as long as possible. Vespa had told me the story of how he'd sent his daughter Athena, the first witch, out onto the Waste when he discovered her magic, even though he was using dark magic himself all along. "When—" I start to ask, but she shushes me with another swipe of her foot.

"You'll see."

The focus shifts to two tables near the blue cylinder. Two bodies are sprawled on the tables. One shines silver, an automaton of beautiful proportions, pistons, and gears. It lies quite still, its metallic eyes vacant, its silver knuckles loose against the steel surface.

The other is a rumpled thing that I hardly know is a girl but for the banner of her long, golden hair, which is so like Olivia's that at first I think it is her. Then I see the scarlet *W* stitched across the breast.

"Athena."

She's asleep, so deeply asleep that I can barely tell she's still alive except that her throat flashes every now and again with her breath.

Then the Emperor appears from the shadows of time, and he is already bent and wizened. He reminds me of the way Charles once was with his dead eyes and grim slash of a mouth, and the dark circle around his lips from eating the raw *myth* of the Elementals. But I sense no Elemental within him. No Grue has eaten his heart. He simply never had one to begin with.

He stoops and brushes the hair back from Athena's temples with surprising gentleness. "Oh, my little girl," he says. "Oh, my little girl. You would not listen to me, even when I warned you. I would have hidden your power away and let you rule by my side. I would have made you my heir if you had shown that you could carry on the Great Work that I have begun. But you would not. And now my plans must be altered. Lucky that Tesla showed me the way."

Tesla? I wonder. *What does he have to do with it?*

He holds up an instrument. I've never seen it before, but I know that it will be used for cutting, and I do not want to see what. I try to turn my head or shut my eyes, but I cannot get away from what's going on inside my own mind. He starts at her forehead and draws it across like a wand or a knife. There's a puff of smoke, a smell of burning bone. I know I'll vomit everywhere if I have to see more.

"Perhaps that's too much for you?" Ximu says too sweetly. "I will move us quickly through this part, then."

Time blurs and shifts. I cannot look at the broken doll that was Athena. I watch the Emperor's back as he lifts something into the open cranium of the automaton. He feverishly connects things with bloodied hands, as if bent on some maniacal knitting project.

There is a whirring click. The automaton's metal eyes blink.

She opens her metal lips. "Faaaatherrrrrrr," she says.

As he reaches to adjust her, I shudder and close my eyes, trying to will the vision away. It shimmers and flashes. I can almost see my little room in Grimgorn. I can almost break free . . .

"No, no—stop! You must see this next part to understand."

Ximu holds me firmly in place.

Next I see the automaton in the glass cylinder, surrounded by magical liquid. She is fully enfleshed. I gag when I realize just whose flesh she wears.

"Stop!" I say. "Please stop!"

But Ximu is relentless. She can force me to see whatever she wants me to see.

When the cylinder opens and the liquid spills out across the laboratory floor, the automaton steps out, smiling tentatively at the man she calls Father. He takes her hand delicately. He helps dress her. I notice that he does not embrace her or show her much affection in any way. She is his Grand Experiment, much as Vespa was with her father. She is the pinnacle of all his art, the ultimate union of science and magic.

There is training—oration, etiquette, dance—all the things a princess should know. And then I see her no more. The laboratory flickers with Elementals tormented, my people fashioned into wraiths and wights, more attempts to make automatons, none of which are ever as successful as the creation of Olivia.

Finally, the images fade from my mind. I am alone in the dark with Ximu again, feeling my stomach roll with horror. Tears stream down my face. I've been weeping a long time without realizing it.

"How . . . how . . . ?" I can't even make the words.

"Do you mean the bit about executing her on the Creeping Waste?" Ximu asks. "A powerful illusion. A ruse, so that no one would come looking for her and he could do as he wished."

It is too horrible. All I can think of is the girl's face as she lay there, before he made the first incision. I'd known her father was evil, but I'd never imagined the depths to which he'd sink. Murdering and resurrecting his own daughter! Forcing her to forget who she'd been to become what he wanted her to be.

I was never able to fully weep for my people, but now I weep and weep and weep. I do not know if I can ever stop weeping.

Ximu laughs. She brushes my tears away, and the pain of that is enough to make me stop. For now.

"So, you see, this girl you care for, she's nothing more than a machine. And she is the key to awakening the army. She is their General, fashioned by Blackwolf in memory of one of the great female Generals of the Old World. John Vaunt stole her out of the crypt when he explored the Bone Palace and spirited her back to his Tower in New London. There he devised his wretched plot for enslaving his daughter to him forever. If she ever disputed him or attempted to rebel against him, all he had to do was shift her programming. Though at the end, even that wasn't working so well. Truth will out, so they say."

"Why?" It's all I can think of to say.

"Why does anyone do anything? He wanted to live. He wanted his daughter beside him. He was obsessed with keeping all the magic and power of this world for himself. Trapped by his own edicts, he had no choice but to do what he did. He waited until all the courtiers who had known Athena were dead. And then he introduced his beloved daughter, Olivia."

The silk has me wrapped so tight, I can't even clench my fists. "And you want to use her to awaken the army so that you can take control."

Ximu nods. "But of course. The army cannot be awakened or used without her. You will help me achieve this. And when I come to the gates and speak the words *Omni fatalis*, you will give her to me."

"No. I will not do this." I am surprised at how calm my voice is.

"You will not?" Ximu says.

Pain clamps my body with delicate pincers. I am wracked with it. I struggle like a worm in my cocoon.

"You will not?"

"No," I say, clenching my jaw.

Light streams through the dark caverns in my mind. She shows me a huddle of Tinkers in cages. She shows me other Tinkers stored in cocoons of silk. I see a girl's face sweet as a rosebud, wrapped in scarlet. I see Uncle Gen leading her *xiren*. The ache I feel inside is deeper than any residual pain from her poison.

"Unless you do exactly as I say, they will all die. Your people have always been excellent building stock—their bones are filled with just enough magic to make many things possible. I have held them against a time of need. But I will not hold them longer if you do not do as I say."

I don't say anything.

"I'll leave you to think on it, then. I am at Euclidea. I will be at the gates in a few days. You know the consequences should you disobey. But have you thought of the rewards if you submit to my design?"

I fall into a dream of such wonder that it exhausts me. Me and my people in the Bone Palace, building objects of such utility and beauty as I've only dreamed. Things that fly without *myth-gas*. Instruments to capture the light of the sun and convert it to light and heat. Ways of harnessing the power of wind and water to broadcast sound. And at the heart of it all, Olivia by my side, Olivia with fingers of silver and jeweled eyes.

"You are a king, Syrus. You are meant to be a king."

CHAPTER 22

Vespa was in the chamber again, looking for the thing she couldn't remember. This time was different, though. There was someone with her. Or rather, there was someone already there. It was as if she was invisible, watching.

A man dressed in rich robes came down the stairs. Torchlight sparkled along the embroidered scales of dragons like Tianlong on his sleeves. Vespa sensed that he was a great lord or king. He was carrying something. Vespa went closer, and gasped when she saw what he held.

A young boy, perhaps Arlen's age. He was just as richly dressed as the king, but he wasn't breathing.

The king carried him to a great sarcophagus, which was painted with Tinker letters and symbols. Vespa couldn't read most of them, though she was intrigued by a prominent symbol at the very center of it. It looked much like the emblem of the Ineffable Watchmaker, a winged clockface. But the clock formed the abdomen of a scarab beetle.

The king set the boy's body into the tomb. He was weeping.

"Sleep well, my son. I entrust my army to you, that they may fight better for you in the next life than they did in this. And when my time is done, then we shall be together again."

He took a key-shaped pendant from around his neck and placed it around the boy's. He took a cuff from his wrist and slid it over the boy's as well. All Vespa could see of it was a flash of gold and brass.

The king kissed the boy on his forehead and slid the sarcophagus lid over him.

Then she watched his form shimmer as he took the shape of a black wolf. He circled the tomb three times before lying down in front of it. He looked out over what Vespa now realized must be a burial chamber, and it was as though he saw her, for his gaze pierced her heart.

She gasped and heard herself cry out. The last thing she saw before her eyes flew open was those amber eyes boring into her own.

The dream disturbed Vespa so deeply that all she wanted was to get out of the palace. She wanted to be in the sun and wind for a while, even if the weather was growing increasingly cold.

She took two books with her—the dream book and the palace history—and decided to scout out a spot. She walked briskly through the halls, marveling at their architecture. It was hard to believe Ximu had built this herself. How the great beast must have labored (or had her servants labor)! She caught herself almost admiring her.

At last she found a small sunken courtyard with a pleasant fountain. The day had progressed sufficiently enough that the stones were warm, and they held in the heat so that it almost felt like the end of summer rather than mid-autumn.

Vespa had hoped to find a spot like this where she could study and practice her magic, and especially after such a vivid dream, it seemed she needed badly to do both. The dream book was again less than helpful. It suggested that those who dreamed of a *scarabeus* were on the verge of a new life. It said nothing about the Ineffable Watchmaker, of course, or a king mourning a dead prince.

The history book was a bit dense. There were long passages loosely translated from the Tinker language that, based on her lessons with Syrus, she wasn't sure were correct. She'd need to see if he could help her understand it; she knew she wasn't very gifted at the Tinker language.

The sadness of the dream still filled Vespa's mind. She decided to try magic instead. A proposition no less frustrating than trying to understand her dreams, she was sure, but certainly something in the here and now.

She wished she could figure out why her magic was so unreliable. Why one day did it seem to serve well and then another not at all? Why did it do that sometimes even from moment to moment?

Vespa had no idea, but perhaps working at what was hardest would be best. She felt she was weakest at illusion, so she started there.

Water was malleable, much more than stone, of course, so she tried shaping something from it. Perhaps a mermaid. She stared hard at it, pulling and stretching at the shape like it was putty. Eyes, nose, fish tail . . .

Someone laughed behind her, and it was as if she'd been plunged into the River again.

All the water splashed back into the basin.

She looked round, chagrined.

"You'll never get it that way, you know, Miss Nyx," Charles said.

"Why not?" she asked.

"Because you're starting off with things that are far too difficult."

Vespa frowned. "I don't see why it matters to you."

He stepped into the garden. "Well, I suppose it really doesn't. Except that I hate to pass up the opportunity to help."

"Yes, we've seen how helpful you've been in the past."

Charles sighed and sat down. "Why can't you let the past go? Surely you've seen by now that I have only the best of intentions. I always did. They just got twisted somehow."

"Oh?" she said.

He ignored her sarcasm and reached for the end of a vine that hung near him.

"Watch," he said.

Charles stared at the vine but only for a moment. Then he looked up at her and smiled. Nothing seemed to have happened, except that when she looked again, the tip of the vine had burst into full bloom. The scarlet trumpets nodded against his fingertips.

He stood. "Start with what is already there. The blossom is within the vine. You have only to make the vine realize that. It is harder to make water realize it should go into a shape that it was never meant to be. You would need something much more powerful—a focusing device—in order to accomplish that. Master that which seems easy before trying something that is hard. And realize at some point that you may need help."

Vespa stared at him, open-mouthed.

"Good day, Miss Nyx," he said.

And then he was gone again, bent on goodness knew what errand.

Vespa waited a while to make sure she was alone again.

Then she went to the opposite end of the arbor and worked at making the vine blossom.

Chapter 23

When I wake, it feels like midmorning, judging from the light coming from between the slats of the shutters. I throw off the covers and sit up, putting my aching head in my hands. It feels like the venom is coursing through my body anew. All I want to do is vomit.

A servant enters the room with scarcely a knock. "The demonstration will begin soon, sir," he says, and begins opening shutters everywhere.

The light blinds me. "Stop!" I shout.

He looks at me as he has at many a spoiled lordling, I'm sure.

"I'm sorry, just . . . please don't open them yet."

"Yes, sir." He bows and plunges the room back into shade.

An hour or so later, bathed, booted, and braided, I make my way up to the demonstration courtyard. My escort leaves me at the stairs. I feel like a stork walking in these strange boots, and it seems like I've entered a great exhibition hall of similarly awkward if brilliantly plumed birds. The women are bedecked with feathers and jewels, and their skirts are wider than those at Bayne and Lucy's wedding masque. I feel somewhat ill, imagining how much all these getups must cost.

In contrast, Olivia wears a simple blue gown and a few glimmering stones around her throat. Her pale hair is held up with ribbons and perhaps one diamond pin. Next to the Scientian nobility she looks almost plain, but I think she looks regal. The only oddity is the knitted stole she wears wrapped around her shoulders and piled high on her neck, but I know she's wearing it to hide her wound. She smiles when she sees me, and I bow quickly to hide the blush I know is coming.

I'm still stunned by the extravagant beauty of this place, so much more magnificent than Virulen was. And yet people here move under the intricately woven arbors as if it's commonplace. In the center of the courtyard a tall, canvas-covered object stands. "What is that?"

"No idea," Bayne murmurs. "Perhaps it has something to do with this demonstration I was told about."

"So, why has this never been the capital?" I can't help but wonder that, looking around at the gilded pillars and alcoves filled with flowers.

"I've read in the Archives that John Vaunt was afraid of the magic here. He came here not long after New London appeared and before the devastation of Euclidea. And that an army of ghosts chased him right out of the city because they didn't believe he was worthy of being a king. So the Architects always said."

The darkness in my mind opens, and I see him—a much younger version of the crabbed Emperor. He is standing before a silver statue at the head of a line of silver statues. He admires it the most. "Bring this along," he says to one of his guards . . .

"Hmph." The dark strands of the nightmares threaten to drag me down. I'm not going to bring them into the light of day.

"In any case, my family came here after the devastation of Euclidea, and here they've remained, to their great fortune."

At that moment, a servant comes by, bearing an ornate tray full of delicacies. A bright orange cluster of berries layered on green icing over a delicate wafer catches my eye. I pop it into my mouth without much thought and then nearly retch.

"Like sea urchin, do you?" Bayne asks. He slips one into his mouth, smiling, as I scowl and barely manage not to wipe my mouth on my sleeve.

I grab at another servant with a tray of fluted glasses, not caring that the pale pink liquor is cloyingly sweet. Anything, anything to get that briny taste out of my mouth.

"I should have warned you," Bayne says. "There will be many treasures of the sea on the menu today, even more than last night."

I nod, wondering if I can slip into the kitchens and somehow find a bit of cold mutton. Somehow I doubt it.

Olivia gestures for us to come to her. People sometimes offer respect, but no one stays to make conversation with her. The room seems to part around Bayne like waves. All eyes are on him, and yet no one wants to meet his gaze directly.

As we get closer to Olivia, I notice that her skin is even grayer than before. Her eyes look weak and feverish.

"Are you well, Majesty?"

Her glance at me says she is not. But she nods instead and returns to surveying the crowd.

"What do you think this demonstration is about?" she asks, looking at Bayne.

"I'm not certain, Majesty. I suspect a show of might, especially after my blustering last night. I apologize."

She's clutching the edges of her stole more forcefully than is necessary. "Are you sure you wouldn't like to sit, Majesty?"

Again that glance, this time filled with warning.

"No. We shall stand until everyone is here."

It's not long until Tesla and Charles, looking dapper as ever, are announced.

Vespa arrives just before everyone is to be seated. I am fortunate to be seated across from Olivia. Bayne, as the new Regent, sits wherever he pleases, which happens to be next to me.

The banquet is even more lavish than before, making the meals at Virulen seem silly by comparison. Suddenly I understand why it was whispered that the Virulens weren't very well-off anymore and needed the alliance with Grimgorn to solidify their future. Compared to the Grimgorns' table, the Virulens may as well have been hosting their gatherings in a Tinker clan car.

The dishes are like scenes from some underwater spectacle. Servants hoist giant clams, out of which flow any number of seaborn delicacies. At first I think they've brought in a roasted, stuffed mermaid until I see that it's part fish, part beautifully sculpted torso. There is also, of course, a nest of Wyvern eggs with a baby just hatched in the center, carved from fruits and vegetables but somehow gleaming with their own inner light. I suspect they've been sprinkled with *myth*. But the crowning jewel is a magnificent cake in the shape of a Kraken, its tentacles wrapped firmly around a great merchant vessel.

Olivia doesn't show any sign of being impressed by any of this, and I have to wonder if she ever saw anything like it in the Tower. Her predecessor wasn't known for putting on such extravagant shows. I'd guess he was too busy spending the treasury on developing new devices to torment Elementals.

Olivia stays quiet, speaking only when spoken to, until there's enough of a lull in the murmuring conversation that she raises her voice and says, "Saint Tesla."

All talk ceases.

Tesla stands and bows. He looks so young that I can't imagine how anyone could ever view him as a saint. "With respect, Majesty, please remember that I am no saint but a humble servant of this noble family, having but lately taken up a post as Chief Artificer."

"Ah yes. Old habits are hard to break, however. Please grace us with the tale of what you are about to demonstrate today."

"Very well, then." He clears his throat and moves over to the canvas-covered tower.

Tesla bows again to his audience. He begins by telling us of his homeland—a place called Serbia—and of how he had lately just come from University and was bound for another place called America because there was a rich man—Edison (another saint, as I recall, though far less important in the Church than Tesla)—who had promised him a great sum of money for his inventions.

But on the way he had met a man—he looks aside at Charles—who had promised him far more than any sum of money. He had promised him freedom and a world full of inexhaustible resources and the time and space to create such things, if only he would . . . Here Tesla pauses.

"Yes?" Olivia says. "Do go on." She coughs slightly and reaches into her pocket for a handkerchief. When she coughs again, I'm alarmed to see spots of what looks like blood before she folds it away. She is worse, much worse.

"Well, perhaps it's best if I just show Your Majesty. That would probably be better than any other paltry words I could summon."

Olivia nods.

"My pleasure, Your Majesty," Tesla says. He goes to the canvas-covered object and pulls off the drape in a flourish.

I glance at Olivia. Her chin rests on her hand, and there's a spot of color on her gray cheek. I think I can see a red weal creeping up over the edge of her stole. I turn my gaze to the tower of welded steel that thrusts toward the autumn sky.

"Steel," Tesla says. "The finest, strongest steel this world can produce, so I am told. It took a great deal of convincing Charles to allow me to have it built here. He was worried it would never come down."

There's a bit of nervous laughter about the table. Everyone else was thinking the same thing.

"But I assure you, it will. And with none of your *myth* or magic. Anyone care to venture a guess as to how?"

"You have a trained Dragon waiting in the atrium?" a lady calls.

"Apparently that is less strange here than one would guess," Tesla says, smiling. "But no."

"Acid from a Sea Serpent!" Vespa ventures.

"You are clever, but I doubt we could convince the Sea Serpent to produce what we'd need willingly. No," he says, pulling a strange device from his pocket, "we will do it with this."

It is so small that I can't really see much but a black box the size of a matchbox or a small cigar case, when Tesla holds it up. It has no distinguishing features. We all look at it, perplexed.

"There's no magic about him whatsoever," Bayne whispers to me. "I don't understand."

Tesla touches something on the box. At first nothing happens. Then the wine in the glasses trembles and the jellied mounds shake. The intricate settings of knives and little forks begin a merry jig about the vibrating plates.

Next the sound begins. A high-pitched whine that makes me want to throw back my head and howl. Vespa claps her hands over her ears. The steel tower begins to sway and shudder.

Bayne stands, throwing down his napkin and clutching the trembling table. "What devilry is this?" he shouts. But his voice is lost in the din.

People cover their ears, the tentative smiles vanishing from their faces.

"Syrus," Olivia says, clutching at me from across the table, "you must get me out of here!" At least, that's what I think she says. Her lips make the words, but the sound from Tesla's device drives out all others. Her face is dark and she's sweating. Her eyes are a terribly wrong color as well—black voids, as if the pupil has swallowed the pale iris entirely.

"Syrus!"

I move around the table, take her elbow, and help her up. She stumbles and nearly sprawls face-first before I manage to catch her and help her out of the Hall. Just as we make the corridor, the steel tower collapses in a heap.

Olivia is half dragging, half hanging on to me for dear life down the corridor toward her chamber. I don't know where I'm going, so I just listen to her sighing directions. Guards are following behind us; two detached themselves from the doors. I hope Bayne and Vespa aren't far behind.

"Almost there," she gasps. "I had to get out of there; that . . . noise . . ."

She trips up the stairs; I see her ankle twist too late. There's an odd, metallic gleam and a ringing snap that didn't sound at all like bone. Unthinking, I sweep her up in my arms and carry her.

She puts her arms around my neck and her forehead into my collarbone like one of the baby cousins I'd carried through the Forest back home. Only this is nothing like that. Her body is cool and soft and strangely heavy. And the smell of her—so strange, like some foreign metal, yet also the faint odor of rot. I ignore the million things racing through my mind and get her into her bed.

"Shall I fetch a physic?" I ask, trying not to notice that her dress is askew or that her hair has come unbound in the process of being carried. I feel foolish for even asking—her ankle is broken!

I try to help her, but she moves away as best she can, trying to cover herself with the blankets. "No, don't," she rasps. "Please don't fetch anyone but Vespa or Bayne."

I frown. "Why, do you think I can't help?"

I look down at the ankle.

Where the foot swings loosely, there are no tendons or bone, just metal and wire. There is blood and rapidly putrefying flesh, but Olivia has a skeleton made of metal, not bone. A memory of a nightmare surfaces—a silver skeleton overlaid with human flesh—and I shudder.

"I think," she says, "only magic can fix this. Or perhaps you're right. Perhaps you are all I need."

She tries to smile, but I can only stare as my stomach sinks into my boots.

The one I love is not human.

Bayne and Vespa come as soon as they can after the banquet.

"Everything is in an uproar," Bayne says as the guard shuts the door behind them. "Are you well, Majesty?"

Olivia shakes her head; I gesture to the dangling foot with its wires and gears.

Bayne and Vespa just stand there with their mouths hanging open. Bayne manages to assume his mask again first, though I can see by his face that there is much more going on in his mind than he's letting on.

Vespa's emotions, on the other hand, are naked on her face for all to see. Tears leak out of her eyes before she dashes them away and comes to Olivia's side to take her hand.

Olivia says it doesn't cause her pain, but I find that hard to believe.

Bayne kneels swiftly by the bedside. "With your permission, Majesty," he says.

"Yes." Her voice is gritty. She pushes a strand of pale hair where it had come unbound back behind her ear. How delicate, how real she looks. My mind races, still trying to understand this. Surely this could not be true. Surely it could not. And yet there's a curious déjà vu here. I remember someone telling me this. I remember hearing that Olivia was neither Elemental nor human.

"Your Majesty," Bayne says, looking up into Olivia's face, "I don't understand."

"Nor do I, Pedant," Olivia murmurs. "Nor do I. Can you fix it?"

"I am no physic, Majesty, nor am I an Artificer of Tesla's caliber . . ."

Olivia's mouth twitches, whether from pain or amusement, I can't tell.

"But you are—or were—an Architect. Use your magic to heal it if you can. I do not want anyone else aware of this, if we can at all avoid it. Vespa, can you help him?"

Vespa looks like she wants to say things that she can't. "I can try," she says softly.

Bayne nods. I don't think I've ever seen him this nervous. Vespa releases Olivia's hand to go stand near Bayne. She puts her hand on his shoulder.

"Let's just try a simple spell of mending first," he says.

I watch the wires and gears as Bayne and Vespa stare at them. Even as they begin to glow, I think I see a way I could put them back together.

Strain etches lines on their faces. I hear Vespa gasp, and Bayne closes his eyes. There's a sudden snap in the air, and Bayne reels back, throwing Vespa straight onto her duff. He rises, clutching at the bedpost, and pulls himself upright. He leans against it as if he were boneless. I help Vespa up.

The glow fades from the Empress's ankle. It will not mend. And where the break is, the flesh around blackens and rots, so rapidly that it's as if a fire has caught and is unraveling her into smoke. The gears and pistons of her calf above her ankle are fascinating.

"We cannot," Bayne gasps.

"I don't understand," Olivia says.

Bayne takes a handkerchief from his pocket and mops sweat from his brow. I help Vespa to a chair, where she sits with her head in her hands. I think I hear her mumble, "The doctor was right."

"What?" Olivia says.

Vespa looks up, surprised.

"We've both been trying to find some way to treat you. Doctor Parnassus told us that we would do better to find an Artificer than an Architect. We had no idea what he really meant. We had no idea there was any other possibility besides human or Elemental." She meets Olivia's eyes, but they are both so distraught that she has to look away.

"And you kept this from me?" Olivia asks.

"I . . . I didn't know how to say it. I didn't know how to ask. Did you know this about yourself, Olivia?"

I look down. The tips of Olivia's fingers are turning black.

Olivia stares at them for many long seconds. Her unblinking gaze is uncannily mechanical. "What are you trying to say?"

Bayne turns back to Olivia, who's looking between them, waiting for an answer. "I repeat what Vespa said. You are not human, Your Majesty."

Vespa puts her head back in her hands. Bayne shakes his head. He seems to contemplate his shoes a long time before saying, "I would you were an Elemental for your sake. Perhaps then we could heal you. But no, you are something else entirely. You are like nothing I've ever encountered. You are a living, breathing automaton."

There's silence for several seconds.

"That's impossible," Olivia says. "I eat . . . I . . . I . . . sleep just like you! I have thoughts and feelings and—" She reaches up to grasp a hank of her hair, as if that would somehow be representative of her humanity, but it comes away in her hand. "Oh my," she whispers, staring at it.

"Do you remember anything about your childhood? Your mother or father?" Bayne asks.

Olivia's face becomes thoughtful. "My predecessor was both mother and father to me. I have never known anything else."

"And do you remember growing up?"

"No," she says slowly. "I have always been this age."

"How far does your memory extend?"

She thinks for what seems an eternity. Finally, she shakes her head with a sad smile. More hair falls in golden curls on her lap.

"There are just fleeting glimpses. Nothing that would suggest I was ever any less than I am now."

"I don't know quite what you are or how your father made you," Bayne says. "But I think somehow he wedded flesh to metal."

Deep within, a voice says, *I know.* I know that her father took her from the army here. I know how he used his dark and ugly magic to weld the body of Athena onto the skeleton of Black-wolf's former general. But how I know that, I have no idea. And if I try to explain how, I literally can't make my tongue form the words.

Bayne continues, "I don't know how he did this, but the magic that kept it all working is dissipating. Perhaps it was the *xiren* poison, or the potion we gave you to purge you of the toxins. Or the demonstration just now. Whatever it is, I don't think I can stop the withering of your flesh . . ."

There's a commotion at the door—the sound of protesting and a thickly accented response, followed by the door thrown wide.

In walks Tesla, smoothing his hair with one hand before depositing the black box he used earlier in his jacket pocket.

Bayne moves to block him from getting too close, but I can see the Artificer's eyes go to the dangling wires of the Empress's broken ankle. Surprise is rapidly overwhelmed by curiosity. He moves to try to take a closer look.

"Shut the bed curtain," Bayne says out of the side of his mouth.

Vespa hurries to comply, but it's too late.

Tesla nods to them, then bows deeply for Olivia's sake.

"Your Majesty will forgive the interruption, I hope," Tesla says. "I had to see if you were well. You left my demonstration in such a rush, and . . ." He looks between all of us.

"I am well enough, Artificer," Olivia says from behind the curtain. "Please allow us to retire in peace now."

"Forgive me that I am so bold, but I could not help noticing your injury. Perhaps this is something I could help fix."

Bayne crosses his arms over his chest. "What can be done has already been tried. I suggest you do as the Empress commands."

Tesla's mouth crimps, but he doesn't seem in the least concerned by Bayne's threatening posture. "Majesty, I can fix things as well as destroy them. I want you to know that. Things that your magic cannot fix."

Suddenly Olivia throws back the curtain. I gasp.

"Can you fix this?" she says, gesturing toward her ankle. "Or this?" She rolls up a sleeve and shows where the flesh has melted from her elbow. "Or what about this?" She pulls back her stole and shows how her shoulder and neck have disintegrated into bloody shreds.

Her mouth is grim and her eyes frantic under her now-patchy hair.

I want to vomit from sheer horror.

Bayne steps aside reluctantly, and Tesla kneels near the Empress's broken foot. He does not touch her in any way, merely gazes upon her circuitry. "This is the most amazing and wonderful thing I have ever been privileged to see," he says. "And I do believe I can fix this, if you will let me."

Olivia looks wildly between all of them. Bayne glowers, still with his arms across his chest. He looks like he wants to drag Tesla out of the room by his coattails. Vespa crosses over to me and puts her arm around my shoulders as if she knows what I'm feeling, though I've not been able to say a word.

"If you think you can . . . ," Olivia says.

"There may be pain," Tesla says. He looks up at Bayne. "I do not understand how your magic works, but might you be able to give her rest and ease?"

Bayne nods. "We can try. It didn't work when we tried healing, but a sleeping spell should be easier. It will at least quiet the flesh."

Tesla stands and bows, moving away from the bed. "If Your Majesty does not object . . ."

Olivia looks at me. As long as I live, I will never forget that wild, gray gaze nor the feeling that we are about to be swept away by the greatest storm any of us would ever face. I want to tell her . . . what? I am not sure that I can say what is in my heart. I go to her, and I clasp her blackened, bloody fingers. She holds my eyes until I feel as though she's looking down into the dark place in my soul. I feel again her heavy body in my arms, her cornsilk hair against my lips. I want to tell her, but my feelings are tangled up in their own impossibility.

"I pray I will see you again," she whispers to me. "There is too much left undone. I must see you again."

All I can do is nod.

At last she looks at Tesla, Bayne, and Vespa. She nods slightly. "Where the Architect falters, perhaps the Artificer may find the way. But if you do not," she says, looking around at each of us, "remember what we stood for. Remember what my Empire was meant to be. Not an Empire of conquest or violence but one of peace and learning. I charge you all by whatever power is left to me that you fulfill this mandate, that you strive to make the Known Lands a realm of peace."

"Olivia," Vespa chokes. She puts her hand over ours. "We will keep your wishes in our hearts forever."

"Lie down, Majesty," Bayne says. "All will be well."

Olivia looks at all of us one last time before she closes her eyes. "I trust you with my life, such as it may be." I think I see the glimmer of tears under her lids, and then one slides down her withering cheek. It leaves a trail of oil rather than water.

Bayne and Vespa stand on either side of the bed. They close their eyes and spread their hands. Magic, soft and somnolent, flows from their fingertips, enclosing Olivia in a misty glow. Tesla looks as though he's trying to figure out how they achieve such manipulations of energy.

Soon Olivia's breath becomes even, and her tortured body relaxes into a deep sleep.

"She will feel no pain now; the magic is enough to at least placate the flesh," Bayne says. "Now see you do whatever it is you must do quickly."

"She must be moved—perhaps if we each take an end of the blanket . . . ," Tesla begins.

"What do you mean?" Vespa says. "Where are you taking her?"

"To my workshop," Tesla says. "I can't very well bring all I'll need here."

All of us are displeased.

"Look, do you wish me to fix her or not?" Tesla asks, looking at each of us in turn.

I want to hit him, but he has a point. I have no idea how much time we have.

Bayne finally bends to take a corner of the blanket and Tesla the other. I steady her in the middle. They lift her so as to keep her hidden in the blankets as much as possible.

Vespa opens the door, and we carry Olivia away down the corridor.

CHAPTER 24 ━━━

The next afternoon, Vespa and Syrus huddled around Olivia's poor, mangled body in Tesla's workshop, trying to figure out what to do. Healing spells hadn't worked. Herbs and other poultices hadn't worked. The sleeping spell was keeping her flesh in stasis, but she couldn't be kept that way forever. Eventually, the spell would wear off.

Besides, the clock was ticking. Ximu was on her way and would likely arrive at the gates any day. Bayne had gone to see to the fortifications of Scientia and to make sure the City was prepared for siege if need be. He also, so he said, wanted to be sure the apothecaries were well stocked against *xiren* poison, if indeed they could figure out a proper antidote. He had forced Charles to go with him, trying to buy them time to figure out what to do for Olivia.

Tesla came to stand beside them.

"Do you happen to know if the Empress received any . . . message with the Phoenix I sent?"

"Yes," Vespa said. "She received it and decoded it, just before the airship exploded."

Tesla nodded. "Things are not what they seem to be here."

"Well, I don't know, this seems pretty bad to me," Syrus said, gesturing at Olivia.

"This isn't the half of it. She is a means to an end. Do you have any idea what she actually is?"

"I don't know what you mean, Artificer. She is our Empress." Vespa said

Tesla shook his head. "Perhaps she is now, but she was much more once."

Vespa looked down at the thick white drape that obscured Olivia from her. "I don't understand."

"If what Charles has told me is correct, she was once the General of the Tinker King's army."

Vespa saw Syrus go pale. He was staring at Tesla as if he had known what the man was going to say before he'd said it.

"Syrus?"

He muttered something and shook his head.

"How is that possible?" Vespa asked.

"Perhaps some magic wedded flesh to metal?" Tesla asked. "I am eager to find out. But what I do know is this: Charles wants that army, and the General is the key. Without her, the army is merely an interesting art installation. With her, it is the most powerful army in the world.

"He entrusted me with helping him find it and control it. Thus far, I have been unsuccessful. When he discovered that the Empress was fleeing here from her enemies, he was ecstatic. Even more so when he realized that she was so vulnerable."

"But how did he know what she was?" Vespa asked.

"He has studied many ancient texts, piecing together the story from them. He knew something like this"—he touched the white cloth near Olivia's shoulder lightly—"was beyond him to recreate. Fortunately for him, I suppose, he had met me."

"And you just went along with whatever he wanted?" Vespa asked.

"What I said yesterday at the demonstration was true. He offered me untold resources to make whatever I desired. I have not yet been able to secure any patron of that caliber. It seemed perfect. I should have known it was too perfect.

"Everything Charles says has the ring of truth to it, but there's always an underlying lie. Yes, there was plague. But it spread unbelievably rapidly and by mysterious means. Anyone who thought they might have the solution to it disappeared or suddenly came down with plague themselves. Charles and I were the only two completely unaffected. Logically, that cannot be a coincidence."

"And so?" Syrus said.

"When I understood the outlines of his plan, I decided to plead for help or at least hope that such a plea would be sufficient warning to your Empress. I had no idea what situation she was in or what she'd be fleeing from. I had no idea what she'd be like. I never expected her to be human," he said, looking down again at Olivia's still body.

"And we didn't expect this," Vespa said. "But she is still very human to us. Will you restore that?" She was challenging him, hoping that he was different from every other Scientist she'd ever met.

"I cannot fully restore that which was lost. I suspect the magic that kept the flesh together has been utterly undone. I also suspect the kinetic energy generated by the flesh is what kept the clockwork wound. I can fix the broken circuitry at the ankle, but I cannot know what else can be done until I can get beneath the flesh and see."

"You are asking us to allow you to take off her flesh?" Syrus said. His voice was cold, but Vespa could hear the anguish underneath.

Tesla sighed. "I know it is difficult to understand. But know this—whosoever controls this automaton controls the army. She is the ultimate weapon, from what Charles says. We must have a care that she doesn't fall into the wrong hands."

"She controls herself," Vespa said quickly. "Unless you give her over to Charles or the *xiren*, she will follow her own destiny. She is still the Empress of the Known Lands."

Tesla nods. "I think we understand one another, then. But I repeat: the flesh will have to come off if you want me to fix her."

Syrus took Vespa by the arm and led her over to another corner of the workshop. The room was vast, filled with canvas-covered objects, metal struts, and tools strewn everywhere.

"You can't seriously be thinking of letting him do this?" Syrus said.

Vespa sighed. She wasn't sure what to think anymore. "Do we have any other choice?"

"Of course we do! We can choose not to kill her, for one thing! If we do this, we're playing right into Charles's hands!"

"I think Tesla is trying to say that we're doing her more harm than good by keeping her this way. Bayne and I know from experience that her flesh cannot be healed. And Doctor Parnassus warned us of the same thing; we just couldn't comprehend it. If she is kept in this state, she is more vulnerable to whatever Charles is planning than if she's awake and functioning."

"I still can't believe this," Syrus said. His dark eyes were as fierce as Vespa had ever seen them.

"Neither can I," she said, putting a gentle hand on his shoulder.

"But I'm beginning to think that if we keep her this way, we are denying her the life she was truly meant to live."

Syrus hung his head.

Then she felt him straighten. He shrugged off her hand and marched back over to Tesla, who was hovering over something on his workbench.

"Who will she be when she wakes up?" Syrus asked.

Tesla's smile was sad and brief. "I have no idea, lad. But I will do all I can to ensure she keeps the freedom to choose."

Chapter 25

I don't know where I'm going when I leave Tesla's workshop. Somewhere, anywhere, other than this.

The girl I loved will soon be gone. In her place will be someone I don't understand. Will she know me when she wakes up? Will she be reduced to only a machine?

Why must everything I love be taken from me?

The rage, held in so long, sweeps over me. I feel a great relief as I give myself up to houndshape. I let the hound take me, not caring that I am in the middle of a corridor full of people hurrying this way and that. I run through them, a white shadow fleeing through corridors of bone.

The black wolf is waiting for me when I come to the courtyard. I make my way over to him. He turns and I follow him, past the giant urns and crumbling statues, past empty temples where my ancestors worshipped the gods they'd left behind.

At last a hall looms before us, glowing like the moon's twin brought to ground.

It feels as though the darkness within me opens wide to the darkness without here. In a vision I see the silver army swarming up and down this hill, locked in combat with Ximu's minions. I see a tall figure watching from one of the balconies above. He is wearing the robes of the Heavenly Dragon. I still cannot see his face, but I know it's Blackwolf.

The wolf leads me up the temple steps. The tall doors with their iron rings are wide-open.

I follow him across a broad porch. He slips behind an empty ivory throne. My rage is slowly transforming into curiosity. He whines and tilts his head.

A set of stairs leads down from behind the throne. He begins to descend, and as he does so, torches flicker with ghostlight. Whispers creep up the stairs, the conversations of a thousand spirits over the centuries.

I am not certain I want to do this, but I follow after him. At last we come to the bottom of the stairs. We pass a chamber from which so much sorrow flows that it nearly pulls me out of hound-shape. But then we're standing on a ledge. Crackling ghostlight illumines a vast pit.

The light skips across the tips of spears and the silver shoulders of an army that stretches farther than I can see. I cannot imagine how much time it took the hundreds who must have dug it to complete it.

In the distance I see a chariot at the head of a column. A chariot where a King might stand. Or a General.

There is an emptiness here, a yearning.

I look around, but the wolf is gone.

All that remains as the light slowly fades again into darkness is the image of the army and its empty chariot flaring behind my eyes.

Chapter 26

Vespa had not slept all night. She was still seeing Olivia's poor mangled body as they slid it onto Tesla's workshop table, still watching Syrus run through the corridors in houndshape. Piskel and Truffler had both been so sad, they were barely speaking to anyone. And Bayne had buried himself in work.

Vespa's heart ached for all of them. For Olivia, who slept her magical sleep in hopes that her friends would be able to restore her. For herself, who just might have lost a friend. And for Syrus, who evidently loved their Empress passionately, far more than Vespa had ever realized.

She couldn't allow herself to think that perhaps Olivia would never wake. She couldn't allow herself to think that after all they had gone through, all they had fought for, that Olivia might indeed have succumbed. It was so senseless.

By dawn she was exhausted with thinking.

She dressed and, wrapping herself in a shawl she'd found in a trunk, decided to go seek out breakfast rather than waiting for it to come to her.

She was surprised to find Bayne in the hall, taking his porridge like a servant. "May I join you?" she asked. She hadn't seen him since the night they'd carried Olivia into the workshop.

"Of course," he said. A servant came quickly, bringing her a bowl of porridge and a mug of steaming black coffee. She cupped the plain mug with her hands, relishing its warmth.

"You haven't slept," Bayne said.

"I suppose I have circles under my eyes."

"Yes, though I gather I shouldn't tell you so."

She shook her head. "Generally not. No."

"What's happened? Has Tesla figured out what to do?"

She took a sip of coffee and realized her hands were shaking. "He wants to flense her, Bayne . . . er . . . my Lord."

"No ceremony here. Flense her? As in . . ."

"Remove her flesh. He says he cannot save it, and he cannot fix her unless it's gone."

Bayne rubbed his chin with his hand. She could see he hadn't shaved in a day or two. "We should talk about this elsewhere. Finish your porridge and then come with me. I'd like to show you something."

"What is it?"

An exasperated smile played about his lips. "You're really not one for surprises, are you?"

She tilted her head. "Not any more."

"In this one case, I'm advising you to live dangerously."

It was her turn to smile. "We should hire a scribe, I think."

"Why's that?"

"To note what you just said for posterity."

He raised a brow, then turned and stood. "Finished?"

She nodded.

• • •

He led her through halls and up flights of stairs, up to battlements she hadn't been able to see from the side of the palace they'd entered a week ago. From up here she could see an old air-car line trailing away toward a distant clearing in the middle of one of the nearest mountains. A white dome rose above the trees.

"We're going there?"

"I suppose I could transport us, but this is actually much more entertaining." Bayne grinned as he slid open the car door. The thing swayed gently from side to side as he gestured for her to step in.

"But . . . won't we be using unnecessary *myth*?" she asked as she stepped into the compartment. She was encased in a bubble of glass stretched over a wood-and-iron frame. She was thankful the floor was solid, even if the walls were not.

He stepped in after her, sliding the door closed. "No," he said. He reached up and touched the roof with a glowing hand.

The car clicked down the tracks, blue sparks spitting out ahead and behind.

"Are you sure? Do you need . . ." She didn't want to suggest he didn't have enough power to handle it, but neither did she want him to waste power they couldn't afford to be without if something happened.

"What is the point of magic if you can't enjoy it once in a while?" he asked. "This is how I used to use it without anyone knowing when I was a child."

"You stole the air-car?" Vespa didn't know why she was surprised. The very fact that he was an Architect suggested he had a bit of a rebellious streak.

"All the time," he said. "It was the only way I could keep my father from knowing precisely where I was at all times. Though, of course, when I learned to use magic, that became much easier."

"I suppose your mentor taught you," she said. She was grateful to think about something besides all her worries over Olivia and Syrus. And Charles.

"No," he said with a rueful smile. "I had to learn on my own when my father called the car back and left me stranded out there." He nodded toward the ever-larger white dome. "Believe me, you do not want to be left alone out there at night."

Vespa looked around uneasily. Beneath them the City had given way to a vast necropolis, filled with monuments and crumbling headstones. The wall that protected the City had fallen in places. It was hard to tell around Bayne's magic, but she thought she saw the telltale shimmer of warding between the fallen stones.

"That is what I've been doing with most of my time lately," he said. "Shoring up fortifications. I don't know what my father was thinking sometimes."

She stopped looking down. They were far from the ground and getting farther as the hill fell into rolling ravines before it met the mountains. It made her nauseated.

She recalled the cars jumping from track to track in the lower parts of the City and swallowed hard. "This doesn't jump the track, does it?"

"No," Bayne said. "More's the pity. I always wanted to see if I could make it fly." He lifted his hand toward the roof of the car again. "Want to try it?"

Vespa remembered the protective bubble they'd used to escape the exploding airship. She wasn't sure which had been more terrifying—trying to make sure the bubble landed safely with its cargo or trying to hold it steady against the *myth*gas flames. "Er . . . no, thank you," she said.

"And here I thought you had a sense of adventure," he teased. He was full of mischief today, as she hadn't seen since they'd fallen in the River together. He seemed to be trying very hard to make her forget their troubles.

"My Lord," she said, "my sense of adventure has been taxed quite enough lately, I'll kindly have you remember." She smiled, despite her haughty tone.

"Then you'd better get ready to have it tasked some more," he said. The boyish grin that lit his eyes made her heart lurch even more awkwardly than the rocking air-car.

She pretended not to notice. She was also pretending not to see just how very far the ground had receded or how fast they were speeding toward their destination.

The mountain soared ahead of them, its sheer shoulders lost in cloud. Here in the lower elevations, if they could truly be deemed as such, the mist and sea wind had conspired to produce a verdant jungle that stretched across the knees of the mountains like an emerald skirt.

"It looks like the perfect place for a Basilisk," Vespa said. The fluttering leaves of the jungle provided the perfect cover for their feathered green scales. Vespa had read in one of the Museum codices that they often waited in the canopy of such forests, draping themselves in such a fashion that unwary travelers would look up and be dead from their glance.

"Oh yes. That and more. But all should be well now. The Elementals here must have heard of your triumph. They'll grant you safe passage, I'm fairly certain."

Vespa didn't feel quite prepared to deal with a Basilisk, even if it did recognize her. She hadn't packed a cockerel in her satchel,

Tiffany Trent

after all. "Fairly certain? You don't reassure me, my Lord."

"I've talked more than one Elemental out of eating you. I'm certain I could do it again, if the situation required it."

Bayne was watching her closely, waiting for her retort. She bit her lip and said nothing.

Then she looked ahead. They were approaching the platform at an alarming speed, and Vespa wasn't sure how they weren't going to run full tilt into one of the twisted trees.

"Perhaps you ought to concentrate on docking us?" she asked.

Too late. The car docked with such ferocity that it threw them together. His arms went round her reflexively as metal shrieked and gears ground.

"Must be a bit rusty," Bayne murmured.

Vespa felt he waited longer than was necessary to let her go, and she truly didn't mind. She wished she minded more.

She disengaged herself as soon as she could. "Sorry," she said, keeping her eyes cast down as they parted.

He didn't say anything but unlatched and slid open the doors. As he helped her out of the car, she ignored the charge that raced up her arm as best she could.

Ancient trees dug into old paving stones like tentacles. Aerial roots and vines festooned their branches. There was a bright flash in the canopy above as a flock of something—birds or sylphids—took flight.

"Were those bluewings?" Vespa asked.

Bayne glanced up. "Yes."

Vespa nodded. Sylphids, then. She'd seen them in one of the Museum bestiaries but had always wanted to see them in the wild. "Is it true what they say about them?" she asked.

244

"That they bestow luck?" Bayne shrugged. "Never was able to squeeze one hard enough to find out when I was a boy. They have a pretty wicked curse."

"Worse than Piskel?"

"Definitely."

"Of course, I let them alone once I realized it was wrong to try to extract good luck from them," he said.

Through the twisting trees she could make out an ivory dome. It was a very familiar shape, something she'd held and examined many a time at the Museum.

She stopped.

Bayne looked at her. "What?"

"That is a skull," she said.

"Yes. So?"

"So, what is a skull of that size doing here in the middle of the jungle?"

"This is where Ximu placed it," Bayne said. "So that the enemy could always see her own failure for eternity."

"Where did you learn that?"

"Syrus. He mentioned something about it being part of the legend of Ximu. We always knew the palace was made of Titan bones, but never knew much more than that."

"We really should have him write some of these things down," Vespa said.

"If we can ever get him to sit still." Bayne gestured. "This way."

Vespa picked her way carefully across the stones while Bayne ambled on ahead. She caught up to him on the porch formed by the open upper jaw and the outthrust nasal bone. The mandible held the skull up. The lower jaw was buried deep in the ground.

Vespa shivered. "Ximu certainly doesn't stint on making things horrifying."

Bayne looked up as he crossed the threshold. "You know, I never really paid much attention to it. I suppose I would have felt differently if I'd known what really happened. Growing up, I was always told that a large creature had died here and a powerful wizard had made the city out of its bones. Nothing more."

Vespa raised a brow. "You didn't question your sources?"

Bayne smiled and shook his head. "Not back then."

"I find that hard to believe," she said. They passed under the arch leading up to the sinuses. Vespa remembered how the bowels of the Tower had been in Tianlong's skull, and how the Heavenly Dragon had expelled it all and shaken free of his earthly confines. She hoped the Titan didn't decide to wake now, though she hardly saw how that was possible. Still, stranger things had happened.

A flood of jagged light drew them onward—the top of the skull had broken in and was open to the sun. She could see stairs curving up the dome and a telescope and other instruments on a ledge under the break. This was the new observatory, relocated from New London. Vespa smiled.

"They say," Bayne said, "that the old King used to come here to think. The light here supposedly provides clarity if you are having trouble deciding what to do about an issue."

"Is that why you brought me here?"

"I don't know if it's true, but if nothing else, it will at least give you a moment's peace," Bayne said.

Vespa didn't want to say aloud that she wondered if there would be many more of those. Instead she said, "Thank you."

She walked to the light, her boots echoing on the stones. Shadows fled in a twisting column through the skylight—birds or syl-phids or something more sinister, she couldn't tell.

The sun poured over her, so hard and bright, she had to close her eyes. There was a feeling of such ancient power here that her bones vibrated with it.

"You feel it?" Bayne said.

"Yes." She was afraid to do much more than whisper. She hadn't felt such power since she'd carried the Heart. It washed all around her in waves.

"This was where my magic first quickened," Bayne said. He was still outside the ragged circle of light. She could only see him as a shadow at its edge. "Some say there are wells of power like this all over the world, places where the magic is thicker than others. And that from these sources flow wondrous things."

"I can see why," Vespa said. It was like bathing in a stream of etheric energy, a current of pleasant fire. It reminded her a bit of how it had been to stand close to the paralytic field. It was all of that and more, without the awful side effects. For the first time in she didn't know how long, she felt refreshed.

She drew in a breath that was pure light. And in that breath a man came to stand beside her, resplendent in Dragon robes. She'd seen him in her dreams—the Tinker King. This time she watched him place the boy in his tomb as if she stood right beside him. He regarded her with sad, ancient eyes. "Bring me my son," he said.

"Who is your son?" Vespa was confused. She was certain his son was already dead.

Then he showed her Syrus's face. "He is the last of a line descended from my sister. I've been trying to speak to him, but there is a curse on him. My old enemy is upon us. There is not much time.

Bring me my son, and I will give you the key to your power."

"I don't . . ."

Before she could say more, she was standing in a tower in Scientia. She was looking out over a classroom of students—her students—to the hustle and bustle and the Winedark Sea tossing beyond. Mostly all she heard was the scratching of quills on paper. She looked down and saw the name of the course: Elemental Magic. Not Etherics or the Ethology of Unnaturals. Magic. She was teaching a class in magic.

Vespa looked down and saw a cuff circling her wrist, and it was decorated with the same *scarabeus* symbol she'd seen on the sarcophagus. It was the cuff the king had taken off his wrist and put on the prince in his tomb. She felt as she once had with the Heart—complete, open, filled with power.

It was a vision. She had never experienced one before, but this rang so true that she knew it in her bones. The king had shown her the future. She would control her gift, and she would teach it to others. Magic would be as common as arithmetic or penmanship. And hundreds, perhaps thousands, of children who would have been abandoned under the old regime or who would have suppressed their gifts at the cost of their own sanity, would be helping the magic to grow.

The magic would be alive and well in such a way as she'd never imagined it could be. It would sing in the breast of every person who walked this world, no longer twisted or denied. And it would begin with her.

"Bring him to me," the Tinker King said again. "Together we can break the curse that is on him."

"I will."

It was such a beautiful, hopeful vision that Vespa reached out to Bayne, wanting him to share it. "Come stand with me."

"I . . ."

She couldn't quite focus on him. "Oh, come, my Lord. Just . . . indulge me for once."

For a moment she thought he wouldn't. And then he was there, sliding into the light. She tried to hold on to the vision she'd just had, hoping it would appear to him, too.

Without any warning, she found herself inside his mind. There was absolutely no sense of things slowly merging, as often happened with their magic. He knew everything she'd been silent about lately, but she had never tried to hide that either. Nothing she felt was a surprise to him. But within him . . .

Vespa gasped in shock. She saw everything he had been hiding, everything that he had tried to keep from her—his wounded pride, his loneliness, his inflated sense of honor, and . . . his love. She understood then that something barred his feelings, something that he clung to. *I swore,* she heard him say again as he had the day of the airship crash.

He moved out of the field of light as quickly as he could. "No more, please. I beg you."

"But, Bayne, if . . ." She stepped toward him, not knowing exactly what to say.

"I told you before: we must leave it," he said, his eyes afire with magic.

"But . . ." She said it almost under her breath, then recovered herself. She had seen the future. And whether he joined her in that future, she felt the truth of her own destiny in her bones. She would teach magic and restore balance in the world. That was more important than anything else. She squared her shoulders. "You must do as you will. We'll still be partners, yes?"

"I wouldn't want the alternative," he said. There was a great weariness in his voice, as if he was tired of his own stubbornness.

"Neither would I," she said.

They meandered for a while longer, but the mirth in their jaunt was gone. Afternoon fell quickly; Vespa shivered and rubbed her arms, wishing for her wrap.

"We should go," Bayne said.

"Yes," she said. "Thank you for bringing me here."

"I wanted you to experience it. I just didn't know . . ."

Vespa mustered a smile, thinking about the vision she'd seen. "It's truly all right. It was wonderful. I would like to come again sometime."

He helped her back into the car, and they rode in silence. She was indeed at peace now. She knew what she had to do.

CHAPTER 27

The banging on my door begins bright and early.

I open it to a guard, who informs me that Tesla has need of me. "Wear your best suit. The Saint does not tolerate slovenliness."

I growl and shut the door to change.

I take Truffler with me, despite the guard's protests. Truffler, of course, can fade into any setting he wishes, but I worry. All the other Elementals have vanished, and I don't believe for a moment that all this *myth* Charles is using is stockpiled. Whatever is taking them could be after Truffler next.

I am thinking so hard about how to find the other Elementals that I barely notice when the guard leads us into Tesla's workshop. Truffler's cry startles me out of my thoughts.

Tesla pulls off old nullgoggles and a laboratory coat he'd been wearing over his clothes. Olivia's silver body is carefully arranged on the slab. Tesla bends over her, dabbing the last drops of acid from her with a heavy cloth. She doesn't appear to be awake. "Come here, boy."

The guard releases me, but I just stand there, staring.

Tesla looks back at me. "Are you going to help or not? Come here."

I force myself to move, because I know I need to see her. I need to hear what he says. It's still just hard for me to believe.

"Come and look at this," Tesla says. There is an eagerness in his voice—an almost boyish excitement.

I'm afraid to look. Seeing Olivia this way is somehow even worse than if I had chanced to see her naked. But if I'm ever to get free of this place, if there is any way we can still save Olivia (though now I truly don't know how), I will have to at least pretend that I'm interested. I will have to bury my rage beneath my cunning. The best hounds do that, too.

"This is the most exquisite construction I have ever seen," Tesla says. He passes his gloved hand over the collarbone and upper arm. With all the flesh stripped away, I can see the intricate circuits and servos, the tiny gears and pistons that had driven her. The mechanisms had been so smooth, the magic that maintained her so seamless, that none of us ever guessed what lurked beneath her flesh. I am intrigued despite myself; must be the Tinker in me.

"Have you ever seen its like? Do you have many of these sorts of things here? I have had many visions of such things in the future of my world, but none of them have been created yet."

"She isn't a thing. She's a person. But no, I haven't seen anything like her." Despite our agreement to trust each other, I still feel wary. If what he said about Charles's plans is true, I'm afraid to trust him with the location of the army.

I look down along the silver length of Olivia's body. In her midsection, right where the navel on a human would be, is a keyhole. A winding key. If she is some sort of clockwork, it's entirely possible that she requires some kind of key to keep her wound. But if that's the case, where might the key be? Her father could have stowed it anywhere.

"Syrus." Tesla leans toward me over the table.

I look into his eyes and see the same earnestness I saw yesterday.

"I want to help you. Tell me how," Tesla says.

"I think we're going to need a key."

And I think I know just the one to ask.

I nearly fall over Vespa as I leave Tesla's workshop.

"I was just coming to get you," she says.

"Oh?"

"There's someone we both need to meet. Lead me to the old palace."

I can't keep the surprise from my face. "How do you know about that?"

"I think someone has been trying very hard to get a message to you. Maybe finally it's getting through."

She explains it to me as we walk, how she'd been having dreams since New London and how those dreams got very vivid once we got to Scientia. She still hadn't realized what they'd meant until this morning.

"Bayne took me to a special place—the observatory in the Titan's skull. And . . ." She seems a bit embarrassed.

"What?"

"Well, I had a vision of the Tinker King. And he told me that you are under some sort of curse and that I should bring you to him."

I nod. I'd had my suspicions about the black wolf, and they'd been confirmed yesterday when he'd shown me the army awaiting its General underground. I wasn't sure why he'd never appeared to me in human form, but I'd assumed that perhaps as a ghost, he couldn't. I'd truly not had many dealings with ghosts. *Nainai* hadn't liked them and was always trying to scare them away as much as possible.

All we can hear in the haunted palace are our own footsteps. There is no other sound. The black wolf is nowhere to be seen, and the ghostlights don't flicker on as we approach the stairs.

"Do you know where we're going?" I ask.

"To his burial chamber," Vespa says.

She makes a light carefully in her hand, and I follow her down the stairs. Instead of going straight toward the pit, she turns left, into the chamber I'd sensed before, the one filled with sadness.

Gold gleams everywhere we look. There are beds and tables and chairs. It amazes me that all this treasure is still here. Why has it not been stolen by greedy Grimgorns? It amazes me even more that this once belonged to a Tinker. What *Nainai* could have done with all of it!

It's not until we near the sarcophagus that I see the form bending over it and startle.

I'm unpleasantly reminded of Olivia as we draw closer. The sarcophagus is open, and a body lies in state there in rotting cloth of gold.

"This was his son," Vespa says to me.

The Tinker King turns. His eyes are amber and piercing as they are in wolfshape. "Yes," he says. "Killed far before his time by Ximu."

"She is coming again," I say.

"She must not be allowed to take this City back." His gaze sweeps us both like fire. I feel terribly unworthy to stand in his presence. He's not just a ghost but a hero, a legend.

"I have brought your son to you so that we can keep that from happening," Vespa says, curtsying deeply to the King.

I look over at her, and I'm about to ask her what she means when his cold hands are on me, the ice so deep, it nearly freezes my heart. It reminds me very much of Charles nearly choking the life out of me once. The fear and anger nearly send me into hound-shape again as it did then.

But these hands reach inside me and find the dark place within. They tug and rip and shred until that dark place no longer remains. The memories flood me. The dreams. The knowledge that I have been spying for Ximu since New London. She is coming for me, expecting me to bring her an army. She is almost here. I can feel her and her army marching across the Plain as if they're the Creeping Waste come to destroy us all again.

The King takes my darkness and replaces it with an iron core of belief. "You are my son now, the last of my line. Only the descendants of the wolf can defeat the great spider."

Something falls around my neck, a cold key by the shape of it. "Take this and awaken my army. They will send Ximu back over the sea at your command!"

"*Xiexie*, my King," I say when I can finally catch my breath from the shock. "*Xiexie ni*."

CHAPTER 28 —

Vespa hadn't yet told anyone about the encounter with the Tinker King. It still felt unreal. But every time she looked down at the *scarabeus* bracelet that now graced her wrist and felt the surge of power from it, she knew it had happened.

She decided to return to the sunken garden she had found the other day and test whether or not such a simple thing could be true. There was cold-blooming jasmine here, but, aside from the trumpet vine that Charles had forced to bloom the other day, everything else was already dreaming of winter. A catwalk ringed the courtyard from above, allowing passersby to take in the heady scents during the proper seasons.

An observant maid who had seen her enter the garden brought tea. "Thank you," Vespa said as she set down the tray.

Piskel joined her from where he'd evidently been snoozing up in the arbor and yawned as he inspected the tray for cake.

She went to the rose garden. She remembered what it had been like trying to coax the vine into bloom. It had happened eventually, but it had taken a great deal of concentration. She spread her fingers against the rose and focused her power through the *scarabeus*. Almost before she thought of it, the rose had budded and bloomed.

She spread her influence wider, and then the entire rose garden was blooming.

Applause from under the arbor made her start.

Charles.

Vespa blushed a bit. She really had wanted to experiment with the *scarabeus* on her own.

He closed the book he was reading, sliding his hands along the cover and setting it down on the wooden bench beside him, before rising to greet her.

She glanced at the title. *Holy Bible*. Without the *Scientific* in the middle. Almost identical to the one she'd seen encased in glass in the Emperor's Cabinet of Curiosities over a year ago and that she had often wondered about since. Presumably, this was a copy Charles had gotten in Old London.

Vespa was filled with questions about Old London and was still incredulous about how he'd gotten there and back again, but she'd rather not ask now. She wanted to be finished with the conversation as quickly as possible.

"Miss Nyx," he said.

"Mr. Waddingly." She looked toward the door, at the catwalk above, anywhere but at him.

"It's very disheartening to me that you still find me menacing," he said.

"I don't think menacing is the proper word."

"Disconcerting, then?"

She shook her head.

The sun glinted in the sandy-blond curls about his face. His brown eyes were full of mischief. He was making fun of her.

"I suppose I can't expect much more, truly," Charles said. "You didn't know me before the Grue took hold. I didn't even recognize myself back then."

"And what were you before you made your deal with the Grue?" It was something Vespa had wondered often in the last year, and even more so since Charles had admitted he'd been too weak to choose other than what the Grue offered him.

"I wanted to be you," he said.

Vespa looked at him in surprise.

"You must understand—as I said before, I came from Lowtown. My father was a tanner. My mother a laundress. We were poorer than poor. And yet I was bright. I showed aptitude for things I shouldn't. Rather than abandon me beyond the Wall, my mother tried to hide it. She paid dearly for a crude dampener, rather like the sort your father gave you in that jade toad. But it didn't work on me.

"An Architect found me in a ditch, nearly dead from eating what filth I could find or trade small charms for, after my father had forcibly removed me from his house. I'd learned to do rough, dark magic to stay alive, but there was still much I didn't know. The Architect took me under his wing. He helped me learn, and he got me a position in the Museum with your father."

"Bayne said you betrayed their order." Vespa knew from both Bayne and Syrus about the fight that had raged through the Archives after Bayne had discovered his dead masters. All of them dead at Charles's hand. It was hard to imagine that this man who smiled ruefully at her and clasped his long fingers in front of him almost as if he were about to recite a poem was the same person who had murdered and enspelled so many with alacrity.

Yet in a way she almost understood. The Heart had given her untold power, and it had been hard to give it up. *What could I have done with the Heart had I been allowed to keep it?* she thought. She had a feeling the *scarabeus* would teach her.

"I did, but it was betrayal out of fear and revenge. They were about to vote me out of the Council. They felt my ideas were too radical, too ambitious. They wanted to teach me a lesson."

"But you taught one to them first."

"The Grue did," Charles said. "It's the custom if one is dismissed by the Architects that one either drinks the little potion they send you the day afterward, or one of them will come take you to the Creeping Waste."

Vespa just stared at him.

"You didn't know that about them, then? They have strict rules for vow-breakers. When Garrett founded the Architects of Athena, he forced his disciples to swear very binding oaths. If they broke any of them, they were expected to drink the potion to erase their memories, or the Architects would come and take their lives. Either way the magic must be forfeited."

"All that for an oath of secrecy?"

Charles laughed hollowly. "Ah, the oaths were much more than that, Miss Nyx. Secrecy, yes, but chastity and obedience as well."

Vespa frowned. "Chastity?"

"Garrett had been Athena's lover. When her father recaptured her and had her put to death, it destroyed Garrett. He made it part of the Architect's Oath that none would love or form lasting ties beyond the Order. Part of that is simple protection; Garrett knew how easy it was to coerce a man when his wife or children were threatened. But they especially forbade congress between a witch and warlock. 'For to love a witch is death,' so the Oath reads. They did not want the business of magic jeopardized by love."

Vespa's heart sank as understanding finally dawned. She remembered Bayne's whisper when they had been in the golden country of their magic. *I swore . . .* and his silence when she'd begged him to tell her what he had sworn.

"He did not tell you?"

"No," she whispered.

"I'm surprised. I would have thought, judging from his marriage to Lucy Virulen, that he had considered himself forsworn. Or that, more logically, he would have considered himself free of the Oath when he discovered all the Architects dead. Either way, I thought he would have told you long before this."

She shook her head.

"I suppose he still considers himself an Architect, even though all the rest of them are dead?"

"Yes."

"Then I am very sorry, Miss Nyx, if I've given you unpleasant news. I know he is your business associate, but I hope you had no further expectations of him."

Vespa was silent. She was not sure how to feel. Buried behind the wall of his oath, she knew that Bayne loved her. But if he could not break the wall down himself, it didn't matter. Even though she had made her peace with it, she still found it a bit hard to bear.

Arms went around her. Tentatively, very gently, Charles pulled her close.

Vespa stiffened at first. Then she realized that this could be a way to get closer to Charles, to understand whether he was still a menace or if he had changed as he said. The cloth beneath her cheek was coarse and yet inviting, like Father's coats had been. And it smelled even nicer. Like warm sunlight and leather-bound books, paper and ink. Gentle, normal things that she could understand. She allowed herself to melt. Just a little.

And yet there was an edge there too. A whisper of power. Something dark and mysterious contained. There was muscle in that wiry frame.

She felt him swat something away—Piskel, from the buzzing sound of it—before patting her on the shoulders.

"There, there," he whispered. "We have suffered so much, you and I. Two people should never suffer so much for magic."

A shadow fell over them from above. Vespa drew back.

And looked straight up into Bayne's eyes. The expression on his face—shock, hurt, betrayal, rage even—struck her almost like a physical blow. But the scorn that followed was almost worse. He didn't bother with the pretense of a nod. He simply retreated, his face like stone.

She wanted to call after him, but she knew better. She looked back at Charles. He smiled. "Oh my. I don't think he liked that much, did he?"

Resignation rose up on the heels of her sorrow. "Most likely not," she said.

The luster went out of the day. She sensed that Charles had gotten what he wanted—a delicate twist of the knife she'd very nearly removed from her heart.

"I'll take my leave, Miss Nyx."

"Thank you. I'm sorry if . . ." She wasn't really sure how to phrase it. She wasn't sorry that she'd doubted him before. How could she not? He had always been an enemy. She had never had the opportunity to think of him differently, and she still wasn't sure she should do so now.

"No need for apologies. I hope that you can forgive me for what I did when I was not myself. Perhaps you will even allow me to be your friend. I realize, though, that the circumstances in which we find ourselves are not the best."

Vespa thought about everything that had brought her to this moment. And now Bayne had seen her in an embrace with Charles. "No, they are not." The sun seemed to have vanished behind a cloud, and Vespa hugged herself, wishing she'd brought a shawl for warmth.

Charles nodded then, picked up his bible, and was off.

CHAPTER 29

She comes to me as has become her habit in the hours just before dawn.

Usually, I am deep in the cave with her, bound in her silk, defenseless.

This time, it's different. It's as though I'm looking into a shimmering lake of fire. I can see a dark shape off in the distance.

A girl cries out to me, and I see her wavering form at the edge of the lake of fire. "Oh, finally! You can see me! I've been waiting for ever so long."

I have no idea what she's talking about.

"Syrus! That is your name, isn't it?"

I pause. I'm trying to place her disheveled hair and scarred features. I don't know her—maybe she's tricking me, using my own memories against me like Ximu does. Perhaps she is one of the drowned ghosts of the palace, a fancy woman who met an untimely end.

"Don't be daft, boy!" she says. "Your name is Syrus?"

I'd recognize that tone anywhere, though.

"Lucy?" I ask.

"That's Lady Virulen to you!" She puts her hands to her face, and when her fingers drop, she looks around in confusion. I feel as though she's seeing things that I can't possibly see. She reaches out, and it's as if there's some sort of impenetrable membrane or wall between us. "Or that's who I was. Once." She looks at me, and her eyes are wild with fear and terror. "Lucy will do."

I look beyond her. "The shadow is moving," I say. I feel compelled to tell her.

She looks behind her and suppresses a scream. "Oh Saint Newton, oh Saint Darwin," she cries. She whirls to look at me, and then I see it—the faint resemblance to that high-bred young lady I once despised. Only this girl has been utterly crushed, nearly dissolved into nothing.

"Please, you've got to help me. This has all been such a mistake . . . such a mistake. If he just hadn't let go of my hand . . ."

He let go of my hand. I remember her words back in the Museum. Those sad, telling words.

"What can I do?" If she is asking to be released from Ximu, I have no idea how that can be done. Charles says he's free of the Grue, but I still find that hard to believe.

"Get me out of here and I swear, I swear . . ."

All I can feel for her is pity as the shadow closes in on her and drags her back into the lake of fire.

I jerk awake, sweating, the blanket wadded between my fists. I toss my hair out of my face and sit there, shaking.

I can still hear her voice. I can feel the terror, a unique terror that only I can understand.

Please, she whispers in the dawn, *please help me.*

I'm so eager to get the key to Olivia and see if it actually works that I forget all about breakfast. I practically run to Tesla's workshop. I haven't forgiven him, not one whit, but if he perhaps has begun to understand what is happening and is willing to help us, then maybe I will be able to forgive him.

But only if Olivia wakes up.

As I approach her on the table, it's still hard to reconcile her with the person she was. But I see that Tesla has finished cleaning her so that she shines, and has repaired the circuitry on her ankle.

Tesla is working at the other end of the shop on some hulking thing that I only dimly saw last time in my rage.

When he sees me, he puts down the tools he's working with and comes to the workbench.

I pull the key from my pocket.

"You found it, I see," he says. "I was about to start pouring a key mold. Only problem with this world—you have to build every single thing you want from scratch. Well . . . some things." He looks around at the everlanterns.

"I was given it," I say. "And I hope I don't fail the person who gave it to me. Or her."

I place the key in the keyhole. I can hear the gears winding and tumbling, the whir of flywheels and cogs and inner workings so intricate as I can't even imagine.

The ticking grows louder, but nothing happens.

"Please, please," I whisper under my breath.

Olivia's eyelids flutter and open wide. She lifts her hands. When she rises and sees her feet, she stumbles off the bench and falls in a clanking heap on the floor.

"Olivia!" I bend down to pick her up, but she moves me away from her with terrifying strength. She puts her hands back on the slab to steady herself. Looking down, Olivia sees the key slowly turning in her belly and she pulls it out, as if she's just pulled out a dagger. Her gears and tumblers keep turning. They should keep going until she winds down, which hopefully will not be for a very long time.

"Syrus?" Her voice doesn't sound like her voice; it's silvery and brittle, not the mellow honey it once was.

But she knows me. She definitely knows me.

"Do you remember what happened?"

Olivia puts a hand to her forehead and seems both repulsed and intrigued by the clinking sound. She also seems to realize at the same time that she has no hair and no skin.

"Yes," she says slowly. "I remember too much." She looks at me with metal eyes. "I remember everything. So many lives . . ."

I look at Tesla. "How is that possible?"

"I don't know," he says. "Perhaps she's developed new memory cells . . . or . . ." He leans toward her as if to pry open one of her panels and discover all her secrets.

"No," I say. "No more experiments or tests. She is still the Empress of the Known Lands."

She smiles sadly. "Thank you for that, dear Syrus. Now, would one of you fetch me a robe?"

In the end, Tesla is able to find her a dusty laboratory coat. She puts that on.

"I suppose I don't really need clothes anymore. It's just . . . familiar."

I want to hold her hand because that is familiar too, but I don't. I want to offer any number of comforts—tea, food, rest—but I realize probably none of those are particularly comforting to her now.

"What has happened?" she says.

I realize that much has happened and yet nothing.

Tesla is better, apparently, at neutral subjects than I am and brings us over to the thing he was working on.

"I have just finished a new invention," he says.

He calls the circulating everlanterns to all focus above the thing. For a moment I'm deeply amused. It looks like a mechanical Kraken.

"I call it the Cephalopod," he says.

"What does it do?" I ask.

Olivia is looking over it, gently touching it with her silver fingertips. I can almost hear the processors whirring, taking in information.

"A little bit of everything," Tesla says. "It can be used on land or in water. It can pick up things, cut things, hold things . . . I envision it largely as a drilling and tunneling engine."

Olivia smiles. "It's a work of art."

"As are you, Your Majesty," Tesla says.

I'm genuinely moved by his respect for her. I would not have expected it. I feared he simply wanted to use her for whatever he could.

He takes us over to another bench. "And here is where I am perfecting my radiant energy device."

Although Olivia's face can now hold no expression, I sense distaste and hesitance in her gaze.

There are antennae all strewn about and another of the little black boxes like the sort that nearly broke Olivia apart.

"Don't worry," he said. "It won't hurt you anymore. I had no idea it would have that effect. I suppose I should make a note of that." And he does, on a little notebook he whips from his pocket.

"What is it supposed to do?" Olivia asks.

"All kinds of things, Majesty. It could potentially give heat and light to all. It could transmit waves of sound around the world so that people could talk to one another from any point on the globe, no matter how far away."

She draws back in disbelief. "That hardly seems possible, Mr. Tesla."

Tesla smiles at her. "I would have said the same of you, Majesty. You are indeed my dream come true."

CHAPTER 30

The slender invitation arrived on a tray in the late afternoon. Vespa had kept to herself throughout most of the day, practicing and reading more books that Truffler had brought her.

Your presence is requested in the Trophy Room at five o' clock.

Somehow the simplicity of it made her exceptionally nervous, as if she was being invited to her own execution. But she let the maids dress her in yet another plain gown and put up her hair with horn combs. She secured the *scarabeus* on her wrist, hoping she wouldn't need to use it.

She was led back to the first room they'd dined in just after they'd arrived at Scientia. Although the refreshments and trappings weren't as elaborate, she was still dazzled by the architecture and magnificence of the Grimgorn collection. She browsed the cases, admiring the handiwork of the taxidermist who had preserved birds and butterflies from all around Newtonia. But at the same time she had to wonder if this was any better or worse than what she had done for the Museum. Many Elementals had nearly gone extinct because of human rapacity. Were other species experiencing the same troubles?

Bayne entered then with Arlen. Though Bayne's clothes weren't evered or too richly embroidered, he no longer wore the Pedant's coat he'd had since she'd known him. He hadn't spoken to her since he'd seen her in the garden with Charles, and he refused to look at her now.

Vespa lifted her chin and stared fixedly at the butterflies in the case. She had no reason to feel ashamed. He had no claim on her, and she had done nothing wrong.

She did look up, though, when Syrus and Tesla entered, escorting Olivia between them. It was the first time she'd seen Olivia since they had agreed to allow Tesla to remove her dying flesh.

To say it was a shock was an understatement. Gone was the golden hair, the deep gray eyes. Gone the pale hands that fluttered at Olivia's throat when she laughed or smiled. There was only silver, folded and hammered into the shapes of a human woman. She wore a dress for modesty, Vespa supposed, but it looked as though someone had tried to dress up a child's toy.

Vespa fought the urge to run. She didn't want to see her friend this way. She didn't want to accept the truth. But it was Syrus's face, the tenderness with which he helped Olivia to her seat, that kept Vespa in the room.

She went up to her Empress and offered her the greatest curtsy she could muster. "Your Majesty."

"Vee!"

Vespa hid her wince. Even Olivia's voice was gone, replaced by something metallic and seemingly inhuman.

But the emotions were still there. Olivia rose and embraced her, and though her arms were heavy and her cheek cold, Vespa realized her friend was still there with her.

"Are you well, Majesty?" Vespa asked.

Olivia nodded, and Vespa could hear the mechanical whir of gears as she did so.

"Much better! Though I hope you don't find me too hideous now to look upon."

Vespa looked into her metal eyes and took one of Olivia's silver fingers in her own. "Never," she said.

Vespa hadn't even noticed that Charles had come in, except when he cleared his throat. She took her seat by Syrus.

"You're looking well, too," Vespa whispered.

"Hard not to when one finally gets some sleep," Syrus said.

"I've called you all here," Charles said rather loudly, "for a very special purpose."

"Execution?" Syrus muttered under his breath. Nothing Charles could do would ever make Syrus fully trust him, Vespa guessed.

"I am immensely pleased to see that Nikola and Mr. Reed have restored Her Majesty to herself. Thank you for that effort. I hope this means we will be able to protect her all the better against what is coming and ensure the future of the realm."

"And just how do you plan to do that exactly?" Bayne asked. "Are we not all precisely where you want us? Spring your trap, sir, and have done!"

Charles looked genuinely baffled. "I haven't the faintest idea what you mean!"

"I mean, the facts do not line up in your favor, Charles," Bayne said. "Consider: There was a great plague, but you survived; you sent an airship just in our hour of need, after a year of not responding to our Empress's correspondence. Yet you knew, in point of fact, what the Empress was and what advantage she might give you were she to come here, did you not?"

"I—" Charles began.

The Empress held up a silver hand. "Enough, my Lord. I can speak for myself here."

"As you wish, Majesty."

"Charles, I do not have the history with you that others at this table have had," Olivia said. "It will be easier for you therefore to tell me the truth, I hope. We were warned before we came here that you had overthrown the Duke and were holding the people hostage. But when we came, we found you a victim of circumstance, a grieving widower who had been thrust into the position of caring for a Duchy. We found you pleasant and helpful. Yet every step of the way you have just been waiting for us to help you find the key, to reveal me for what I truly am, yes?"

There was a long silence. Charles's gaze darted between them like a frantic bird.

"I am Your Majesty's most humble servant!" he said. "If I was otherwise, would I have been as pleasant and helpful as you say? Would I have returned the Duchy to its former heir?" Charles looked at Bayne. "And while the facts may not be in my favor, my Lord, I had nothing to do with that wretched plague. I loved your sister. I would never have harmed her or this City. What was begun in Old London was completed by your sister. I am not the man I was."

Now it was Olivia's turn to be silent. Vespa could almost hear the gears turning.

At last she said, "Over the centuries I have seen many men like you, Charles. Men who wanted power. Men who tried to do good and could not because their love of power overruled them. Do not be one of those men. They never end well."

Vespa watched Charles carefully. He bowed and lowered his

eyes. She sensed nothing amiss. No curl of the lip, no craven hypocrisy, as he said, "I shall endeavor not to repeat history, Majesty."

When he straightened, he met all of their gazes. "But you must all endeavor to do the same. Whether you will it or no, your freeing of the Heavenly Dragon has unbalanced the world. Now you must set it right."

"And so we will," Syrus said. "When the battle is won and my people are free . . ."

"You are a fool, Tinker." Charles said it without menace, but Syrus rose in protest. Olivia put a hand on his arm and forced him to sink back beside her.

"If you kill Ximu," Charles said, "you will only make matters worse." He looked at Bayne. "You of all people should know what happens when those who deal in magic circumvent the Great Law."

"And you should know your history better, Charles. The Great Law was set in place after the binding of the Umbrals. It affects only those who swore to uphold it."

Charles laughed, and it reminded Vespa of his former self. "You truly think that killing an Umbral that has been here since the foundation of the world will not unbalance the very essence of magic? Look what setting Tianlong free did!"

There was a long silence.

Syrus spoke up in a small voice. "There is also another thing to think about: Lucy Virulen."

"How so?" Bayne asked.

"She came to me in a dream, after the Tinker King lifted Ximu's curse. She told me that she wanted to be free, that she'd had no choice but to join with Ximu to survive."

"Ximu cursed you?" Bayne asked.

Syrus's fingers danced over the old wound on his neck. "Yes. She has been using me to spy on all of us, trying to force me to give Olivia over to her. Until now." Olivia laid a silver hand on his arm in silent sympathy.

Charles ignored this information as if it was not new to him. "If you kill Ximu," he said, "you will almost certainly kill Lucy."

"But you killed the Grue," Vespa said, "and you lived to tell about it."

Charles shook his head. "No. I was able to weaken him enough to separate from him without lasting harm to myself. There's a difference."

"So, what are you suggesting?" Bayne asked.

"Separate Ximu and Lucy. Trap Ximu for all eternity, so that she is alive but can no longer do any harm."

Everyone spoke at once. Olivia called again for quiet.

"Let us think about this, and how it might be done. If Lucy is truly repentant, then we should do our best to help her, yes?"

"How can it be done?" Vespa asked.

"Quite honestly," Charles said, "I don't know if it can be done here. But I do have the formulae for the purgatives I took. The other thing that will be needed, the final thing, is a literal shock to the system."

"As in some sort of blast of etheric energy?" Bayne asked. Vespa could see he was still incredulous.

"Yes, in a manner of speaking. Though Tesla can summon it up via radiant energy fields, as you saw in his demonstration."

"So," Vespa said, "we feed Ximu these potions, then shock her, and that should somehow free Lucy?"

Charles nodded.

"But how do we get the purgatives into her?" Olivia asked.

Charles smiled. "We will need bait."

CHAPTER 31

Vespa finds me in Tesla's workshop, of course. Olivia and I have been working together on one of Tesla's radiant energy transmitters. She's quite skilled at such things, having regained a memory of helping her former King in building the army and their weaponry. Tesla's making several transmitters, enough so that we can cast a net of energy across the city and see if it will actually power everything without the use of *myth*. If it does, we may be able to keep Ximu's army at bay more easily than we've thought. Tesla is out installing some of the others in a small net as a test.

Olivia holds the panel open with her metal fingers so that I can reach inside and weld the plates together according to Tesla's plan. She can withstand much more heat than I can and has greater strength. It still is so strange that I can barely allow myself to think about it, except that her metal eyes are looking at me and she is smiling her silver smile.

I realize Vespa is there when Olivia nods toward a point behind me.

I feel a bit of dread in the pit of my stomach for some reason. I think I know what Vespa has come to ask about. I really don't want to say yes.

I slide the face shield from my head and turn.

When Vespa hears the sparking of the welder stop, she also turns to face us. "Syrus. Olivia."

Her voice seems overly cheerful.

I try not to sound sullen. "What?"

"Syrus," Olivia whispers. Even her whispers now have metal in them.

"I'm sorry to interrupt, but may I speak with you for just a moment?"

Vespa wrings her hands for a second, as if she's rehearsed this but suddenly has forgotten how to begin. "Look," she says, "I know that none of us really like Charles. I don't like him either. But I think that he has a good plan, perhaps the best plan we've yet come across."

"You mean the one about trapping Ximu in the strongest paralytic field ever created so that she's just biding her time until someone lets her loose?" I ask.

Vespa purses her lips. "Not exactly."

"Well, that is what will happen, you know."

"But you'd rather kill her instead?" Vespa tilts her head, and her eyes are sharp and defiant as the day she pulled the banshee alarm on me.

"Look, that isn't really what I'd prefer. I'd rather not kill anything if I can help it. But it seems to me the risk of doing otherwise is too great."

"How so? You know better than anyone what happens when things are thrown out of balance," Vespa says.

I grit my teeth. "Yes, but—"

"So, how will killing her solve anything?"

"She'll be dead. She won't ever come back to haunt us again."

"You know it's not that simple. When something with as much power as she possesses is destroyed or mortally wounded, the entire world can fall out of balance. Who knows what Ximu caused when she killed the Titan and turned her into a palace?" She says it with great confidence, but again it sounds as if she's been rehearsing all this.

"You do see what he's doing, don't you?" I ask.

"Who?"

"Charles."

Olivia is still listening, but she's also gathering more wire for the interior of the antenna. She likes to stay busy, and she can do more than one thing at a time quite easily.

"What?" Vespa asks.

"You really don't know?" I need to do something with my hands, so I grab a greasy spanner and start wiping it down with a rag.

"Enlighten me." She puts her hands on her hips, like one of the old Tinker junkwives back in the trainyard.

"He's manipulating you to get what he wants. He wants something. And you are not seeing the entire picture."

"He's had a change of heart," she says. "He's trying to set things right."

"I doubt it!"

Vespa sighs. "He's doing it because he understands. He knows everything the Grue knew. And what the Grue knew was that manipulating the balance created chaos and in that moment, he could seize control. He didn't care, though, if the rest of the world suffered for it. Charles realizes that now."

"So?"

"We don't know what the consequences could be if we destroy Ximu. She's been here since the very beginning. Like Tianlong. We've seen the results of releasing magic into a world hungry for it. Now we need to try to restore the balance that we unwittingly upset. Killing her is not the way to do it."

I sigh. I start arranging all the tools from right to left, the way my uncles once did in their stalls. I have no idea why, except that I really can't bring myself to answer her.

"Besides," Vespa adds, "you yourself said you dreamed that Lucy begged you to be freed. Have you no compassion?"

Finally, I manage to say, "Why does this decision rest on me?" I look over at Olivia. "Shouldn't it rest with her, truthfully?"

"Well, yes," Vespa says, "but I think Olivia sees the logic of what I'm saying."

Olivia nods. "Yes. And though it is ultimately my decision, I think you have much at stake, Syrus. Your family is feeding her spiderlings. Your uncle is leading her assassins. This has the most to do with you of any of us."

If it's possible, her metal eyes go blank, and I can see that she's scanning her distant past. "My army chased her into the sea once. I can do it again. But many people died even then. If we can prevent that, I would welcome it."

She's right. There is really nothing more to say.

Olivia puts her hand on my arm in wordless sympathy. I remember a day when that hand wouldn't have been silver or heavy. A day when I wouldn't have been able to hear the winding of her gears or the occasional clink of her joints. This is Ximu's fault.

"I'll do this for you," I say, looking at Olivia.

Olivia shakes her head. "Not for me. For you. For your people. Taking life will never restore the lives of those lost. But you have the chance to both restore a life and halt the evil of another. I know you'll do what's right."

"Then with your blessings," Vespa says, "we can begin our plan."

We both nod.

CHAPTER 32 ——

I don't trust him as far as I could throw him," Bayne said. "I'm sure he's hiding something from us."

"Well," Vespa said, "that's understandable. We've hidden things from him, too." She couldn't believe she was defending Charles. Never in her life would she have imagined that was a possibility. "But he's agreed to help now. The least we can do is cooperate on our end."

"What does that mean exactly?" Bayne asked.

"We give him the energy he needs, help him distract Ximu long enough to get Lucy free before we shove the giant spider into our own web."

"And what of the Tinkers and the *xiren*? Will they be free when Ximu is trapped? Or will they go on?"

"I don't know," Vespa said. "But Syrus has agreed to help us."

"He has?" Bayne raised a brow. "I'm surprised. It seems as though there are many details missing."

"But it's the only choice if he wants to save them! If she dies, they'll die too."

"So Charles has said." Bayne unfolded himself from the battlements and turned to look out over the mist-covered mountains.

He was as distant and remote as the heights, it seemed.

"I don't see what other choice we have. Everything else he's said has been true." She couldn't tell him how much Charles had helped her with her magic. How he had taught her to start small and work up to the bigger things. She knew the *scarabeus* was helpful too, but Charles also made magic comprehensible in a way that Bayne never quite had. Though she couldn't bring herself to say so. As ever, though, it seemed as if Bayne picked up on her thoughts.

"What is his hold over you?" He turned back to look at her.

She forced herself to look him in the eye, though it felt like she was being shot full of angry darts.

"Nothing. I just think . . ." Vespa swallowed, hating the words that crowded the back of her throat.

"What?"

"I think we have to trust him. We have no choice."

"There's always a choice, Pedant Nyx," Bayne said. "The question is whether we're making the right one."

"Well, in this case, I think this is both the only choice and the right one. And we really will need your help to make this work."

"Very well, then. But the moment he diverges from the plan, my compliance will be withdrawn. And I will come prepared for that moment. Understood?" He crossed his arms over his chest, and the ducal signet on his finger winked at her. He made it so difficult to argue with him. And yet so easy all at once.

But this answer was better than she'd been expecting.

They all met in the courtyard of the ancient palace. The autumn sun struck hard on the paving stones, making Vespa want to seek shade behind one of the great statues that lined the square. She wished she'd brought the bonnet the maid had tried to give her.

Tesla was pacing out the dimensions of the trap. "You will need to lure Ximu here," he said. "If we set up the field in this courtyard, this will be the strongest place. Any other place and she might still be able to pull free."

"But what will happen to Lucy?" Syrus asked.

"If we're fortunate," Charles said, "the division field I set up here will be enough to separate the two. It would help if we could some-how get the potions into her before this, but the ways in which we could offer it seem less than fair."

"Such as?" Bayne asked.

"Well, a person willing to sacrifice himself for the cause could drink it so that she'd feed off him, for instance. But I doubt anyone here is quite that noble." Charles smiled darkly.

Vespa tried to offer a solution instead. "How about putting out a goat or a cow laced with it?" She said in an aside to Syrus, "Does she eat goats or cows? Do the legends say anything about that?"

Syrus stepped forward.

"I'll do it," he said. "She expects me to give her Olivia anyway. I will go to her and offer myself."

"But Syrus," Vespa said, "won't she kill you when she's realized you've betrayed her?"

"I think the prospect of the key will be enough to satisfy her."

"But will she still not kill you? If you don't give her the key . . ." Vespa trailed off.

Syrus held up two keys. "I always carry a spare." He grinned.

The two keys looked identical; the difference was that one had the patina of age and the other did not. The other difference was that Vespa could feel the magic coming off the old one and nothing from the new. "She'll sense the difference. There's magic in the old one," Vespa said.

"I was hoping you might help me with that."

"You don't have to do this, Syrus. Really . . ."

He looked at her, and she could see the resolution in his eyes. "You said this was my decision. Well, now I'm truly making it mine."

Vespa nodded. She couldn't smile, though. It was far too deadly a situation for Syrus to put himself in. But he was a man now. No one could make his decisions for him.

"Yes, all well and good. Now that's decided, can we move on, please?" Charles asked.

Vespa rolled her eyes. Sometimes Charles and Bayne were too alike for her comfort.

"So, we lure her away from the army, and she hits the division field here," Charles said, standing near a spot that Tesla was sketching onto a tablet.

"And then?" Bayne asked.

"And then we have her, my Lord Duke," Charles said. "And here she will stay, held for all eternity."

"You're certain?"

Bayne looked between him and Tesla.

Tesla answered, "If my understanding of the schematics that are on archive here are correct, this is how the first Elementals were held at the Museum of Unnatural History."

Piskel began grumping about and settled on Syrus's shoulder with a thud.

"What's the matter?" Vespa said. She had been worried that Truffler and Piskel might not want to help them capture Ximu, remembering the old days of the Museum and New London.

"He says that's the case unless you're a sylph," Syrus said, patting the sylph gently.

Vespa could imagine the strain Syrus was feeling. Just thinking about him going alone to face Ximu was terrifying enough for her. She remembered how she had felt when Charles had taken her up to the Machine. She knew that terror of inevitability, that slim hope that what she believed in so desperately would come to pass.

They went back to pacing out the paralytic field. Tesla positioned the thin antennae he and Syrus had developed together. "This will be a perfect way to test the design. If it can withstand holding this kind of power, it should be able to service the entire City," Tesla said.

Bayne nodded, but Vespa saw how he looked at Charles. She knew that he was still trying to figure out what secret plan Charles might be masking behind this one. He was still sure he would be caught unawares. But he went along with it—they all did—because there was nothing better that could be done.

"It will have to be right," Vespa muttered under her breath to Truffler. "It will just have to."

Truffler took her hand in his, and silently they watched the rods being set into place.

CHAPTER 33

The hour I've set for myself finally comes. The others know I'm going but not exactly when. I don't want to have to say good-bye. Besides, I'll be back. Ximu will only take a taste, because she'll want me to give her the army. I know this. All is as it should be.

But if that's true, why are my knees knocking together so badly, I can barely walk?

I know she's in a cave at the base of the mountains. Scouts have seen her army positioning itself between the City and the mountains, and occasionally the hybrids have tested the strength of the gaps in the walls. She's waiting. It will be almost a relief to go to her; her call has been so strong lately that it's nearly impossible to refuse, even with the curse broken.

The potions clank in my satchels as I walk. There's no point in shifting to speed this up. I will take my time. I want to feel the sea wind on my face, to feel the moonlight falling on me, silver and perfect as Olivia's smile.

Olivia.

I wanted to say good-bye to her. I almost did today in the workshop but then stopped myself. She would have offered to go with me, and we cannot afford for Ximu to get hold of her.

Then over my own soft clinking, I hear the sound of footsteps. I think perhaps it's the Grimgorn guard, but as the sound grows louder, I know it for what it is.

There's no point in hiding, so I just stand and watch her. She's wearing a hooded cloak, but occasionally the moon tricks out a flash of silver.

"You didn't really think you could leave without my knowing, did you?" Olivia asks.

"I didn't want you to worry. And I also didn't want to put you in danger. You should go back, Olivia. I'll be back soon enough." Even I can hear the false cheer in my voice.

"How will you get back on your own, Syrus? Ximu can be swift when she wishes, and the *xiren* even swifter. Barring some Elemental with wings, I'm the only one who can outrun them."

I consider protesting again—the foolhardiness of it, the terrible danger—but I simply do not want to walk this road alone. "Walk with me, then," I say, and she slips her cold hand into mine.

It feels as though the entire world is silently watching as we pick our way through the tombs and graves of Scientia.

And then I notice those amber eyes watching me from a little hillock under a twisted tree.

Blackwolf comes to me, and though he cannot speak in this form, he puts his head under my hand. The touch of his ruff comforts me, and together we three walk down the hill, his strength flowing into me. It would be almost easy if I was just going into battle. If, like the stories from the Old World that *Nainai* sometimes told, I went into the heart of the cave with my spear to kill the darkness that lived there.

But this is a different world, and we must learn to dance with the darkness. After all, it is only a reflection of our inner selves. If we try to kill it, we are killing a part of ourselves. What are the stars without night? What is life without death?

We must give ourselves up for lost and, in so doing, find ourselves. I think *Nainai* said that to me once long ago. As I hold Olivia's hand, I never knew what it meant until now.

There is no guard at this gate. Bayne has pulled all the defenses in tightly, protecting the inner City as best he can.

Blackwolf stops.

"*Xiexie*," I whisper. He closes his eyes and bows his head. And then he is lost in the shadows once again.

My legs tremble so hard just before this last part of the journey that I'm afraid I'll fall down.

Olivia is watching me from the shadows of her hood. "Don't worry," she says. "I'll be with you. I'll keep you from harm."

I manage to smile. "Shouldn't I be saying that to you?"

She shrugs. "You seem to have forgotten that I'm the General here."

I down the two potions quickly, their bitter taste making me want to spit them back out. Charles said I would feel no effects from them, that my bond with the hound is different from that with humans and Greater Elementals. Still, it makes me feel even more nervous and sick, and for a moment I press my forehead against the rusting iron bars and wish I did not have to do this.

Olivia puts her hand on my shoulder in wordless sympathy.

But then I think of my people and the long slavery we have endured, always changing masters but never changing fates. Whether they know it or not, they're waiting for me to free them. And Lucy, too. Even though I disliked the girl, Vespa is right—she does deserve compassion for the terror she's gone through. Only I can change their fates.

I slide out between the bars, and Olivia follows suit. I've spent enough time deliberating, and I suck the last potion down. I can feel them bubbling together in my stomach, fizzing out along my veins.

At the mouth of her cave I go a few steps ahead of Olivia so they will see that she is under my command. The *xiren* come to collect us.

"Finally, you've seen reason," my uncle says.

I smile wearily at him. I will carry the charade on as long as I have to. "Take me to her, then. She will want her prize."

Ximu is in the darkest, dankest, foulest hole I can imagine. The smell makes me gag.

Whatever you do, don't vomit, Charles had said.

That admonition and knowing Olivia is at my back keep me going.

Lucy's warped face greets me out of the gloom.

"Took you long enough. You are a resistant little thing, for a mortal. I was beginning to think I'd lost you."

I want to say something brilliant, something heroic, but instead I take the false key out of my bag and shove it with a trembling hand in her face. Vespa's magic gives it a lovely, warm glow. I pull Olivia around beside me.

"Good," Ximu says. "Very good."

I wait on her to pounce, to drink of me in her triumph, as she so often has in my nightmares. But she does nothing. She is waiting on me.

I step forward. "Give me what you promised, then," I say

through chattering teeth. "Make me *xiren*. I am your weapon, and this automaton will do whatever we say."

She rubs her little forefeet together and the scarlet fangs emerge, poison dripping.

"This," she says, as she leaps toward me, "is going to be a very good day."

She bends me backward, nearly breaking me in half in her eagerness. She doesn't bother winding me into a cocoon first. She simply dives into me, as if she hasn't fed in centuries.

The last thing I see is Olivia's face and a great shining sword that has grown in her hands.

Chapter 34 ⟝

Alarms were sounding in her sleep. And something was shaking her. Something was wrong, horribly, horribly wrong.

"Vespa, wake up!" Truffler was saying in a hoarse, terrified whisper.

"What? What's wrong?"

She tried to put on her clothes, but he kept pulling at her.

"No time! Syrus! Olivia!" he said. He was practically hauling her out of the door.

Vespa only managed to get on her dressing gown and boots before they were outside and running toward the courtyard.

"What did they do?" she said, her stomach filling with dread.

Truffler shook his head and moaned in answer. Which was not really an answer, but she gathered it was the best she was going to get.

She saw Bayne racing across the courtyard with a little star beside him—Piskel. Just over the dark edges of the buildings they could see a line of light. Vespa couldn't tell if it was dawn or fire.

They met running up the stairs to the old haunted palace.

"Do you know what's happening?" Bayne asked. He carried a satchel, and she heard things clinking around in it.

Vespa shook her head, barely able to breathe. "Something to do with Syrus and Olivia, but I don't know what."

"I fear this cannot be good."

Silver gleamed in the moonlight, and they realized it was Olivia bending over something.

"Olivia," Vespa said.

Syrus was on the floor, the bite wound on his neck still oozing blood and venom.

"By Athena," Bayne whispered, kneeling next to him. "He went off and tried to do it alone, didn't he?"

Olivia nodded. "I sensed he might do it tonight. I went with him, and we pretended that he was giving me over to her. I waited until she'd drunk enough of him, and then I cut him free and ran with him. They are behind me, though. I'm certain they'll soon be here. Can you help him?"

It was an innocent enough question, but Vespa felt ashamed by it. They had not been able to help Olivia when she needed them. But she trusted them, nonetheless, and was absolutely without bitterness that no magic could have saved the person she'd once been.

"Based on the knowledge I've been gathering lately, I hope I have just the thing," Bayne said. He reached into his satchel, uncorked one of the vials, and poured something that smelled strongly of licorice down Syrus's throat.

Syrus spluttered and coughed and gasped. Then he rolled over and threw up.

Syrus wiped his mouth on his sleeve just as Bayne tried to hand him a handkerchief. He took it sheepishly. "I hate doing that. What's happening?" Syrus asked, looking around at all of them. His eyes stayed on Olivia. "You saved me, didn't you?"

Olivia smiled, nodding.

"You shouldn't have done that," Syrus said. "She could have gotten you."

"You shouldn't have tried to go without telling me," she said. Alarms rang out, drowning anything else she might have said.

Bayne coughed rather uncomfortably. "In case you hadn't noticed, there are sirens howling out there. We're under attack."

"What do you think is happening outside?" Vespa asked.

"Some of the forces are at the front gates, but I've kept back several regiments in the graveyard and along the inner walls. They still may not be enough, though," Bayne said. "She's coming from that direction, yes?" he asked, looking at Syrus and Olivia.

"Yes," Olivia said. "She was behind me, coming through the graveyard."

"Is there anything we can do to slow her, to make sure Tesla and Charles are in position?" Vespa asked.

"Put up as strong a defense as we can with magic," Bayne said. "Or . . ." He glanced over at Olivia.

"Don't you dare," Syrus said.

"What?" Olivia asked.

"Do you have any memory of this place?" Bayne asked.

Olivia looked around. "Yes." She walked out onto the terrace, her metal footsteps clanging against ivory. "I have defended it often enough before."

"You lived here once, as General to the King's army," Bayne said.

"I know," she said. "That's why everyone wanted me. I was a weapon to them."

"Bayne, no," Syrus said. "Don't . . ."

Olivia turned back toward them. Her eyes couldn't be seen in the pre-dawn gloom. "It's all right, Syrus," she said. "Where is the army? Still beneath this hall?"

Everyone was silent.

"Where is it?" she asked again.

"Yes," Syrus said. "Beneath us."

"Then let's go there."

A shudder passed through the entire palace. "She's coming!" Olivia said. "Down here." They hurried behind the throne, down winding stairs in the dark. Bayne sent out a flare of light as they neared the bottom of the stairs, keeping them from tipping into the pit. A chasm yawned away from them. Thousands of silver bodies and pointed weapons caught and reflected the light back to them. An army indeed worthy of a king.

"I remember this," Olivia said. "I remember . . ." She turned to all of them. "This way."

They were at the deep end of the pit, which sloped upward. Vespa noticed that the walls of the pit were lined with row upon row of clay jars large enough to fit a human child inside.

"What are those for?" she whispered.

"Those are funerary urns. They contain the souls of those who swore to fight eternally for their King," Olivia said.

"Oh."

"There is a great door that way," Olivia said. "My chariot is there."

Vespa shivered at the way she said it. Moment by moment as they traversed the pit, Olivia was sounding less like their Empress and more like the General she had once been.

Finally the slope of the pit reached level ground again, and they could step in among the warriors themselves. As they wove through the motionless army, Vespa could have sworn that she heard a click, like a strange awareness coming sharply into focus.

But there was also another sound. A scratching sound, a drilling sound from the wall in front of them.

"Hurry!"

They got Olivia into her chariot. There was a place for her feet, and she stepped into it. There was another almost inaudible click.

Vespa didn't know what to make of it. Anything else like this she'd seen in New London had been *myth*-powered. But this wasn't powered by *myth* at all. She hoped they would figure it out quickly, because otherwise they were going to be sitting ducks in just a few short moments.

The drilling and tearing sounds became more persistent. Then Vespa saw daylight. The wall in front of them had started to crack.

"Olivia," Syrus said. "You don't have to do this."

She reached out a hand to him and took his trembling fingers in her own.

"The old King has shown his favor of you by giving you my key. He has made you his son. Let this be the everlasting symbol of my love for you. I am abdicating in favor of you. I will be your General. I will protect you and your family for generations to come. The name of the Tinker King will be honored throughout all the Known Lands. But you must consent to let me go. You must consent to be my King."

Syrus was speechless as she pulled him close and kissed him. Vespa looked away, unable to bear the sadness between them.

Olivia murmured something Vespa couldn't quite catch.

For several heart-stopping moments there was nothing. No movement, no sound but the resolute drilling and tearing, and the light growing brighter.

Then there was a ticking, the sound of clockwork resolving itself into a rhythm. Olivia's metal eyes grew very bright as she let go of Syrus's hands.

"Now," Olivia said to Vespa. "Use the *scarabeus* to call the souls into the warriors. Their souls will restore their life force."

For this, Vespa had been practicing, she realized. Learning how to focus the power of the *scarabeus*, how to use it to control and magnify her own power. She just prayed her magic was enough.

Bayne said, "I will feed you what strength I can."

Vespa nodded, and Bayne took her hand. She could feel his strength flowing up her fingers, focusing into the *scarabeus* and casting outward.

Syrus's voice strengthened hers with the proper pitch, even if it carried no power. Piskel and Truffler hummed along with them in the old language, weaving their magic with Vespa's and Bayne's.

Vespa was aware of all the souls lining the pit, souls that preferred to continue their long slumber, souls that did not want to be called. Vespa pulled at them with all her might. She reached out and took hold of Bayne's power, so fast and so hard that it sent him to his knees, clutching at the chariot's edge with his free hand.

"Rise," she said. *"Rise and be counted. For the dawn has come, and war is at our door."*

The shadows stretched and tore like taffy. Vespa felt the very fiber of her being flowing off in thousands of directions, seeding the souls with the compulsion to rise and honor the oath they'd sworn. One by one, they did her bidding. One by one, the army came to attention.

Vespa nearly wept with joy and exhaustion. Bayne managed to stand again.

Then the wall was torn away and harsh morning light streamed in on them, blinding them after the relative darkness of the pit.

As her eyes adjusted, Vespa's heart quailed at the scene that spread before them. Ximu had broken through the outer wall. Grimgorn soldiers were scattered like bowling pins. A platoon of hybrids was lined up behind *xiren* Captains.

"Thank you very much for providing us with our new army," Ximu said. "I wasn't quite certain you could do it, but I had faith that my little Tinker spy would help me win the day. This charade can finally be at an end."

Bayne laughed bitterly. "I think you'd better reconsider."

"Oh no," Ximu said. "I am quite sincere about this farce being at an end."

"Agreed," Bayne said. "No, I mean the army. It's ours."

Ximu laughed. "I am pleased to see that your acumen has not improved one bit since last we spoke."

"Yours hasn't improved much either," Bayne said.

Syrus said almost to himself, "Don't toy with her. Not now."

Vespa caught his eye, and the haunted look he gave her made her squeeze his shoulder in understanding. "He's buying us time to recover," she whispered. "We are all drained to the core."

"Enough of this!" Ximu shouted. "Give over control of this army or suffer the consequences!"

"I think your armies and your City belong to me."

The spidery minions, even more hideous by day, charged them. *Xiren* followed them with their long-handled blades.

"Now is the time," Vespa said to the General, hoping perhaps to urge her and the army forward.

The General turned her head toward Syrus.

Another sound rose beneath the clanking sounds of Ximu's hybrids, a heavy thrumming like the sound of drums coming toward them.

Then the first of the Cephalopod's tentacular arms snaked round the corner. One of the pincer arms reached out and tried to grab Ximu, but she swatted it away.

The cockpit came fully into view, a glass bubble that encased Charles. His attempts to seize Ximu seemed futile. Vespa watched in horror as one of the energy guns burned bright before it discharged a shot that smoked on Ximu's hide.

"Wait! That wasn't—" Vespa began to shout. Then she saw that the shot had mostly been a buzz of energy meant to goad her.

Ximu took the bait, grinning at them, and followed Charles while her hybrids and *xiren* swarmed through the gap. Scientian reinforcements were attempting to come up through the smoke and rubble of the wall, but they were hampered by the *xiren* and the hybrids who waited to slice them down at the breach.

"You can handle this?" Vespa asked Syrus and Olivia. "We have a spider to catch."

They nodded. Syrus had tied himself upright in the chariot. Bayne handed him a sword he'd rescued from one of the weapons caches in the walls. "Good hunting, then."

"And to you," Syrus said.

The General urged the metal horses forward, and Vespa saw that beside them in the chariot rode the ghost of the Tinker King.

Vespa took hold of Bayne's hand, feeling the signet ring press its Wyvern emblem into her palm.

"Not far to go, luckily," he said.

And then they were standing on the porch above the courtyard, watching as Charles drew Ximu on around the corner.

Tesla was waiting in his little cage at the far end of the courtyard, ready to press the button on his black box and bring the radiant energy net to life.

From the other side of the building they could hear the sounds of the army fighting the hybrids and *xiren*. A few moments was all they had before the enemy would follow their Queen. Hopefully Olivia and Syrus could hold them off for a while. All they needed was just a few seconds. A few seconds would change everything.

So Charles had said.

Charles and Ximu were at a standoff. He was backing slowly toward the spot they'd designated, but he needed her to go in first.

She was clearly waiting on something.

"Now's the test," Bayne said. "Now we find out whether we were in her web all along."

Vespa nodded.

Charles lunged forward. He managed to grab Ximu by the leg, but attempting to drag her bodily backward wasn't going to work. Another odd-looking tentacle snaked out and latched onto the Shadowspider Queen's abdomen.

"What is he doing?" Vespa asked, looking at Bayne frantically. "This wasn't part of the plan!"

Ximu howled in pain. Her life energy was being pumped into a swelling bag that formed the Cephalopod's head.

"I hope he's merely trying to weaken her," Bayne said.

They watched helplessly as she wrestled the Cephalopod,

drawing it in close to her, biting the glass cockpit where Charles furiously worked the levers.

Vespa watched them dancing back and forth, ever closer and ever farther from the division line.

The Cephalopod was smoking and making sad moaning sounds as its hydraulics began to fail while Ximu attempted to detach its lamprey cable from her side.

Finally, in one last great heave, Ximu rose and threw the Cephalopod straight into the trap zone, tearing a wound in her side.

The machine flipped on its back and scored a line through the pavement, glass and parts flying everywhere. Vespa screamed as she saw Tesla dive from the control booth just before the crumpled Cephalopod skidded into it.

All was still for a moment, with Ximu nursing her wounds at one end of the courtyard and the twisted wreckage smoking at the other.

Then they saw Charles trying to extricate himself from the mess. He was still in the trap zone.

"Damn it," Bayne said. "I'm going to go help him. Be ready on my signal. Can you feed power to the field if I ask it?"

Vespa nodded.

Then he was gone.

"Bayne!" There was so much more she'd wanted to say, to warn him about. Even if she could get the field working without Tesla, no one could be in the field when Ximu stepped in; they'd be trapped forever, too.

Ximu began creeping toward them, her scarlet fangs erupting from Lucy's poor, leering mouth. Vespa thought she might have seen tears in the monster's eyes, but she couldn't be certain.

Bayne was trying to pull Charles out, but it looked like his legs were stuck.

Tesla had risen from behind one of the guardian statues and was pointing his device at the antennae.

"No!" Vespa shouted. She closed her eyes, expecting to hear the dreadful whine that had nearly shaken Olivia apart at the demonstration a week ago. Or the vast energy that had made all the hairs of Vespa's body stand on end. But she heard and felt nothing.

Dimly she heard Bayne calling her.

She opened her eyes and saw that Tesla was standing there in complete dismay, pointing and pressing and getting no response.

Vespa saw Charles and Bayne exchange words, and then Bayne stepped back and saluted Charles. He turned and faced Ximu.

"No," Vespa said, walking down a few steps. The din of fighting came from around the corner; Olivia's soldiers were being pushed into the courtyard by the relentless *xiren* and their hybrid army.

Bayne looked up at Vespa and gave her a deep bow.

And she knew what he wanted her to do.

Radiant energy and etheric energy were the same. They were just called by different principles. He wanted her to call down the energy and trigger the field with her magic. And he would support her in it.

But if she did that, he would be trapped.

Ximu was about to step over the division line.

Do it, Bayne said in Vespa's mind.

She opened her heart, the place that she had thought so empty and powerless since she'd given the Heart back to Tianlong. She opened that place and let pure love flow out, the love she'd only ever briefly known in the golden country of magic.

The *scarabeus* magnified it into a great wave that flowed outward from her. And as Ximu leaped over the line, the love burned through her. It cleaved something from the ancient spider, and then it sparked into a net of brilliant energy, like a sun come to rest on the stones.

And trapped there, a giant insect in amber, was Ximu. She seemed smaller than she had been, or perhaps it was just a trick of the light. But as Ximu slowed and settled in the paralytic field, Vespa heard the sounds of fighting begin to cease.

"Bayne," she said.

The ancient hall of the Tinker King seemed suddenly filled with echoes.

Through the wavering of the field Vespa thought she saw a dark shape, perhaps more than one.

She started to run and then realized she didn't have to.

The *scarabeus* flared, and in a moment she was on the other side of the field.

Bayne was helping up a disheveled girl. A girl who had once had porcelain skin, snapping black eyes, and flowing black curls. And the spoiled personality to match. A girl, who, in another world it almost seemed, had briefly been Bayne's wife. She let go of his hand when she saw Vespa and wavered uncertainly.

"Lucy," Vespa said. She opened her arms.

Lucy hesitated one more moment before falling into them.

"Forgive me," Lucy whispered. Even her fine voice was gone.

Vespa looked across her shoulder at Bayne. His gaze was knowing, loving, and a little bit sheepish all at once.

"I'll try," Vespa whispered.

And after that, the light somehow became too bright, the scents and sounds too overwhelming. It was as if her blood had all been drained out of her and replaced with air.

"I think I'm going to faint," she whispered with the deepest embarrassment.

And then all was dark.

CHAPTER 35

M y heart pounds until it almost burns in my chest, not just from fear or hope or any of those things, but from that last moment when Olivia's metal lips touched mine.

I can hear dreadful noises from the courtyard beyond. I'm praying to all the clan mothers this means that things are going well when there's a roar and a burst of power so strong, it rocks the chariot nearly off its wheels. Piskel tumbles arse-over-teakettle off my shoulder and fetches up against the chariot wall. He stands woozily, moaning and clutching his head.

Then his entire expression changes. He zips away, but it's as if he's flying through honey.

"Fine. Leave us in our hour of need," I say. Even my voice sounds slow and funny. All around us the silver army fights the *xiren*, immune to their poison and magic.

I feel the wave of resonance when it starts, and I'm wishing that I could be on the other side of the wall to see it. I want to see Tesla's experiment realized. But the way this feels is different from what I imagined when he explained it to me. It feels very much like magic. I see the light spread above the roofs like a new sun. Everything burns, and the hybrids slow and still, falling over dead. The golden markings of the *xiren* dissolve, and the darkness seeps from their skin. They all stand looking around them as if they've just woken from a long nightmare. From across the courtyard I see Uncle Gen shake his head and drop his long-handled blade as if it burns him.

In the light, souls depart—the army's, the newly dead, even what little piece of soul Charles had regained. All are departing like motes of fire in a golden storm for a country that is beyond the imagining of any witch or scientist.

I feel a tug beside me, and I realize that the Tinker King is leaving, too.

"My son has at last returned. Let your reign be filled with joy, my King."

A heavy coat settles around my shoulders. I look down and see dragon stitching up and down the sleeves. It's the mantle of the King. I look up into Blackwolf's face, his true face, and I see it's as kindly as any of the old grandfathers who used to smoke around the fires in the trainyard.

Then he, too, is gone. I bow my head, disbelieving.

The light slowly dies.

I am left standing alone in a courtyard of statues, the King's robe heavy as all the burdens of life around my shoulders.

Then Gen is smiling at me over the edge of the chariot, and he says, "Don't get too comfortable in that fancy robe, boy. We've still got work to do."

I'm thinking of all the Tinkers who are still in the caves, delirious with venom, waiting for the nightmares to end.

Olivia smiles at me. "Whenever you're ready, my King."

I nod and pull Gen up beside us.

"So tell me the truth," I say as we make our way through the rubble and round the corner to try to find Vespa and Bayne. "Did you really choose to serve that old she-demon? Or were you just saying that to convince me?"

Gen shakes his head. "*Waisheng*, half the time I never even knew my own name. It was like walking in a dream. I said all kinds of things I was trying desperately not to say. Every time I thought I'd warned you away, I realized I'd only just tried to draw you in. I'm glad you never believed me."

I'm about to answer when I see Ximu trapped in what looks like a glowing piece of amber. I knew they'd done it, of course, but the sight is still an overwhelming relief.

Then I see Bayne and someone who must be Lucy holding up another person. Vespa.

I leap off the chariot.

"Is she all right?"

Lucy won't look any of us in the eye. She hangs back a bit. I suspect it will take a long time, if ever, for her to be fully healed.

"She will be," Bayne says. "I think we all will be now."

"Then may I have your permission to seek out my people in the caves? My uncle says many there are still in need."

Bayne smiles. "You're the King, my Lord. Do as you will, and take whatever you may require to do so."

He bows to me. And that is perhaps the most surprising thing of my life—that a Duke would bow low to a trainyard melonhead like me and call me King.

Chapter 36 ━

When Vespa woke, she was blind at first. Over her eyes was something cool and dark that smelled of lavender. She lifted her hands and pushed it off, and then realized her hands were bandaged too.

Faces resolved slowly. Syrus. Truffler. Piskel.

Her heart nearly stopped when she realized there was no Bayne.

Then he was there, a bouquet of flowers in his hand.

Tesla stepped forward. "It should have worked," he said indignantly. "I've never had any invention of mine not work before. It's very odd. I must find out why it didn't work."

"I'm sure you will," Vespa said. "Olivia?" She looked around for her.

"Is making sure no Tinkers are still trapped somewhere in the caves," Syrus said.

Vespa looked at Bayne again, trying to read him. She could sense nothing from him, though, neither regret nor anger nor . . . anything else.

Tesla took Syrus by the arm. "I think these two need to speak alone," he said.

"Inexcusably impolite way to treat a King," Syrus said with the ghost of a smile.

They shut the door behind them, laughing.

"King?" Vespa said, raising a brow.

"Yes, quite the surprise. Probably for him more than anyone else. Olivia abdicated in favor of him, and Blackwolf named him his successor. He is the first Tinker King in generations. And he has much work to do, if all the people we've rescued from the caverns are any indication. Ximu seemed to have a propensity for collecting Tinkers."

"And Lucy and Charles?"

"My, you're full of questions, aren't you?"

"I'm just getting started." Vespa smoothed the coverlet over her stomach and patted beside her. "Do tell."

Bayne seated himself gingerly so as not to crush her.

"I'm afraid Charles didn't make it. At the last second he sacrificed himself. I'm still rather amazed. I think Lucy is quite damaged by her experience. She'll never be the same, and perhaps that's a good thing."

"And what about you?"

"I have been formally reinstated to the family and officially proclaimed Duke."

"Ah," she said. She looked down at her bandaged hands, moving restlessly on the covers. "Bayne, there's . . ."

"Vespa," he began at the same time.

They both laughed.

"You first," they said.

More laughter. She didn't think she'd ever seen his eyes sparkle so much.

"Look," Bayne said, sliding off the bed and kneeling beside it, "this is rather a big, lonely place, and I find I'm much in need of . . ." He took a deep breath. " . . . well, you."

Vespa watched him for a long moment, unable to say a single thing. "What about your vows?" she finally managed.

"As I think someone astutely pointed out, the Architects are no more, and thus I am no longer bound by their vows. I would like to make some new ones," he said. And his voice was soft and steady as it had been that day his words alone had kept her safe from the Sphinx.

But she would not let him get away that easily. "Such as?"

"Marriage vows," he said. "Vespa, I hardly deserve to ask this of you, and I deserve you even less, but . . ."

"Oh, stop talking, you stubborn fool," she said. She pulled him into her arms as best she could, which was awkward considering the flowers and the bed between them. But his arms slid around her, and his lips met hers almost before she could murmur, "Of course the answer is yes."

As his lips moved on hers, that longed-for golden country opened wide before them. This time, neither of them made any move to leave.

CHAPTER 37

At midnight I go out to see my city. I know so little of this place or the Kings of old, but it stirs some primal memory—part of the hound within. I wander through the Bone Palace. I can still feel Blackwolf here, but it's like the warm presence of someone sleeping. He has at last gone to his rest, and the troubles that tormented him have dissolved with Ximu's capture.

But mine, it seems, have just begun.

I climb the battlements, which have mostly all been repaired since the attack of the *xiren*. The mountains that ring the City are white-shouldered in the moonlight. Clouds heavy with snow are moving in off the sea, and the first flakes fall even as I watch. The harsh salt wind matches my mood, and I exult in it.

Some would say that I have triumphed. Some would say that I have done more than could ever be imagined, though somewhere I think *Nainai* may be smiling and saying, "At last you did what I thought you would all along." It is no small thing to wake up and find oneself King. But it is even greater to realize that all along all you wanted was to be King in one woman's eyes.

That happened. But not in the way I had intended.

The courtyard below is filled with the King's army, row upon row of silent statues. I know I have but to speak the word and Olivia will rouse them and lead them to battle. But I also know that I won't use that power. I will do everything to keep from using it. There is something terrible about such perfect, swift compliance. It reminds me far too much of the Raven Guard for my liking. We must find a way to live together in this world, all of us.

I go down to the courtyard, and the snow freezes through my boots as I walk out onto it.

Olivia steps out of the line of her regiment to be with me. She prefers to stay out here, she says, the better to guard us all in the nights.

"My King, you seem deep in thought tonight."

I sigh, wishing for things that cannot be.

You will find your love, she had said. But I know no other, better love than this.

"Tell me a tale of the Time Before," I say, "when you led the armies of Blackwolf, and my people were as numberless as the stars."

She smiles and takes my hand. "Let us go somewhere warm, and I will tell you of a Time That Will Be."

Acknowledgments

Thanks go to the usual suspects—my very patient and tireless editor, Navah Wolfe; agent, Jennifer Laughran; publicist, Anna McKean; and the design team headed by Chloë Foglia.

Big thanks to Ysabeau Wilce, who has been my rock through this draft, and encouraged me to think big and small in all the right places. Thanks also to the many friends and family both near and far who have supported me throughout this process.

Finally, I want to say how much I appreciate the brilliant readers who buoyed me along the way with their cheer, flowers, little gifties, and reviews of undying devotion. I'm proud to know so many of you personally. Though I was very ill through much of the writing of this book, you're the reason I kept going, even when I thought I couldn't.